PRAISE FOR
MANUEL VÁZQUEZ MONTALBÁN
PEPE CARVALHO SERIES

"Montalbán does for Barcelona what Chandler did for
Los Angeles—he exposes the criminal power relationships
beneath the façade of democracy."
**—THE GUARDIAN**

"Montalbán writes with authority and
compassion—a le Carré-like sorrow."
**—PUBLISHERS WEEKLY**

"A writer who is caustic about the
powerful and tender towards the oppressed."
**—TIMES LITERARY SUPPLEMENT**

"Carvalho travels down the mean calles
with humor, perception, and compassion."
**—THE TIMES (LONDON)**

"Does for modern Barcelona what
Dickens did for 19th century London."
**—TOTAL**

"Carvalho is funny … scathingly witty about the powerful.
He is an original eccentric, burning books and cooking all
night. Like Chandler's Phillip Marlowe, he is a man of honor
walking the mean streets of a sick society."
**—INDEPENDENT (LONDON)**

CALGARY PUBLIC LIBRARY

APR  -  2012

"I cannot wait for other Pepe Carvalho titles
to be published here. Meanwhile, make the most
of *Murder in the Central Committee.*"
**—NEW STATESMAN (LONDON)**

"A sharp wit and a knowing eye."
**—SUNDAY TIMES (LONDON)**

"Splendid flavor of life in Barcelona and Madrid, a
memorable hero in Pepe, and one of the most startling
love scenes you'll ever come across."
**—SCOTSMAN**

"An excuse for a gastronomic, political,
and social tour of Barcelona."
**—THE GUARDIAN**

"An inventive and sexy writer... Warmly recommended."
**—THE IRISH INDEPENDENT**

"Pepe Carvalho's greatest concern is with his
stomach, but when not pursuing delicacies, he can
unravel the most tangled of mysteries."
**—THE SUNDAY TIMES**

Born in Barcelona in 1939, **MANUEL VÁZQUEZ MONTALBÁN** (1939–2003) was a member of *Partit Socialista Unificat de Catalunya* (PSUC), and was jailed by the Franco government for four years for supporting a miners' strike. A columnist for Madrid's *El País*, as well as a prolific poet, playwright, and essayist, Vázquez Montalbán was also a well-known gourmand who wrote often about food. The nineteen novels in his Pepe Carvalho series have won international acclaim, including the Planeta prize (1979) and the International Grand Prix de Littérature Policière (1981), both for *Southern Seas*. He died in 2003 in Hong Kong, on his way home to Barcelona.

**PATRICK CAMILLER** has translated Che Guevara's African diaries and, from the Romanian, Norman Manea's *The Black Envelope*.

# MURDER
## IN THE CENTRAL
# COMMITTEE

# MANUEL
# VÁZQUEZ
# MONTALBÁN

## TRANSLATED BY PATRICK CAMILLER

 MELVILLE HOUSE
BROOKLYN, NEW YORK

 MELVILLE
INTERNATIONAL
CRIME

## MURDER IN THE CENTRAL COMMITTEE

First published as *Asesinato en el Comité Central* by
Editorial Planeta, S.A., Barcelona

© 1981 Manuel Vázquez Montalbán

Translation © 1984 Patrick Camiller

This edition published by arrangement with Serpent's Tail

First Melville House printing: January 2012

Melville House Publishing
145 Plymouth Street
Brooklyn, NY 11201

www.mhpbooks.com

ISBN: 978-1-61219-036-5

Printed in the United States of America

1 2 3 4 5 6 7 8 9 10

Library of Congress Control Number: 2011942039

To Josefina Sallés just because
and Javier Alfaya as agreed

We have freed ourselves of a blind faith in science, but now we feel stronger than ever that faith to which Marx was referring when he said that communists are capable of 'storming the heavens'. When that faith grows cold and doubt creeps in, one begins to cease being a communist. That is the truth.

—Irene Falcón, quoted by Jorge Semprún in *The Autobiography of Federico Sánchez*


But death suddenly shows that the real society is lying.

—Georges Bataille, *The Theory of Religion*

## Author's note

Since he can foresee a perverse tendency to identify the characters in this novel with real persons, the author would like to state that he has confined himself to the use of archetypes, although he does recognise that we real people sometimes behave as archetypes.

**Archetype**: Sovereign and eternal type which serves as an example and model for the human will and understanding.

—*Dictionary of the Royal Academy*

# Dishes and parties

**Arroz de Arzac**  a rice dish named after a famous restaurant in San Sebastian
**Bacalao**  a stew of salted codfish
**Butifarra**  a distinctive Catalan sausage
**Capipota**  a dish made from head and leg of pork
**Chinchon**  an aniseed-based alcoholic drink
**Chorizo**  a hard pork sausage
**Cocido**  a popular stewed dish made with various ingredients
**Fabada**  a rich Asturian stew made from beans and pork
**Fesols**  Catalan word for beans
**Horchata**  a popular drink based on ice-cream
**Kokochas**  cheeks of hake
**Orujo**  a grape *eau-de-vie* akin to the Italian grappa

**FUE**  Communist-Socialist student organisation in the 1930s
**Movimiento Obrero**  literally workers' movement, the section of the trade-union movement in which the Communist Party has traditionally played a dominant role
**PCE**  Partido Comunista de España, Communist Party of Spain
**PSOE**  Partido Socialista Obrero de España, the Socialist Party of Spain
**PSUC**  Partido Socialista Unificado Catalan, the semi-autonomous Communist Party in Catalonia
**UCD**  Union Centro-democratico, the main centre-right coalition which headed the transition from the Franco regime. Now virtually defunct
**UGT**  Union General del Trabajo, the trade-union federation in which the Socialist Party has traditionally played a dominant role

# MURDER IN THE CENTRAL COMMITTEE

Santos absent-mindedly shuffled the folders. By pretending to do something, he avoided the obligation to greet everyone as they arrived.

'These were left untouched by human hand at the last meeting.'

The secretary pointed to a forlorn heap of folders piled at one end of the display-table. It was covered with dossiers and brand-new folders in which members of the central committee of the Spanish Communist Party would find the agenda, an outline of the general secretary's political report, and the full text of an intervention to be made by the leader of Movimiento Obrero.

'In my time people gave their life to be on the central committee. Now they haggle over every weekend.'

Santos smiled at Julian Mir, the chief steward.

'I wouldn't go back to those times.'

'No, Santos, nor would I. But I get sore when I see how inconsiderate certain comrades can be. Some travel seven hundred kilometres by train to come to the meeting, while others stay put in Argüelles, half an hour away by taxi.'

'So, what shall I do with the folders left from the last meeting?'

'Put them with today's.'

The girl did as Santos said, and Julian Mir returned to his duties as chief steward, casting expert eyes over the movements of his red-armbanded subordinates.

'We'll have an unpleasant surprise one of these days. I don't like this place.'

Santos met Mir's critical ill-humour with a nod that could have indicated either agreement or disapproval. He had been using the same gesture with Mir ever since the days of the Fifth Regiment. Then, Julian had never liked the evening shadows, which had seemed pregnant with Franco's soldiers, nor the morning light that opened the way to advance parties of *Regulares*. Later, he had not been fond of the Tarn fruit groves, which seemed to have borne the shape of German patrols ever since the Pleistocene. Later still, he had not liked his missions inside the country, although he carried them out with the haughty assurance of a Western film hero.

'Many problems?'

'Four fascists died of fear,' Mir had invariably replied on his return from a trip to Franco's Spain.

He had always been like that. Probably born that way, thought Santos, and he was suddenly surprised that Julian Mir had once been born: so long ago; too long. The time was now stored in his stiff white hair and his old athlete's musculature that made him look like a chicken spoiling for a fight.

'I don't like this place.'

'Here we go again. Where would you like to hold the central committee?' asked Santos.

'There are too many little offices dotted everywhere. That's what I am complaining about. There should be a fine central head-quarters like every proper Communist Party has got. Does it seem right to you? Just yesterday, the Anabaptists from Torrejón de Ardoz held a convention here. Look at what's written on that poster.'

'I'd have to put my glasses on.'

'Oh yes! You've been losing your faculties ever since you became a pen-pusher,' Mir said. 'I can read it all right: "The way of the spirit in the path of the body", by Yogi Sundra Bashuarti. That was here yesterday. I can't tell anymore whether this is a central committee meeting or a gathering of fakirs. Communists in a hotel – as if we were tourists or underwear salesmen.'

'You're in a right old mood.'

'And one day they'll sneak in a commando disguised as a tropical orchestra. Sometimes you can even hear the music from the dance-hall.'

'It's quite atmospheric.'

Santos left Mir to his ill-humour and immediately received a feverish hug from the comrade-mayor of Liñán de la Frontera. He had not lost his faculties. His memory was still fresh clay on which all the Party's faces were engraved; and his arms still responded with Herculean strength to the Soviet hugs which more distant comrades used to test his already aged frame.

'Why do we hug like this?' he once asked Fernando Garrido.

'Probably since the civil war,' Garrido had shrugged. 'Any parting or meeting was very emotional.'

'I think it's Soviet influence. They always greet each other like

2

that. At least we didn't pick up their way of kissing.'

'Don't mention that, man. When they gave me a kiss on the mouth, I never knew what to do: kick them in the balls or let myself be had.'

Garrido was clearly late. The comrades were standing in circles outside the meeting-room and would remain there until the charged opening of the door announced Garrido's entry. The circles would then open like eyes to contemplate once more the ever miraculous incarnation of the working-class vanguard in the person of the general secretary. Santos decided to inspect the meeting-room one last time before Garrido entered beneath the invisible mantle of History. Standing in the door, he could hear behind him the rising, digestive-like rumble of conversation as he looked at the lonely conference room of the Hotel Continental. Its prophylactic, symmetrical concentration of tables and chairs, lacking the warmth of leather or fabric, surrounded the table of power at which Garrido would sit, flanked by two executive committee members on either side.

'Is the sound all right? Have you tested the recorder?'

The heads of those responsible nodded to Santos.

'Who's sitting next to Fernando today?' Leveder asked.

'Martialay, Bouza, Helena Subirats and I.'

'The unity of the men and lands of Spain.'

'Martialay won't be there as a Basque, but as the Movimiento Obrero leader.'

'I know, I know, it was a joke.'

'A bit worn, though.'

As Santos replied to the ironic young man, he mentally went over his background: Paco Leveder, lecturer in civil law, part of the Democratic Union batch. 'He'll make a good parliamentarian,' Garrido had remarked when he heard him speak at the Ivry college, made available by the French Communist Party for a secret meeting with university staff from Spain. Now he was just a parliamentarian.

'He's not the only one. Some forty per cent of the central committee are missing. A sense of punctuality is the first thing to go when you become legal. Anyway, weren't you absent without apologies from the last meeting?'

'I phoned Paloma to say I had to attend a public function.'

'You know that central committee meetings are more important than even a Party function,' Santos said.

3

'You'll be telling me next that the central committee is the Party's highest leadership body.'

'I don't think I need to.'

'Does "the land to those who till it" mean anything to you? Or "all power to the soviets"?'

'They did before you were born.'

'You certainly preserve yourself well, Santos.'

He left Leveder with a smile. Answering all the greetings and witticisms directed to him by various groups, he moved ever more softly towards the door from which Julian Mir was indicating Garrido's arrival. As if everything had been calculated by an all-powerful chronometer, he replaced Julian at the door just as it was framing the body of the general secretary. Fernando Garrido smiled and moved forward, moved forward and smiled. He waved and spoke briefly with one group after another, as if reciting a speech timed to last the exact distance between the doors of the entrance-hall and the meeting-room. The circles opened and even broke apart as some comrades insisted on a handshake with Garrido, hoping for a confidential word or offering one of their own to the general secretary, who, devoid of secrets himself, indulgently inclined his head to listen. Yet he did not linger as he walked between Santos and Julian, drawing in his wake two stewards who barely left room for Martialay in the narrow human passageway. Garrido made a special stop to receive the crushing embrace of Harguindey, twenty-one years and a day served in prison with the superhuman obstinacy of the time. Garrido survived Harguindey's slap on the shoulder. He told a joke to Helena Subirats that produced a roar of laughter more like an ovation.

We still can't believe that we are able to meet, Santos thought; that Fernando is here, that a van-load of policemen are protecting the side-entrance to the hotel.

He respected the halts in the procession and yet tried his best to hurry it along. At one point he stopped so that Martialay could keep up with them.

'We weren't able to circulate your speech before today.'

'As always.'

'Nearly always.'

Garrido had had his hair cut, and he left behind the scent of after-shave lotion mixed with traces of a recent shower. Who could have imagined him like that? For a moment, Santos thought he was following the young leader who, during the meetings to prepare for October 1934,* had said to him: 'Leave everything and follow me!' Santos had followed, through forty years of war, exile, imprisonment, false identities, and even Crimean holidays and strategic poker-games with the Soviets.

'Santos.'

'Yes, Fernando.'

'I'd like to have a word with you and Martialay before the meeting begins.'

The three went into the room, and Julian Mir closed the door behind them.

'I still don't quite understand,' said Garrido, 'why we put off seeing the socialists.'

'It's only a fortnight to the union elections,' Martialay argued, 'and we have to keep our distance. The going will get rough; the PSOE will have its fingers in the UGT campaign.'

'Anyway, if there's a question of intervention at the meeting, it should be answered rather ambiguously. Clear-cut positions are often a cover for obscurity and vacillation.'

'I thought everything was clear.'

'That's why it may be unclear. What's your view, Santos?'

'There's no need to draw back from the meeting with the socialists. It will seem just as logical for us to go ahead as to call it off.'

'That's right.'

'Strikes me as a byzantine problem.'

'You're always saying that you don't want to be a Party transmission-belt. Well, nor can the Party be a transmission-belt of yours.'

Martialay shrugged and went to find his place at the table. He immediately plunged into the typewritten waters of his coming speech.

'He's nervous.'

'He has reason to be.'

Garrido took a cigarette from his jacket pocket as if it were one huge packet of cigarettes. 'He seems to take them out ready-lighted,' an interviewer had once written.

'You won't be allowed to smoke,' Santos reminded him.

'And then they say I'm a dictator.'

* October 1934: date of a working-class insurrection in Asturias.

He put the cigarette back into his pocket:

'Right, let's get started.'

Santos opened the door and went to sit on Garrido's right. From there he could see the central committee members as they made their noisy, chattering entrance.

'Nearly a plenum. They're obviously expecting something. Did you see the thing in *El País*?'

'Those people are still polite when they screw us. But *Cambio 16* has gone back to its headline: "Trade-Union Blackmail".'

Garrido stood up to greet Helena Subirats.

'Your *La Calle* interview was very good.'

'I'm glad you liked it. I'm still smouldering at the way the interviewers reduced everything to simple schemas.'

Santos was the first to call for quiet, followed by a chorus of older and disciplined members. He then tapped the microphone, and its tubercular, electronic cough proved more effective than the 'ssh!' of human voices.

'The agenda is in the folder in front of you.'

Sixty per cent of those present thought it necessary to check. Julian Mir ushered in a four-man crew from Televisión Española, who bathed the platform and the first four rows of tables in a flood of light. Like an animal incapable of modulation, their camera devoured reality with a single steady sound.

'You can stay if you like,' Garrido proposed as the TV men were saying goodbye.

'That would be very interesting, but we've got to film the opening of the PSOE executive meeting.'

'Go, then. But you'd find out more here.'

'I don't doubt it.'

'Meetings of communists are always more exciting.'

Santos supported Garrido's jokes with his smile. Martialay continued to wrestle with the written sheets of his intervention. After the TV men left, the doors were closed and silence settled in the room.

'Let's get it over quickly, because you know I can't keep going without a smoke.'

Laughter.

The lights went out, as if the laughter had been badly received by the gods of electrical energy. A thick, unmistakable pall of darkness hung over the room.

'Those Workers' Commission people are always on strike,' Garrido remarked. But the microphones did not pick up his joke.

He wanted to say it louder, but he could not manage it. An icy pain crossed his English-wool vest and drained him of life.

When the lights came back on, Santos was the first to realise that the scene had changed. It was not normal for Fernando Garrido to be slumped over the files, his mouth open and his eyes glassier than the thick-lensed spectacles fallen across his face. Santos rose as if something had painfully rubbed against his legs. The other communists stood in turn, stupefied, wondering what had happened. Then they rushed forward, overturning chairs as they went, to discover the reality of death.

The will to awake was enough to wake him up. He switched on the radio, which was already fully tuned to *Spain at Eight*. 'Profound national and international repercussions of the assassination of Fernando Garrido, general secretary of the Communist Party of Spain.' Grief and sympathy at home and abroad. And the profound repercussions? The Spanish government has denied that troops are confined to barracks or that the Brunete armoured division has carried out special manoeuvres. The head of government has met with the secretary-general of PSOE and José Santos Pacheco from the executive committee of the Communist Party of Spain. Superintendent Fonseca has been appointed by the government to head the investigation into Fernando Garrido's murder.

'That bloody Fonseca strikes again,' Carvalho said to himself as he switched off the radio. Fonseca's gleaming eyes, lidless and watery. The smooth, blood-thirsty little rabbit. Superimposed on him, the image of Fernando Garrido twenty-five years ago – walking the gravel-path of a house beside the Marne, surrounded by young students who had come from 'the interior' for the 1956 summer school.

7

'If the Spanish bourgeoisie is not prepared to assist our plan for national reconciliation, we shall not hesitate to pick up our guns again and set off for the mountains.'

'Which mountains?'

Garrido looked at him with a smile on his lips, but his eyes were cold and hard behind the glasses.

'What are you studying? Haven't you learnt yet that Spain is one of the most mountainous countries in Europe?'

The others laughed and dispelled the tension. Now and again, however, Carvalho saw Garrido staring at him in a kind of silent warning from afar. Look out, kid. Don't try to be smart. This is a serious business. During the rest period, when he wanted to be alone in the refreshing shade of the ash trees, Carvalho was accompanied by an old leader bearing all the scars of life and History. Such an exemplary life, it was implied, mocked the student's petty irony which, a few minutes earlier, had deflated something as dramatic as the to-be-or-not-to-be of the Spanish revolution.

'You think it funny that Garrido should be talking about the mountains. But just seven or eight years ago, we were still being hunted there like animals. Even today, a communist in Spain is tortured and sentenced to a hundred years in jail.'

Carvalho was too young to excuse himself, but too full of admiration to let it rankle. He heard the old comrade out and followed all the other meetings without a word of sarcasm. The regime would fall that October, and a woman comrade reported that the Party was now so strong in Barcelona that it could place the city in a state of siege. The influence of Camus, the young Carvalho thought. But he said nothing and examined the woman with the interest one has for a species on the verge of extinction.

'I could see it myself, and the Barcelona comrades will bear me out.'

This they did, rather unenthusiastically, as if they could not do otherwise, creating a bond between objective and subjective conditions through the dose of subjectivity required to believe what they were saying. Then came the embraces, the farewells, the songs:

I must go down to the harbour
And up to Tibidabo go.
There to shout with my people.

Yankees out! Death to Franco!
The blood of Spaniards
Is not the blood of slaves!

The songs were not well sung, because only the course organisers knew the words. Whenever they sang, the veteran communists therefore had to summon up the notorious voluntarism of youth.

Young Guard, Young Guard
Give them no peace or quarter!

Carvalho had shown that you could not go to such a course in the spirit of Machado's watchword: 'Doubt, my son, even your own doubt.'

Spring has at last appeared
On the wings of a dove.
The people's voices rise up
Over the Spanish land.
Long live the Barcelona strikes!

I must go down to the harbour
And up to Tibidabo go.

That was precisely what he did nowadays. He went down to the harbour in the hope of relaxing between a tiresome wait and a tiresome, sub-criminal investigation. Up to Tibidabo he went, in search of the Vallvidrera hiding-place from which he could contemplate an older, wiser, more cynical city, with nothing to offer the youth of today or tomorrow. That was the only time he had seen Garrido during his Party days. Twenty-five years later, he had gone to see him at a rally and merely discovered that the years had left their mark. He's right at the top of middle-distance bull-fighting, a dark-skinned young dude sardonically remarked in the disguise of someone at his first communion. 'Where the hell were you in that summer of fifty-six?' Carvalho asked with his eyes, although he did not have the slightest hope of a reply. The thousands upon thousands of people who had come to the rally might have been the fruit of years of spiritual exercises in France and catacomb activitiy inside the country. But Garrido's speech was the same as ever: he was still suggesting that the bourgeoisie should reach a pact of progress if it did not wish to see a return to fascism or to face the danger of pre-revolutionary chaos. Enough communists were present to place the city in a state of siege. But what should be done once a city was already in a state of siege? Seated next to Garrido was the comrade who, twenty-four years earlier, had laid siege to cities with her imagination and her desires. Her name then had been Irena, but now she was called Helena Subirats, complete with an MP's certificate and soothing declarations.

'No dictatorship, not even of the proletariat.'

He switched programmes to see if any expanded on the Radio Nacional report. A local radio station was trying to interview José Santos Pacheco, who had unexpectedly arrived in Barcelona on the first plane from Madrid. Santos did his best to dodge the questions, but he merely succeeded in dodging the answers.

'Is it the crime of a fanatic or the beginning of a vast plan to destabilise democracy?'

'Look, no one knows anything yet. Ask the government. It's an act against democracy.'

'Why have you come to Barcelona?'

'I've been coming here often for some time.'

'What do you make of the appointment of Superintendent Fonseca to head the official investigation?'

'It's a bad joke. Fonseca is still remembered by communists as one of Franco's choice hangmen.'

Fonseca used to offer cigarettes half-way out of the packet, his arm half stretched out, his voice half raised. Those eyes were as if wounded by reality, full of water and threats. Carvalho remembered him walking along the corridor, whimsically looking at the latest police haul and asking his Barcelona lieutenants for a running commentary.

'That one?'

'José Carvalho. A dangerous red.'

Fonseca managed to close his eyes in disgust as the lieutenant landed a punch in Carvalho's unsuspecting stomach.

'You and I are going to have a long hard talk,' he said as he continued his inspection of the day's bag. 'We've got the whole night ahead of us.'

'This is war, boss.'

Biscuter had switched on the transistor and was listening to a live report from the Communist Party's mortuary chapel in Madrid. Thousands of *madrileños* had already passed in front of Fernando Garrido's mortal remains, while the impressive police presence had been backed up by a deployment of troops in the outer suburbs.

'Excuse me, an opinion-poll for Radio Nacional. What do you put the murder down to?'

'To international fascism – what else?'

'But how do you explain that he was killed in a closed place, where the only people present were communists, members of the central committee?'

'In the only way a good communist can explain it. It was international fascism.'

'Are you a Party member?'

'Yes, I have been for a long time.'

'Did you know Fernando Garrido personally?'

'I had the honour of shaking his hand on more than one occasion. I was a branch delegate to the 1978 congress.'

'That was when there was a fight between Leninists and non-Leninists. Could that have anything to do with the murder?'

'You can't know us very well. We don't go around killing each other. You watch too much television or you've seen too many American films. Which radio did you say you're from?'

'Radio Nacional.'

'Well, it doesn't surprise me then.'

'Well said, you old chump!' Biscuter shouted.

'What's it to you, Biscuter?'

'It's a dirty business, boss. You've got to admit Garrido was a nice old fellow.'

Biscuter had not even had time to rub his eyes or to put the office table in order.

'Are you having breakfast here, boss? I've got some fantastic butifarras and a few fesols left over from yesterday.'

'I can't think *and* eat breakfast.'

'Does the radio stop you thinking?'

'I'll think about it.'

Carvalho picked up the phone and dialled a number, all the time wrinkling his nose as if the number smelled bad.

'Señor Detras? I'll hang on.'

'I'm not a communist,' someone else was saying on the radio, 'but I have come to say farewell to Garrido because I am a democrat and what they have done is too unspeakable for words. It's an assault on democracy. Who did it? The CIA? The Russians? You'll soon find out, what with all the crap, if you'll pardon the expression, that there is in politics.'

'Señor Detras? I'm Carvalho, the detective. Your girl is in a stage-actors' commune performing *The Caucasian Chalk Circle* at Riudellots de la Selva. She's fine. They only do one performance a day. Out of the question. I won't go looking for her: that's your business. I'll send you the bill. The play? It's decent. Rather subversive, but no nudity. Don't worry yourself. Right. It could be a lot worse. In my last case like yours, the girl was in Goa with one hell of a diarrhoea. She had to be repatriated on a Caritas plane. At your service.'

'Listen to what this guy's saying, boss! Listen!'

'There's got to be an end to this political nightmare. I'm not against politicians as people, but I'm against them as politicians. Since Franco's death, politics has descended on us like the plague.'

'I'd like some breakfast, Biscuter, but not that dreary stuff you were offering. Bread and tomato, some well-truffled Catalan sausage, a few split olives, a jug of cold red wine. Mild things. I'm full of toxins.'

Biscuter installed himself in the kitchenette lying off the corridor to the toilet. He whistled contentedly or repeated the order to the tune of *Three Coins in a Fountain*. Carvalho switched off the radio and began arranging the papers on his forties-style desk, whose layers of varnish had failed to highlight its wooden colour and instead formed a kind of brilliantine for furniture half-way between neo-classicism and inter-war functionalism. He picked up a sheet of paper on which Biscuter had written: 'Important visit at eleven.'

'Why is it an important visit?'

'Because they told me so.'

12

'They told you they were important?'

'They said it was a very important and confidential matter. They even asked if you would be completely alone.'

Noises came up from the Ramblas. Carvahlo looked out of the window. Two or three hundred people, their arms linked, were marching in rows down the street. 'The real terrorists are you, the fascists!' and 'Brother Garrido! We shall not forget you!'

'Here, Biscuter.'

'Twenty thousand pesetas! What's this for?'

'Buy food for two weeks. Just in case.'

'Things are going to blow up. That's what I was already thinking.'

'Maybe nothing will happen, but look at the queues starting to form in the food-shops.'

A little queue of women with baskets jutted out of the corner shop.

'Use the same plan as when Franco died. Fabada the only ready-made meal. It's the only one that keeps well in tins.'

Biscuter passed his fingers through the few red hairs left on his skull, rubbed his hands, bent his legs and geared up his body for the energetic activity required by the situation. His weak chest was drawn in so as to accentuate the resolution of a pair of childlike, gangliate shoulders. Before going out, he put Carvalho's breakfast on the table and left the bottle of ice-cold orujo by the wine-jug.

'Looks like you'll need this, boss.'

Biscuter produced a wink by means of a rash muscular movement that nearly paralysed half his face. He threw himself into the urban jungle, equipped with his mental parachute and that desire for adventure which anyone had to have in order to work with Carvalho. The detective ate his breakfast without thinking about the food. He had chosen a meal that required no reflection and almost no conscious attention. A breakfast that could discreetly accompany some transcendental meditation. Not even ham would have been the right choice, for it demands a critical, judicious sense of taste. Catalan sausage, however, adjusts to mechanical tasting and artless chewing. It did at least have to be truffled if its flavour was to surprise Carvalho from time to time, as the patches of truffle suddenly burst its smell in his mouth cavity and set up sharp sensations at the tip of his nose. Whatever the meal, it was always necessary to leave some time for dialectics, based on either the flavour or the texture of the food. With much less time for reflection, Brillat-Savarin wrote his *Physiology of Taste*. He was a man both famous and stupid – qualities which, Baudelaire noted, 'go very well together'. As for the sickly little drug-taker Baudelaire, he only drank wine or smoked drugs to worry his mother and punish her for marrying another man.

'Write a doctoral thesis on something so arbitrary that it rules out any thesis or antithesis, and then change jobs,' Carvalho said to himself as he held a little piece of truffle in his mouth, soaking up all its aroma and transforming it into a mere obstacle that the tongue would drop into the doubtless horrible depths of the stomach. He poured wine down his throat until he felt his stomach machinery to be well lubricated. Then he filled a glass with the orujo that lay attractive and threatening like a bare-toothed animal.

'You won't do me any good, you swine.'

And yet he drank it down in one go and felt a cold fire rise from stomach to nostrils – the same contradiction, after all, as that expressed in any vanilla ice soufflé.

'If you like we'll come back later.'

One of the men nodded towards the food still on the table.

'I'd already finished.'

'It's the best time for breakfast.'

He had never heard him say anything so cheap. Carvalho remembered him twenty-two years earlier, standing before the military court on a charge of rebellion. Then Salvatella had declared that he recognised only the courts of the Republic, not the one trying him. Evidently disturbed by his lack of respect, the military judges increased the sentence demanded by the prosecutor. But as he left the courtroom, Salvatella still tried to make a salute with his handcuffed hands, while Carvalho and a number of others were pushed out by local policemen. Salvatella turned to his companion and introduced him to Carvalho:

'José Santos Pacheco, member of the executive commitee of the Communist Party of Spain. My name is Floreal Salvatella. I belong

14

to the PSUC executive and the PCE central committee.'

'Mine is on the name-plate downstairs.'

'We didn't need to look at that. We were sent by Marcos Núñez, a comrade who knows you well.'

'Yes, we met now and again when we were trying to solve the mysterious killing of a manager.'

'A tough case, was it?'

'So tough that they all wanted to kill him but he died by himself.'

Santos Pacheco looked as if he had stepped out of a press cutting or a TV news flash. In the background behind Garrido, and now in the background behind Salvatella. Tall, sunburnt, hewed by life into the form of an old, grey-haired mariner, he bent a little to hear the two Spaniards condemned to the average height of 165 centimetres. Salvatella, however, was only a memory of that nearly young prisoner whom Carvalho had seen sentenced to a hundred and twelve years. You've put on weight, Floreal; not from prison, it would seem, but as a result of time and legality. They only sat down when Carvalho suggested it, and even then they did so with the prudent reserve used by every communist to show that he is nothing like the prefabricated image of an uncultured, soulless brute. Salvatella kept his eyes on Santos, who took up the offer and played soloist with the tone that he might have used to open a Party meeting. It was a firm, level voice, as if he were trying to make it exactly like the voice of anyone else present.

'I don't think it's hard to guess why we're here. First of all, I'd ask you to be as discreet as possible about our conversation, however it may go. If necessary, I'll claim professional secrecy.'

'It's an almost forced secrecy. I never talk to anyone.'

'As a preventive measure?'

'No. I just think it's obvious that if what other people say does not interest me, then nothing I can say will interest them.'

'You'd go a long way in politics. Those who talk least usually have the most successful careers.'

'In politics, as in bed and everywhere else, you must never allow any doubt to creep in.'

'I've come on more or less official business. We would like you to help us investigate the murder of our general secretary. The government has appointed an unsatisfactory investigator against our express wishes, and it has been accepted that we should have one of our own, whose complete freedom of movement is guaranteed by both the Party and the government. If Superintendent Fonseca had not been given the case, we might not have taken this step. But that alone is enough to show that the government will try to use the investigation to get at us. I don't know if you are familiar with Fonseca's background.'

'I am. And you know it.'

'Yes, that's true. You are one of Fonseca's thousands of past victims.'

'A mere trifle. I was hardly even an insect in Fonseca's zoo.'

'Any effort to bring down the dictatorship was worthy of praise. Anyway, you know who Fonseca is. You know he started his career as a Franquist infiltrator in our party; he cost us a very great deal in the forties, including four shootings. I won't beat about the bush anymore. We're here on business and you have only to name your price.'

Salvatella seemed to be busy digesting what Santos had said, while Santos himself looked at Carvalho with an encouraging smile on his lips, as if he had already received a positive answer.

'What do you want me to do? To find the murderer or to help you cover up the murder?'

'Maybe we were given the wrong information. But they told us you uncovered murders, not covered them up.'

'This case is beyond my powers. I'm used to starring in black-and-white films, and now you're offering me a 70mm super-production with governments and police departments at the centre. In Madrid, too. I'm tired of travelling. I know Barcelona like the back of my hand, but sometimes I find even this city unbearable. Imagine me in Madrid, among the skyscrapers, functionaries of the old regime, ex-functionaries of the regime. I'm apolitical – let's get that straight. But I can't stand the little moustaches worn by functionaries of the old regime, ex-functionaries of the regime.'

Santos looked to see what was in Salvatella's eyes. His smile told Carvalho that he knew Santos was lacking in humour. Strengthened and forewarned by his comrade, Santos returned Carvalho's look in the form of a complicit smile.

'Madrid is no abstraction, and you can't generalise about functionaries. I can see that you swallow all the clichés current in the provinces.'

'I neither swallow them nor refrain from swallowing them. But Madrid is not what it used to be:'

'In 1936?'

'No. In 1959, when I lived there. Take the prawns at the Casa del Abuelo. Excellent and ridiculously cheap. Just try finding them now.'

'Ah, so it's a question of prawns.'

Santos's eyes shifted left and right, as if he were trying to work out exactly how the disappearance of prawns from the Casa del Abuelo fitted into a conversation about the murdered general secretary of the Communist Party.

'There are some first-class shellfish restaurants,' he burst out with a certain relief.

'But what do they charge?'

'Obviously shellfish are expensive.'

'There's some of everything,' Salvatella chipped in. 'When I go to a central committee meeting, I sleep at Togores's place – you know, the Perkins one. He lives near the Sports Palace, in Calle Duque de Sesto. There's an excellent and fairly cheap shellfish restaurant in the area. It's always full. And if you walk around a bit, you can find some very nice pubs. The local near Togores's place is really quite impressive: María de Ceberos, it's called. Have you ever tried the lamb kidneys that woman makes? Absolutely delicious. The simplest thing in the world: salt, pepper, under the grill, a squirt of oil and lemon. Of course, they have to be very fresh *lamb* kidneys.'

Either you're play-acting or you're a man after my own heart, Carvalho thought. He noticed the clear disorientation of Santos, who was trying with a smile to enter into the gastronomic complicity.

'I can't really answer you. It's a long time since I've been in Madrid, but on my last visit I wandered through the Asturias district. There's now a cafeteria where there used to be a pub, and they serve you Madrid-style tripe made with stock-cubes and some horse-meat chorizo.'

'Well, tripe's another story. It has to be admitted, and it's not just a provincial cliché . . . ' Santos shrugged at Salvatella's allusion.

' . . . that much has been lost. The same is happening to Madrid-style tripe as to Asturian fabada. It's tinned. Tinned.'

Salvatella harshly pointed out this objective truth to Santos Pacheco, as if he were showing him the very wound made by Mercader's ice-pick in Trotsky's skull.

'I don't like tripe,' Santos said defensively.

As I thought, Carvalho said to himself.

Santos shifted awkwardly. But for fear of displeasing Carvalho, he did not dare to bring the conversation back to the original theme. His mounting irritation focused instead on Salvatella; on that traitor who, before Garrido's corpse had even grown cold, could launch into a trivial conversation about prawns, tripe and grilled lamb-kidneys. So he lay in wait, with a cold, admonitory stare that Salvatella met just as he was beginning to speak.

'There's no tripe like in . . . Anyway. If you come to Madrid, we'll have plenty of time to discuss and eat tripe. Don't let's get away from the purpose of our visit. Besides, we're disturbing you. You have to work as well. We'll agree to the price you set. We'll find you the best hotel in Madrid, whichever one you like.'

'Why me?'

'Because you're an ex-communist. Because you know who we are, what we're like, where we come from, and where we're going.'

Santos spoke with passion; even, one might have said, with a moist warmth in those eyes which harboured the immortal remains of his friend and comrade Fernando Garrido.

'An ex-communist is either an apostate or a renegade.'

'It's enough for us that he's an apostate.'

Your conduct has been judged improper. The leadership has asked us to set up a cell court and to decide in the first instance whether you should continue to be a member. Carvalho saw himself interrupting the rhythmic movement of his brush across the yellow canvas-sheet. He left the word 'amnesty' half-written and turned to that callow, larva-like economist:

'You've improved a lot if you're willing to accept help from an apostate. But I'm not even that. I'd almost forgotten that I was once a communist. Just like I'd forgotten that I worked for the CIA for four years. Did you know that?'

'We did,' they said almost in unison.

Carvalho leant against the back-rest of his revolving armchair:

'I warn you. I make no reductions on grounds of nostalgia.'

'We'll pay whatever is necessary.'

It struck Carvalho that Salvatella had to arrest the spontaneous movement of his hand towards his wallet.

'Will you be long in Madrid, boss?'

'As long as necessary.'

'What shall I do with all that food?'

The office seemed half-full of tins, sausages and salted codfish.

'Keep yours here, and take the rest up to my place in Vallvidrera.'

'What if there's trouble? One of my mother's brothers was a travelling salesman. The civil war caught him in Aranjuez, and nothing more was heard of him.'

'Times have changed – people too.'

'When I was a kid and my mother was still alive, she often used to cry thinking about her brother.'

'People used to cry much more than they do now.'

'True enough, boss.'

All he had left now was to say goodbye to Charo.

'I'm off.'

'Where to?'

'I'm leaving Barcelona for about a fortnight, I guess.'

'Just like that, over the phone?'

'It all happened very quickly.'

'Right, dear, don't waste any more time.'

And she hung up.

'If civil war starts and I don't come back, share all the food with Charo.'

'I'd already thought of that, boss. Call me if you need me.'

'I'll miss your cooking, Biscuter. I'm going to a town which has given no more than a stew, an omelette and a dish of tripe to the gastronomic culture of our country.'

'What omelette?'

'Uncle Lucas's. If the Lorenzo brothers call about the revolving-door patent, tell them to try again in a fortnight.'

The Ramblas were about to start channelling people in search of restaurants and snack-bars. Casual strollers and groups of pensioners were making way for the newspaper kiosks. A slow-moving, garrulous and more cheerful mass of people were shaping up for the gastronomic mysteries concealed in the dark side-streets where new restaurants appeared every day – one more proof of the democratic pluralism made available by the liberation from domestic gastronomic paternalism. At the height of the crisis of patriarchal society, heads of families were out in search of new restaurants, their hearts thumping at the forbidden adventure of a cream sauce with Olot truffles, dishes with tights and black, transparent underwear, four-course oral-genital meals in which the tongue is ready for the polyvalency of aromatic herbs and quick-fried dishes enlivened by bites of pine-kernel.

'Have you got a surprise that will help me leave the city for a while in a really memorable way?'

The pork-butcher on Calle Fernando pointed to a rosé wine:

'It's just come in from Valladolid: a natural rosé.'

'I'll have it with a shellfish risotto.'

Carvalho was drawn to Les Quatre Barres by the 'burnt-garlic angler-fish', but the street was full of idle young whores and the four restaurant tables were about to be taken by Generalitat civil servants, whose reconstruction of Catalonia began with the reconstruction of their own palates. Nor was there any point in going to the Agut d'Avignon, where tables were reserved with as much notice as Jane Fonda gave in booking her civilian flight to the moon. Besides, Carvalho did not want to give the owner the satisfaction of turning away customers, in the manner of an Iranian who gives, withholds or raises the price of oil. And so he preferred to walk to the Boquería, with the aim of making a soup from two kilos of fish and molluscs. Afterwards he picked his car up from the Garduña parking lot and went to have a bacalao at the Pa i Trago eating-house near San Antonio market. There, at least, civilised human beings could breakfast on a capipota with mixed vegetable sauce at nine o'clock in the morning.

Between a fine relic of those legendary pre-war bacalaos from Terranova and a dish of Catalan-style tripe with beans, Carvalho rang Salvatella at the PSUC central committee offices.

'I'm going to Madrid early tomorrow, but I'd like to have a leisurely chat with you. Why don't you come to dinner at my house?'

The man at the other end was very busy that evening. He had to explain the decisions of the last central committee to a suburban branch meeting and then prepare a speech on the new electoral bill that was to be debated in the Catalan *Parlament* in two days' time.

'You can imagine what the branch meeting will be like after Garrido's assassination.'

'I think there's an order of priorities, and a discussion of my activity is now at the top.'

'Of course.'

'I was thinking of making a shellfish risotto, very much like arroz de Arzac.'

'Arzac's made with kokochas.'

'Also with clams.'

'It could be a very interesting risotto. I'll go to the branch meeting and then accept your invitation.'

'We're fated to understand each other.'

He gave Salvatella the directions to his house in Vallvidrera. Without giving time to the woman whose nipples and mascara-hardened eyes urged him to hurry, Carvalho rang his agent and neighbour Enric Fuster.

'Are you interested in supper with a communist?'

'Depends on what it is. Anyway, you know I don't vote communist.'

'Shellfish risotto.'

'Wine?'

'Viña Esmeralda or Watrau, depending on whether you feel young or mature.'

'Young till death.'

'Viña Esmeralda, then.'

'Is the communist from the tedious or the nostalgic faction?'

'The gastronomic faction.'

'They don't know what to do to win votes. I'll come. Dinner-jacket?'

'Dark suit.'

Against all the rules of taste, Carvalho wanted to take leave of the district by consuming a horchata at the best ice-cream parlour in Barcelona, the one in Calle Parlamento. But the metal containers were dry, and the place was as forsaken as a public urinal; the glazed-tile parlour illuminated by the neon light of a dark evening. He started on the Calle de la Cera Ancha, walking between gypsies who had brought their stools and brandy-laced coffee to the bars of the Ronda and the corner of Calle Salvadors. In the 1940s he had watched the same gypsies, or their parents, dancing and generally surviving around the doors of the Bar Moderno or the Alujas – watched them from the balcony of a house constructed in 1846, two years before the *Communist Manifesto*, in a clear gesture of historic optimism on the builder's part. The street divided into the Calle de la Botella and the Calle de la Cera Estrecha, where the Padró cinema had ceased to cater for old people, gypsies and boisterous children and become a kind of film club. How you have changed, Padró of Barcelona! Repopulated with cosmopolitan immigrants, Guineans, Chileans, Uruguayans; boys and girls in flower and marijuana, trying out post-marital, pre-marital and anti-marital relations; counter-cultural bookshops where the nazi Hermann Hesse lies next to a manual of some yogi from Freguenal de la Sierra. Denuded ever since the disappearance of the shady street-traders and Pepa the lottery queen, the district has no heroic remnants other then the Padró fountain; the Romanesque chapel half-hidden between a local school and a tailor's shop, its apse formerly shared by an alcohol merchant and a blacksmith; and the condom shop – La Pajarita – which may be declared a historical monument or building of national interest if Jordi Pujol, president of the Generalitat of Catalonia, grants the request that Carvalho has been thinking of sending one day.

The approach of winter was apparent in the rapid nightfall over the Vallés, while on the other side of Carvalho's house, Barcelona received night on a sea displaying various forms of pollution and an uneven division of the first city lights. Carvalho envisaged a cold journey, a stranger's sojourn in a town where he had never been happy or unhappy and which suddenly appeared in the desolate landscape as a papier-mâché miracle worthy of Las Vegas or Brasilia. While the fish were cooking on the stove and imparting their aromas to the broth, Carvalho furiously washed the clams in a resolute struggle against the sand lurking in their grooves. They seemed more like fruits of the earth than of the sea, especially when they opened in the steam to show the toughness of poor clams, so different from the unwholesome purity of the richer species delicate in both colour and health. By contrast, these clams required teeth, serious chewing, before they divulged the deep flavours hidden in their coarse textures. He heated the rice in a pan of already sautéd onions, strained the fish broth and threw away the residue. Then he filtered the milky bouillon left by the clams and waited for the valves to cool before pulling out their cooked and humanly reduced flesh. Raw molluscs are boundless creatures: only the warmth of death gives them a determinate limit and volume. He prepared a good amount of garlic and parsley. After all these preparations, the meal could be finished as soon as the guests arrived.

He went to his room, took a suitcase from his dream-deep wardrobe and filled it with five changes of clothes, a toilet bag and a bundle of Canary cigars given him by the client before last. Next he examined his pistol and tested the spring on the clasp-knife four or five times. He sprawled on the bed, one eye on the ashes in the fireplace, the other on the ever brighter city lights. He tested his muscular reflexes by seeing if he could jump straight to his feet. Two movements were needed, and so he lay down to try again. He finally succeeded and went up to the bookcase full of empty spaces, collapsed sections and books deformed by lack of support or the asphyxiating pressure of larger volumes. He took down Engels's *The Housing Question*, and one look at 'Part Three: Supplementary Remarks on Proudhon and the Housing Question' convinced him that it deserved the fire. He tore the book in three, fanned the pages out so that they would catch fire more easily, and began to construct a building of twigs and branches on the ruins of one of Engels's most inadequate works. The fire rose like a persuasive tongue, and it suddenly occurred to Carvalho that quite a few days would pass before the ceremony could be repeated. Time would thus work in favour of the passive resistance of his library to being burnt at a punishment velocity proportional to the number of useless and inadequate truths it contained. He decided to allow himself the gratuitous act of burning a book in the fire of no appeal. He did not choose at random, but looked on the shelves of literary pedagogy and criticism in order to surprise an anthology of Castilian so-called erotic poetry by two citizens, Bernatán and García. He convicted them of an excrutiating selection that managed to desex even the last piece of skin lending itself to the most unimaginative eroticism.

The flames swallowed the book with relish, and Carvalho lay down again, satisfied that men of the future could now avoid disorientating information about the erotic customs and abuses of twentieth-century Spain. The telephone rang.

'José Carvalho?'

'Yes.'

'For your own good, we advise you not to act foolishly.'

'You mean the book-burning? Who are you: Bernatán or García? Or maybe Engels?'

'Don't play the clown. Leave the dead in peace, particularly the ones you know. He got what was coming to him. You won't be warned again.'

It was a policeman's voice from a Bardem film – assuming, of course, that Bardem had been allowed to use real policemen. Carvalho poured himself a glass of cold orujo and went to open the door for Enric Fuster.

'Here are some Villores truffles perserved in cognac.'

'What's so special about the truffles from the village of yours?'

'The aroma.'

Fuster rubbed his hands at the glowing fire, and then tapped his temple when he saw the charred frame of the fire-eaten book.

'Have you seen a psychiatrist yet?'

The agent held out a bill for the processing and payment of income tax.

'Haven't you got the wrong client? You mean that isn't Pujol's bill?'

'*Vertumnis, quotquot sunt natus iniquis*, said the great Horace.'

'A word of warning. If you want your bill to be paid, you will have to act as witness to my meeting with a CP big-wig. Whatever happens, you must play the role of witness and then keep as quiet as the grave about what you hear. That's not just a manner of speaking. They've just threatened me over the phone.'

'What have you got yourself into?'

'Garrido's murder. I'm investigating it for the Party.'

'You're coming along, Pepe. You'll end up an extra in one of Le Carré's novels.'

'What do you think of the whole thing.'

'There may be five or six hundred motives for the murder, and a couple of million candidates.'

'A locked room, with all the entrances guarded by stewards. A hundred and forty central committee members, of whom a hundred and thirty-nine could be the murderer. That's all there is to go on. Unless someone slipped in, killed Garrido and left again. The likeliest solution is that the murderer was in the room and used accomplices to fix the lighting.'

'What does the Party say?'

'They refuse to accept that it was an inside murder.'

'Sounds like an English mystery.'

'A typical case of murder in a room locked from inside with no other exit. But in an English mystery, the murdered person is the only one who appears in the room. In our case, he has a hundred and thirty-nine companions. Sounds more like a Chinese or Galician joke than an English detective story.'

Salvatella pressed the bell as politely as he offered Carvalho what, in his view, was a modest yet interesting present: a facsimile of the first issues of *Horizons*, a cultural review published clandestinely under the Franco regime. Carvalho mentally promised to burn it sometime around 1984, along with George Orwell's novel. As they were crossing the gravel yard, he told Salvatella of Fuster's presence.

'Don't worry. He's my partner. I have no secrets from him – professional secrets, that is.'

He stressed the work 'partner' as he was introducing the two guests, and Fuster's faint eyebrows pointed at a Mephistophelean angle behind the loosely balanced spectacles that kept him looking like a Sorbonne student unfairly afflicted with monastic baldness. He had no idea what Fuster and Salvatella discussed as he reheated the rice in the sautéd onion, adding the clam juices and enough fish stock to cover the risotto by a finger's depth. He let the mixture boil for ten minutes, then lowered the heat while continuing to spread the clams over the rice, and finally added a garland of chopped garlic and parsley. In the meantime, Fuster served Salvatella with chilled sherry and almond-stuffed olives. Their conversation covered in great detail the boundary between Castille and Aragon, a privileged slice of the world where Fuster had been born and which he had left to study in Barcelona, Paris and London, in a journey he would have liked to be without beginning or end. For his part, Salvatella asked with great interest about the anti-Catalan features of Valencian nationalism. One would have said he was taking notes, except that his hands were busy holding the glass that Fuster filled with the zeal of a self-important waiter and hunting down the evanescent almond-toothed olives. A little later, he praised the choice of Viña Esmeralda and showed his erudition by mentioning the wine-book written by its producer. He sat truly ecstatic after eating his third forkful of rice in its rich sauce of clams, garlic and parsley.

'It's the antithesis of Valencia-style rice. Simplicity as opposed to baroque,' Salvatella concluded. And Fuster's nodding gave his conclusions a definite stamp.

'Are you communists always communists? Now, for example, while you are digesting a supper I trust you found agreeable?'

'Probably, although not the way you think. I'm here because I am a communist. That is what brought me here. I'm happy to be with you both. We are joined by a pleasant common experience. The possibility of conversing. But if you start asking me questions about the Party, I'll react as the Party man I am.'

'And you will say what you think is in the Party's interests.'

'The Party is interested in finding Garrido's murderer. It was an act against the Party, the working class and democracy. So there is no conflict between what you want to know and what I ought to tell you, although I warn you that I can't be as useful as my PCE comrades. It's a sister-party of ours, but still another party. It corresponds to different realities.'

'Suppose it was a crime of passion: a personal vendetta, for example. Or suppose it was a political crime. Why? What for?'

'To blacken the Party; to leave it without its historical leader of the last forty years or so. Does that seem petty to you?'

'It doesn't seem enough unless it was, as you say, the first move in a process of destabilisation to change the political system. That's assuming it was the work of the right. If that was not the aim, then it seems an act out of all proportion. Senseless. You're not a threat to the right for the moment. You're a potential or latent threat, but they don't need to wipe you out. You're not even an alternative

26

government.'

'You underestimate us,' Salvatella said. 'We may not be so important in numbers, but we are in qualitative terms. When a dictatorship comes to an end, the only really organised forces are those which have systematically fought against the dictatorship. In the case of Spain, that means the communists. We're indispensable, then, in any left-wing strategy or any process of democratic consolidation. Quite naturally, the socialists are growing on votes that correspond to "invertebrate" social tendencies. Our votes correspond to "vertebrate" social tendencies. It's harder and, in the short term, less profitable to vote for us: it requires a higher level of political consciousness and greater capacity for political action. Besides, you shouldn't forget that we support and influence the main trade-union force in the country.'

'For the moment.'

Salvatella cheerfully accepted Fuster's qualification.

'Okay, for the moment. Union elections have been announced, and there will undoubtedly be a fierce struggle between the workers' commissions and the UGT.'

'They could have tried to kill Garrido in the street or to discredit him by whipping up a campaign or causing problems in the Party. It wouldn't be the first time. Why go for an assassination, which puts the whole country on the brink of the abyss? Why a scenario that puts the blame on the Party as a whole?'

'Have you read today's papers?'

'I've glanced at them.'

'You should look at the Madrid press, which is directly linked to political and economic pressure-groups. They already take it as proven that the communists are to blame. "Communist Patricide" – that's the exact title in *Ya*, as you'd expect from the paper of the Church and the right-wing Christian-Democrats. *ABC*, holding a candle for banking capital and the royal household says "Settling of Accounts in the Central Committee". And what about political trend-setters around the palace? Well, *Cambio 16* headlines with "The Struggle for Power". *El País* has a well-known ex-communist on its editorial staff and did attempt a rational account of the events. But it could not refrain from morbid insinuations between the lines: "Growing Opposition to Garrido in the Party".'

'Was it growing?'

'Garrido was subject to argument but also beyond it.'

'Like the Pope in Rome.'

'Or like the general secretary of PSOE, or the chairman of the UCD, the SPD or the leader of the British Conservative Party. Leaders are not arbitrary creatures of fashion or destiny. They stem from a process of natural selection corresponding to each party's needs.'

'Were you at the central committee meeting?'

'Yes.'

'Was everything normal until the murder took place?'

'Quite normal.'

'And then? What did you think when you saw Garrido's body on the table?'

'Everything, except that he'd been murdered. Then I formed part of a cordon to prevent people from entering or leaving the room. We checked that everyone there was a central committee member.'

'Go on.'

'Then it began to be your problem.'

'In the late fifties, you were sentenced to more than a hundred years' imprisonment in Barcelona. Released at the end of the sixties. What then?'

I went underground until the Party was legalised in 1977. It's a pretty commonplace story in our party. More than five centuries of imprisonment are brought together at every meeting of the central comittee.'

'Have you always been a professional?'

'Not always. I have been since 1941, when I began to organise partisan activity in Roussillon. I'm a professional in Lenin's sense of the word. My job is to make the revolution. First in the mountains, next in prison, and then on street-corners with the collar of my raincoat turned up. Now I sit behind a table drafting a full-scale amendment to an electoral reform bill.'

'Have you built up any grievances against the Party?'

'Against myself?'

'You're not the only one in command.'

'Above me is the central committee, which decides as a collective body. Neither the executive nor the general secretary does more than interpret the decisions of the central committee.'

'Sounds like a fairy-story.'

'You know there are sometimes witches in a fairy-story.'

Salvatella laughed uncontrollably, as if he were freeing himself from a collective language and recovering his own capacity for speech.

'The communion of the saints, the forgiveness of sins, the redemption of the flesh, everlasting life,' Fuster recited.

'Amen,' Salvatella concluded. It was obvious that he considered the meeting at an end, for he held out his hand, expressed thanks for the meal, and told Carvalho that the 'comrades' would wait for him at the airport at whatever hour he came.

'How will I recognise them? Will Santos be there?'

'The less you're seen with Santos the better. They'll be watching the services from Barcelona to Madrid.'

Carvalho kept his most dramatic news until last.

'They've threatened me over the phone that I'll be killed if I don't drop the case. As far as I am aware, Santos Pacheco, you and I are the only ones who know about our link-up.'

Salvatella took some time to reply.

'They may have followed us.'

'You were more efficient underground.'

'Sometimes. Not always.'

He had read a good deal on the subject; rather like a sick man who devours books on his illness or a death-cell prisoner who eventually knows more than his lawyer about the penal code. No one is more like an ex-communist than an ex-priest. To sin against History or against God – what is the difference? The literature had methodically classified the various possibilities. Koestler or the renegade. Orwell or the apostate. Bukharin or the self-immolator. Carvalho's case would never be the object of study, perhaps because it was typical of periods when History is lived without great dramatisation and people break with their world or steer their life along different axes. Left the Party to become assistant in Spanish at a mediocre Midwestern university. Recruited as a translator for a State Department bureau. Given the offer one day of working on special intelligence missions. Soon saw himself in the mirror as a CIA agent who

29

would travel half-way round the world, accumulate five-year postings and perhaps eventually return home as a pensioner. During interrogations at the Brigada Social headquarters, he never felt himself to be the hero of his own history, but always a part of the machine that had to resist and fulfil its mission so that the machine should not break down. When they hit him, or when Fonseca called across the room 'You deserve to be dropped' as they held him out of the window, he felt secure in his own lack of importance. The cries that came from nearby rooms, if someone opened the door, filled him with a sense of fatality about a situation that left him no possibility of choice. Later, as the police-van was driving him to prison, he took a cigarette from Cerdán and suddenly realised from his handcuffs that he was handcuffed too. A guillotine-like anguish sliced through his wrists. Cerdán was a leader. A promising leader who had assimilated the Party language and allowed the Party to recognise itself in him.

'At least I won't be tried for breaking discipline,' said Carvalho as he slumped on the straw bed in the cell he shared with Cerdán and a Maquinista* worker whose collar-bone had been broken under interrogation.

'Forget all that. It was a misunderstanding.'

'What would you have sentenced me to?'

'These are hard times, Pepe. If you're hard on other people's lack of understanding, you must also be hard on your own.'

The son of a bitch had an answer for everything. Six weeks before the condemnation of Stalin at the Twentieth Congress, he had refuted every single point of Carvalho's critique of Stalinism. Then he forgot his Stalinist past with the speed at which children forget their little sins. Let a hundred flowers bloom! For realism without bound! While Carvalho contemplated the cell ceiling as a continuation of the wall-framed sky and the wall-framed sky as a continuation of the cell ceiling, Cerdán organised a short course of lectures dealing with Ricardo's influence upon Marx. He also explained to the workers how the 'peaceful, nation-wide twenty-four-hour strike' fitted into the fall of fascism or rather the 'assault on the first-level contradiction', as it was fashionable to say at the time. Cerdán spoke through the nose to other priests of the spirit; but when he addressed the working class, he seemed like a primary

* Maquinista: a large engineering factory in Barcelona.

school teacher explaining that a table has four legs or that balls are round objects.

'When I get out, I'll ask to be "released" and perhaps go to work in a factory. Marx said that you cannot understand people's problems if you don't eat their bread and drink their wine. What will you do? A university career seems to me a sign of individualist egoism, of evasive self-centredness. What will you do?'

Carvalho turned his eyes down from the ceiling or sky to watch Cerdán doing his regular morning gymnastics in the tiny space between the heap of litter and the Maquinista worker's wretched bed. As well as doing gymnastics, he ordered books on modern algebra and mathematical logic and started to learn German. He ate nothing that did not contain the necessary protein and vitamins for him to be fit for the 'peaceful, nation-wide twenty-four-hour strike'.

'Imagine it lasts twelve hours. Or thirty-six.'

The Maquinista worker laughed, clutching his stomach with one hand and his collar-bone with the other. But Cerdán merely clenched his teeth in a friendly sort of way – a gesture worthy of recognition and much more agreeable than the unfriendly clenching of the teeth through which he rose to the requisite level of consciousness and launched into a long speech on the identity of the individual, class and historical morality.

'It's not good to spread defeatism among the workers – particularly not here,' Cerdán said in an aside, perhaps in the showers, when the leader turned to the icy jet with the parsimony of a watchmaker.

Afterwards he would dry his short, white, muscular body, topped by a sad, bird-like head cropped in the German style, hunting down every drop of water that could upset his internal thermostat and damage his machine for thought and revolutionary action. He must have had some mysterious influence over his own body, for when he used the bowl shared by the three cell-mates, his shit smelt the least of all and only bothered them with a final whiff of liquorice that Carvalho put down to the cod-liver oil sent by his family to sustain him as a young animal sick with mental plenitude.

'Prison is not a desirable place to be. It doesn't prove your fighting qualities. But it's a necessary experience in the life of a revolutionary, and it has been of great advantage to you.'

'In what way?'

'Your behaviour outside raised people's suspicions. You were

31

even seen one day leaving Via Layetana,* and word came down that you were being watched as a possible informer.'

The bolts and keys, so definitive after roll-call, rang faintly in the back of his memory. While waiting in the prescribed position for a warder to inspect their cell and close the door, Carvalho muttered:

'Go on.'

'I put you in quarantine. I told some comrades to be on their guard, although I added that it could be a mistake. Now it's all cleared up.'

They had known each other for five years, sharing all the anxiety of underground work. The hapless feeling as you left home with a bundle of leaflets and knew you might not return for five or six years. Five years of swapping false-bottomed suitcases, of greeting contacts from abroad and seeing them back across the same border-tunnel, of distrusting everything outside *Mundo Obrero*** and Radio España Independiente. Five years discovering Sartre, Marx, Brassens, Shostakovich, Mayakovski, Lefebvre, Pratolini, Ostrovski, Sholokhov, and so on. When the warder had finished the inspection and locked the door, Carvalho waited for Cerdán to turn round before saying:

'You really are the biggest son of a bitch.'

Cerdán answered with a condescending smile. The kind of smile we use with people who, however much we do for them, will never quite reach our own level. A month later, Cerdán was moved to Burgos, and Carvalho could not avoid a final hug straight out of a Soviet film. Cerdán walked down the corridor with a commendably martial air, even though he had been forced to wear a huge, grey prison-suit stitched by stapler.

In the paper which a stewardess gave him on the flight to Madrid, Carvalho read that Justo Cerdán had been questioned in connection with the murder of Fernando Garrido. There followed a biography of the PCE dissident, now a leader of the radical extra-parliamentary movements and a fierce critic of Garrido's reformism. Although he was not thought to be directly implicated in the assassination, the man once groomed as Garrido's successor

* Via Layetana: location of the Barcelona headquarters of the political police.
** *Mundo Obrero*: newspaper of the Communist Party of Spain.

32

apparently still had a strong influence on broad sections of the Party. It was therefore possible that the murder had involved an inner-Party conspiracy to break the sizeable mandate of a leader judged disastrous by the most left-wing sections of the organisation.

He had been expecting a reception committee headed by some ex-worker turned Party-functionary, but he was actually met by two boys straight out of a punk-dress comedy. If they did not call him 'dad' or 'man' it was not for lack of inclination but because they had cautiously adapted themselves to their assignment from the leadership. It had been necessary to use them in order to throw the Anti-Terrorist Squad off the scent and to transfer any suspicion of the newcomer to the Drugs Squad. The young men tried to behave well and even suggested a bocata in the airport bar in case he had not had breakfast.

'I prefer sharper poisons – ones that work faster.'

Their sense of humour was quite different, separated from Carvalho's by twenty years of linguistic degeneration. So he did not try out any Hollywood dialogue from the thirties or forties, but resorted to the kind of questions asked by a Japanese executive.

'Fermín knows that,' one of them answered.

'No, you'd better ask Fede's cousin.'

'But he's not in Castelló anymore.'*

'Ask him later, when we change cars.'

The Bajaras motorway offered its architectural display to the traveller, condensing ten years of the nation's complete confidence in its architects, such as had never before been granted to any similar priestly group. As it reached the Torres Blancas heights, the car turned sharply right and zigzagged between small vehicles full of mothers who had dyed themselves blonde in order to justify their children's fair complexion.

'Are all the children blonde in Madrid?'

'I don't know why everyone's coming out the same.'

---

* (Calle) Castelló: then the location of the PCE headquarters in Madrid.

'Some contamination.'

'No doubt.'

The car stopped.

'Go into the snack-bar and you'll see a girl sitting reading *Diario 16*. Tell her who you are and she'll go with you.'

The girl was eating a sandwich with a small glass of wine; not at all bothered that she was the only person sitting among a mass of breakfasters.

'Did you have a good trip?'

Their run in the SEAT–850 was the occasion for a pleasant chat about the rain that fell much less often in Madrid than when she had been a young girl. She had nice legs, even if a bit thin, and a fringe allowed her face to begin with two magnificent, ring-shadowed eyes, as plaintive as her thin, Audrey Hepburn figure accentuated by a black-and-lilac dress.

'Which hotel did you book me into?'

'One near the Opera, but I'm not taking you there. Santos is waiting in a private house.'

The main slogan on the walls was: Comunistas, Asesinos.

'The Fuerza Nueva spent the whole night painting those,' she told Carvalho. 'Yes, call me Carmela. Is the traffic this bad in Barcelona? You Catalans have a reputation as better drivers.' It was a long time since anyone had referred to him as Catalan. 'Barcelona's different – like Europe. Isn't that what they say?'

'I didn't think people said that anymore.'

'Oh yes! Particularly if you talk with a Catalan. I don't know why, but they do say it.'

Carmela stopped the car outside a chalet on the Jarama road. She got out, looked right and left, and asked him to follow her through the iron-gate leading into a garden completely covered by the trunk and bare scaffolding of a willow tree. She said a few words to a man with slanting shoulders who was walking up and down the entrance-hall with his hands behind his back. She then climbed a granite stairway, so nimbly that Carvalho had to take two steps at a time to keep up with her. Behind the upholstered, gold-locked door, Santos was waiting together with an old strong-man who eyed Carvalho with the professional suspicion of a sergeant-major.

'Señor Carvalho, may I present Julian Mir, our chief security man. We'll just have a quick chat to fix things for the immediate future. Then Carmela will take you to the hotel, and we'll start to move as soon as you give us word.'

Carvalho wanted to see the scene of the murder, a ground plan of the Party centre, a chart of the seating arrangements at the central committee, and have all available information about everyone present on that day.

'Is that all?'

'That's all for the moment.'

'Before the morning's over, I have to introduce you to the government contact-man between yourself and Fonseca. Nor will it be possible to avoid meeting Fonseca. You'll travel around Madrid in Carmela's car, accompanied by her alone, or so everyone will think. In fact, another car will be following you with two comrades. It'll be the two who met you at the airport. You can't see them from the window, but they're parked up there round the corner. You can contact me or Julian through Carmela, at any time of the day or night. Here, that's for your initial expenses.'

Santos handed him an envelope, and Julian Mir asked him to sign a receipt for fifty thousand pesetas.

'We'll keep you a long way from Party headquarters. Apart from Fonseca's boys, there are at least two or three parallel services sniffing around. We know about them from the government contact-man himself. Nothing can be done to stop them.'

'Those people only stop strike pickets. That's what they're for.'

Carvalho wondered whether Mir's irritability was just a passing mood or part of his usual way of looking at an uncontrollable reality.

'I was threatened over the phone. They didn't say why, but it seems obvious.'

Mir nodded, as if Carvalho's words confirmed his earliest suppositions. Santos closed his eyelids in a gesture of agreement, and it was then that Carvalho noticed how white his hair had become.

'Salvatella told me something about that over the phone.'

'Something? No, he'll have told you all. Who's in the picture about what I'll be doing?'

'The secretariat of the executive committee. That is, six people in Madrid and Salvatella in Barcelona. Apart from Salvatella, who acted as a go-between, none of our comrades in the Catalan leadership has been informed.'

'So?'

'All our phones are tapped, now more than ever.'

'The government?' Mir complained.

'Who knows? The government is more nervous than we are – at least it seems like it. I feel they have tightened up security and put an anti-coup plan into motion. Fernando's murder could be a signal. Anyway, we haven't mentioned your side of things on the phone. They must have followed us: that's the only explanation. When they saw us get in touch with you, they must have guessed what we were up to.'

'Who?'

'If we knew, we might have the answer to Fernando's murder.'

'I warned you,' Mir shook his finger accusingly.

'We took every precaution – just like when we were underground. Not that we thought our mission would remain a secret for long, but we hoped to gain enough time at least for you to reach Madrid without any problems. Don't be too worried. Your escort will be armed. We even have authorisation from the government.'

'This is all going to complicate the economic question.'

Mir looked at him as if he were an exploiter of the working class. Santos, however, kept one of his eyes half-closed, trying to calculate how much Carvalho's life was worth.

'We'll leave that until you present us with the bill. That shows we're confident that we can pay and that you will live to receive the money.'

'I don't know where, but some years ago I read that you were optimistic people.'

Santos did not allow the perfect exit and retorted just as Carvalho was leaving the room:

'Anyway, remember that no one can look after you better than yourself.'

'*Tú*, Carmela, who do you think killed the old man?'

Carmela smiled with relief at her passenger's use of the familiar *tú*.

'Well, I don't know, because we hadn't been killing much lately. Things were getting a bit dull. A real drag, starting with all the par-

36

liamentary stuff. Do you understand?'

The car proceeded down Calle Serrano. The numerous taxi-drivers assisted their advance by banging on their steering-wheel, while with the other hand they conducted a conversation with their fare. The girl's driving was affected by her surfeit of tasks: to show that women are good drivers; to get Carvalho to his hotel as quickly as possible; and to check that the escort-car had not been caught at some traffic lights.

'It's real heavy weather being followed in this town. I'd like them to make an American ganster film in Madrid!'

'Do you work at it full time?'

'Do I look like a professional taxi-driver?'

'No, I mean a Party full-timer.'

'Well, I get thirty-six thousand pesetas a month for full days and occasional nights, with no guaranteed holidays, no benefits and so far no social security. If you call that being a full-timer, I guess I am one. Sometimes I also stick up posters for nothing and lend them the kid.'

'What kid?'

'My son. He can be carried, and I take him along to all the demonstrations in favour of divorce and abortion. So they can see on telly we also have babies when we have to.'

'Does the little one mind?'

'He copes with everything. Like when I take him to a demo against squid rolls and what he likes are frankfurters. No, but seriously . . .'

She turned back to the realm of historic responsibilities. With her grave eyes and a voice like that of the tsar's messenger, Mikhail Strogov, she said to Carvalho:

'I work at the central committee, and I've been given this job so that everything should look more normal.'

She was wearing some whitish tights, as if to flesh out her almost over-slim legs, or to cover blue-veined branches like those which showed through the translucent skin stuck to her cheek-bones. Almost forcibly stuck, one would say, so that room should remain for her well-painted excessive eyes, swallowing up an inevitably small nose, and a pair of cheeks which, when she smiled, had to ask the mouth's permission before leaving a thick furrow tight as a bow string down to lips that were continually being moistened by a small tongue. A shop-window full of cheeses replaced Carmela's face. At the end of the street, the square on the right was dominated by the squat torso and tall legs of the Opera building, one shoulder higher than the other and undoubtedly narrow in compass.

'Escalinata,' Carvalho muttered as the car reached the steps leading to Calle Escalinata.

'You know it?'

'I had some friends there many years ago. A painter, his patroness and her daughter, just arrived from Egypt.'

'It's getting interesting. Was the girl a mummy?'

'No, she was a flamenco dancer. She specialised in sevillanas, which were much liked in Egypt.'

Lost in thought, Beethoven showed not the slightest intention of waving from the plaster perch where he stood like an animal in a music-shop window. The road opened on to the Plaza de Oriente, with its enveloping Goya-like skies, but only for an instant. For Carmela then circled the back of the Opera and reached the square, pointing her car towards the billboard for *Kramer versus Kramer*.

'There's your hotel. To start with, we booked you a room for a week. It's under the name of Selecciones Progreso, Ltd, not the Party. Look, it's very difficult to wait for you here in the car.'

'Don't wait for me.'

'Not on your life! You're my responsibility, and anyway they're following us.'

'I'd like to visit the memorial chapel.'

'There's no chapel, pal. The Party is said to have priests and even bishops, but we don't yet set up memorial chapels for general secretaries.'

'I'll just drop off my suitcase. Do a trip round the block.'

The Hotel Opera blended the neatly bricked dignity of an English or Dutch hotel with the historical collage of the square. The exterior did not have the somewhat dusty ochre of Aragon brickwork, but resembled the new houses in Amsterdam, Rotterdam or Chelsea which seek to simplify volume without losing the visual rhythms of traditional architecture or falling into the sharp visual intolerance of concrete. The hotel formed a corner that offered apologies to declining neo-classicism and particularly the hunchbacked Opera palace, which looked more like a storehouse for Vopo electric truncheons on the Unter den Linden. He left his case with a bellboy, who seemed rather unsure of the day ahead, and returned to the warmth of the car and Carmela.

'There was going to be trouble if you didn't come back. Those two saw me set off round the block and started flashing their lights. I told them to get lost. They could have thought a bit more or have had some respect for another's initiative. So, it's to the memorial chapel, as you put it?'

'Where is it?'

'We didn't have anywhere suitable on hand. Nearly all our places are in blocks of flats – you can imagine the rumpus there would have been. So we've been given the entrance-hall to the Cortes. I'll drop you off and wait in the Plaza de Casanova, just on the corner of Carrera de San Jeronimo. But don't stand in the queue, because you won't get through in time and we have two appointments this morning.'

She circled the Opera again and drove into the heavy, Frenchified Plaza de Oriente. As a check to French stylistic dominance, the street separating the edges of the palace and the square had been called Calle Bailén, its function being to watch, question and cancel out the palace. The route along the Gran Vía, Alcalá and the Paseo del Prado displayed all the normality of city life, hardly affected by the police jeeps and armoured coaches parked at every major intersection on the Plaza España, the Callao and the Red de San Luis.

'A lot of cops, eh?'

'They've formed a ring round the Cortes in case some extremists try to stir things up.'

Carvalho got down and walked uphill towards the dark lions that framed the entrance to the Cortes palace. He kept parallel to the line of mourners forced to hug the façades at the constant urging of the police. A sergeant caught him by the arm and took him to one side, aggressively insisting that he could not remain in front of the staircase but must either join the queue or go away. From the pavement on the other side of the street, he saw the queue as an animal moving compact into the palace and leaving with its skeleton shattered, as if something had happened inside the building to break its cohesion. Nothing missing: not the tears, nor the stiff posture of scornful yet curious onlookers, not the semblance of being there in passing or by chance.

'What have they got there?' asked one sharp-eyes with enormous hair-filled nostrils.

'Communion hosts.'

He lowered his nostrils and drew his teeth back into his mouth.

An official black car stopped and let out an ex-minister of culture. All around were microphones and hovering notebooks from which Señor de la Cierva's mighty senatorial head emerged; probably declaring that, in spite of all the political rivalry, he still recognised the great loss.

'Who's that?' asked sharp-eyes, this time in the hope of really finding out and regaining the friendly attention of the caustic stranger.

'A ghost from the past.'

'You should say: "I've come to pick up my passport – Señor Plasencia is expecting me." They'll take you straight up.'

Anyone with the slightest knowledge of its functions, past, present and future, is always impressed in passing through the gates of the State Security Office. But if the guard clicks his heels at the statement, "I've come to pick up my passport – Señor Plasencia is expecting me," then a royal mantle immediately falls over one's shoulders and the halberdiers seem to shout the echoing announcement: Pepe Carvalho . . . Pepe . . . Carvalho. Looking over his glasses, Señor Plasencia rubbed his chillblained hands and led him away from the bustling offices, where clerks quizzed the sports pages of the morning papers and someone was asking: 'Do we have diplomatic relations with Outer Mongolia?'

'Outer Mongolia. That's all I wanted to hear!' Plasencia grumbled peevishly as he looked up at the little lift descending with asthmatic slowness.

'Do you know where Outer Mongolia is?'

'Between the Soviet Union and China.'

Plasencia gazed with admiration and opened the lift door for him.

'Very few people would have been able to say that.'

Plasencia watched him sideways, with a huge eye trained and deformed by suspicion. Carvalho was obviously not a Mongol or a Chinese. Maybe Soviet? As far as Plasencia was concerned, Outer Mongolia had for years been a prohibited entry in Spanish passports, a country forbidden by His Excellency, who must have had good reasons. It seemed to him that people had no right to know anything about a forbidden country, and someone who even knew where it was could not be quite honest. They came out into a wide, yellow-tiled corridor with green paper on the walls and almost no doors. There they were met by a sluggish-looking man with pointed ears and a sack of potatoes under each eye. Plasencia slightly bent his head towards Carvalho, and the other man eyed the merchandise as if obliged not to believe what he saw.

'Carvalho?'

'Yes.'

'Your identity card.'

'I've already seen it.'

'Four eyes are better than two.'

Feeling upset with his colleagues, the man with the rings under his eyes pored over all the details at the speed of an East Berlin Vopo or a barely literate child.

'Your mother's name?'

'Ofelia.'

'Was she foreign?'

'No. Galician.'

'Doesn't sound Galician to me.'

After Plasencia grunted and left them, the other man finally relaxed.

'Follow me,' he said, turning his back on Carvalho and continuing along the corridor up to a window that looked onto a peeling wall of an inner yard or alleyway. Just as he seemed on the point of throwing himself out of the window, the functionary half turned through a door that led straight to a short flight of stairs. They arrived in a square-shaped room where the lift was the only door. They stood inside and the man pressed the lowest button of all. Carvalho calculated that they would be going down to the last of the underground storeys. The lift opened on a reception room furnished and carpeted in the style of an inter-war *wagon-lit*. Everything smelt of dampness, and the passage of time was discolouring the joints of every object as if it was there that the general decomposition first signalled itself. An usher took Carvalho's particulars, while his companion with ringed eyes pointed to a young man with a look of a television announcer, waistcoated, lacquered in both hair and smile. When someone opened the tall, leather-padded door,

Carvalho saw that he had reached his destination. Santos stood up at almost the same time as the minister of the interior, and another waistcoated young man was introduced as the assistant of some obscure deputy chief executive of the government presidium. The minister fired the opening shot: he was the first to be concerned about the speediest possible clarification of what had happened. Señor Pérez-Montesa de la Hinestrilla had been personally appointed by the head of government to form a tripartite body that would assure closer collaboration among the government, the Communist Party and the minister of the interior. Pérez-Montesa de la Hinestrilla gave a cordial smile, as if he were trying to sell a Ford Granada or a country house in Torremolinos. Santos gave a resumé of the situation in the most impeccable end-of-congress style. The three looked at Carvàlho, waiting to hear what he would say.

'It might be useful for us to make a list of those who did not kill him.'

The waistcoated young man burst out laughing, while the minister of the interior took a long time to understand and Santos bowed his head in dejection. Such a stab of humour had not been expected. A prominent Adam's apple began to speak above a tweed waistcoat:

'The government has naturally been considering all kinds of possibilities. Although it is prepared to accept the results of any other investigation such as yours, it intends to push the process of its own right through to the last minor detail, however disturbing this may be. For what is at stake is no longer just the government's credibility, but the credibility of the democratic process and of the state based on autonomous regions.'

Carvalho had read a newspaper article which suggested, not without truth, that Madrid writers were keen on reviving the baroque. It was a mental problem reflected even in government executives.

'Which possibility is the government considering more than others?'

Pérez-Montesa de la Hinestrilla drew in air, sharpening his nose and whole face to a point. He then plunged into two sheets of woolly talk and finally concluded that the government was considering no more than the traffic on Castellana Avenue. The minister of the interior fully corroborated the facts:

'No more, no less.'

Santos tried to apply historical materialism to the concrete situation and dialectical materialism to the situation in the abstract. Carvalho grasped this when he saw the old communist squinting in silent exasperation. Carvalho was told that he could depend on Pérez-Montesa de la Hinestrilla and Superintendent Fonseca at any time, really at any time.

'Why did you pick Fonseca?' asked Santos.

'He's our best officer, and the best officers are needed for the most difficult cases.'

The minister of the interior thrust forward his face and shoulders with a dissuasive power apparent in his shiny, smouldering eyes.

'I won't allow my officers' competence to be challenged, nor my own competence in selecting them.'

'The challenge won't come from me. But Fonseca . . . '

The minister struck the table with sufficient self-control that no one could say he banged it.

'Santos. We've talked about this a thousand and one times. Just as many of us have forgotten about it, so you ought to do the same. Fonseca is our best officer.'

Pérez-Montesa de la Hinestrilla acompanied them to a corner of the reception room and was eager to exchange impressions away from the minister's presence. Speaking in a low voice, the young civil servant tried to excuse the minister's rigidity:

'He's a very nice guy, but a little rusty. If only we had a thousand like him. He was in the Blue Division* and, take my word for it, he's more anti-communist than God himself. But he's a democrat. His feelings are those of a democrat, and he'll play the democratic game right to the end. As I told you yesterday, Pepe, you can trust us. Things are in good hands.'

Pepe went up to Santos, who was deep in an ocean of perplexities. Then Santos, Carvalho and the man with rings under his eyes went into the lift.

'Who's the guy with the waistcoat?'

'We'll talk about it later.'

They passed through other hands and along other corridors until they were left alone outside an office marked 'State Security Brigade.'

---

* Blue Division: a special division sent by the Franco regime to fight alongside the Germans on the Eastern front during the Second World War.

'I'll leave you here. It's too much for me to meet Fonseca. I'll be in the Continental after lunch so that we can go over everything.'

'Who's the guy with the waistcoat?'

'One of fifty thousand democrats the UCD wheeled out overnight to fill state positions. He's the son of I-can't-remember-who and was in touch for a bit with our Party at university. In this city, guys like him come by the thousand.'

'Madrid is a city of a million waistcoats.'

Fonseca stood up behind his powerful table and came to meet Carvelho with one small hand outstretched. Carvalho barely brushed it, weighing perhaps the work of time on that discoloured, straight-edged countenance with its lidless eyes and darting pupils.

'How are things, Señor Carvalho?' Whenever he stopped speaking, he pursed his lips as if to ask pardon, or perhaps just compassion, for something or other. 'Sánchez Ariño, my main assistant. The great Dillinger, as he's known here. I'm sure you already know all about him. And this sprightly Andalusian is Pilar.'

Sánchez Ariño waved a playful greeting across the room with his fingers, while the sprightly Andalusian woman managed to form a smile through a crust of make-up and rouge, at the risk that her mascara-covered eyelashes would become stuck forever.

'Your reputation has travelled ahead of you.' Fonseca was now looking at him with his arms folded over a small pot-belly that looked like a tumulus on his otherwise thin body. 'The famous Pepe Carvalho.'

He continued to look at him as if begging his autograaph.

'You are much more famous than me.'

'Mine is ill-fame. Just because I do my duty. My vocation has always been to be a policeman. I'm one of those who believe in a vocation, and I completely agree with what Marañón said on the subject. I had the good fortune to be a disciple of Marañón and Ortega. Don't be surprised. I'm older than I look. The civil war found me in the Complutense. Would you like a drink? A smoke?'

He had the same way of tightly gripping the pocket, in case he changed his mind at the last minute and decided it was more useful to leave the prisoner frustrated. This time, however, he was serious. And when Carvalho said that he only smoked cigars, Fonseca offered the packet to Sánchez Ariñó instead. Without taking his bulging eyes off Carvalho, the elderly adolescent waved no with a hand bearing a shiny golden ring in the shape of a Comanche's head. Fonseca checked his initial impulse to sit across the table and beckoned Carvalho into one of the leather armchairs next to a window facing the Puerta del Sol. Sánchez Ariñó kept to Carvalho's right, seated or reclining on a corner of the table that supported the sprightly Andalusian's typewriter.

'Pilar,' Fonseca said gently without looking at her. Pilar rose and walked out of the room, leaving behind the scent of magnolia essence that saturated her abundant flesh beneath a lilac dress and a cover of loose flowing hair dyed jet-black.

'You must be in a hurry, and so are we. I must confess that I was against the idea of a parallel investigation from the very beginning. The minister tried to persuade me by referring to the circumstances. What circumstances? you will doubtless ask. Or perhaps you won't.'

'Which do you prefer? That I ask or don't ask?'

'Don't let's get sidetracked. That folder, the third one from the right, is concerned just with you. And you know who I am. If I agreed to your investigation, it was so that no one could ever say Fonseca was guided by clichés or *a priori* judgements. I'm a professional. I used to persecute reds, and now I do the same with yellows. Tomorrow, it'll be the crimsons.'

'Or back to the reds.'

Fonseca and Sánchez Ariñó exchanged glances. The superintendent leant towards Carvalho and spat out in a crumpled voice:

'That's a good one! They've already got the country by the balls, and they won't let go this time.' He nervously pointed to his flies. 'Times are changing.'

Fonseca smiled serenely. His features softened, as if they bore no relation to the contorted face of a few seconds before. He was the same as ever: a great play-actor who could hit someone in the face and then immediately kneel down and ask forgiveness, begging that he should no longer be forced to act in that way.

'I'd like to know how far the investigation has got.'

'We're making a systematic comparison of the various statements made by central committee members. District police officers recorded them that very morning at the scene of the crime, although top people from the State Security Office were also present.'

'Yourself?'

'Me? No. I was called in later. I followed the course of the investigation from this office. I don't meddle where I'm not asked. I've been that way all my life.'

In 1940 the young Ramón Fonseca Merlasca had entered into contact with the underground organisation of the Communist Party of Spain. No one had tried to attract him, but he was well received because he had been an active FUE member when at university in 1934. He showed great courage on his first Party assignments, in conditions where the slightest delay could mean a firing-squad. In 1941 he gradually moved up to a high position in the Madrid network: he was given responsibility for contacts with abroad and even proposed for the district committee. The growing underground activity made the government nervous at German demands for an immediate clean-up and allied embassy pressure for information about repressive measures. Fonseca could have thrived in the Party and reached the central leadership, but he obeyed his new instructions to demolish as much as possible of the Madrid apparatus. His face would never be forgotten by the men and women who paid with decades of imprisonment for the success of this operation. Those who had paid with their lives had, of course, no memories left. When, many years later, the Party spread throughout Spain and had to face regular police crack-downs, many recognised Superintendent Fonseca as that infiltrator who quoted from Lenin's *What is to be Done* or *State and Revolution* with the fluidity of an expert and the conviction of a fanatic. Now it was an ageing, tired fanatic who kept his eyes on Carvalho, trying to make out his code of behaviour and to guess what he was thinking about Fonseca himself. A smile of mockery mixed with self-pity was dancing on his lips:

'They did it themselves. There's not the slightest doubt. It's a struggle for power.'

'A struggle for power in a party broken by the murder? That makes no sense.'

'They'll soak it all up. In fact, they no longer knew what to do with Garrido. He was a symbol for people over fifty or sixty, but he was meeting more and more opposition among younger ones. If that wasn't the motive, then it was a family-type settling of accounts in the KGB. Because it is plain for all to see that Garrido was a KGB agent.'

'What about his anti-Soviet attitudes?'

'Look, Señor Carvalho, I'll let this little kid explain all about that. Come here, Sánchez, and get going on what we've talked about so many times.'

'What for?'

'What do you mean? You'll understand once you start talking. We have to convince our friend here. Everything has to be explained to him. Now, dialogue! Action! Aren't we in a full democracy?'

'Come on, this is pointless,' he motioned to the file on Carvalho.

'He's referring to your past. Sánchez has this theory that once a red, always a red. Give the gentleman a chance. He has an interesting life-history.'

Sánchez Ariñó sighed in resignation, straightened himself and began to pace up and down.

'The KGB has a special department of anti-Soviet propagandists who are quite capable of speaking in public if such a demonstration serves the interests of the USSR. In Italy and Spain, for example, and all the countries of eurocommunism or some such euro shit. The communists who make public declarations against the USSR do so because it is not in the USSR's interests to give the impression that pro-Moscow communism is being established in Europe or any advanced capitalist country. It counts on capitalism being so thick as to believe the divergences and to accept the euro-alternative. It will then be able to reap the fruits – for instance, a non-aligned European foreign policy. All that's ABC. I don't see why you made me go on, don Ramón.'

'Let's suppose your TV scenario is right. Why bump off Garrido when he's playing so well?'

'Something must have gone wrong. Maybe he started to believe it, and the murder was a way of destroying both the dog and the rabies. The whole party is affected, deprived of authority, and the Soviet Union can either manipulate what's left or use a more docile political platform.'

'Is that your initial assumption or the result of an investigation you have not even begun?'

'It's theory,' Fonseca smiled, striking his knees with both hands. 'The investigation will be practice.'

47

'What about other motives? A personal score, a provocation by the right wing or by some secret service, not necessarily Soviet.'

'It's possible. You see? You, too, start from presupposition. It's your theory. And your theory frees the Party and communism from any blame. You're beginning the investigation with a clear political bias. Your investigation will be a mere practical ratification of your theories. In fact, you can do it more easily than I can. You'll show your little masters to be in the right, while I have to produce conclusions that satisfy the government, the opposition and God knows who else. For democracy has to be saved, and you can't screw democracy. Obviously not.'

Sánchez Ariñó let out a high-pitched laugh, which seemed to escape through a chink in his dignified bearing.

'What are you laughing at, eh?'

But Fonseca succumbed to a similar attack, wrapping his mouth with a hand that contained all the fire of suppressed laughter.

'Look, you're making me laugh. What will this man think? That it's all fun and games?'

'Well, chief, you say some strange things . . .'

They split their sides until tears came into their eyes. Carvalho stood up and went towards the door.

'There's one other thing.'

Fonseca had conquered his mirth in the middle of the last joke. As he turned round, Carvalho saw him gravely, and in a mockingly superior way, hold out a sheet of paper full of notes and telephone numbers.

'I want you to be able to reach me at any time of the day. So that no one can say afterwards . . .'

'Is it true that shots have been fired outside the Cortes?'

'Move on, madam, I know nothing about it.'

Carvalho overheard the exchange as he was leaving the State Security Office. When he asked Carmela the same question in her car, she merely said 'yes' with her eyes.

'Not in the Cortes itself, no. But there were shots in the Plaza de Canalejas. From a car and in the air. Trying to create atmosphere. It happened yesterday in four or five parts of Madrid. And this morning, some toughs were knocking people about in Malasaña and the literature faculty. Have you seen this?'

She handed him a copy of *El Heraldo Español*. The leader of Fuerza Nueva stated: 'He who lives by the sword shall die by the sword . . . The crimes of a criminal ideology are turning against those who hold that ideology.'

'There are huge blasts in every paper. The Socialists have brought out a special issue of *El Socialista*. Not an inch is wasted: there's a poisonous eulogy of Garrido which argues that he unsuccessfully tried to democratise the Party and that he could not prevent the trade-union movement from growing more radical and escaping its control. He was therefore a victim of the contradiction between desire and reality. They're after us. They're all after us.'

It has been said that the worst thing that can happen to someone with persecution mania is to be persecuted in reality. Carvalho tried to work out how many years Carmela had been a Party activist. It couldn't have been very many, and yet the whole catacomb culture had rubbed off on her, perhaps to the musical accompaniment of rock culture, itself at home in cellars and darkness.

'Where do you want to eat? I've heard you have posh tastes.'

'Take me to some bars.'

'Are you serious?'

'Serious.'

'Okay. We can either do Argüelles or stay around here. Calle Echegaray and all that.'

'Let's get out of this area. I've seen a lot of it already.'

Carmela parked on a zebra crossing at the Plaza del Conde del Valle de Suchil. She pushed her glasses back and struck out along Calle Rodriguez de San Pedro.

'What would you say to stuffed onion?'

'Stuffed with what?'

'Meat. They're doing some at La Zamorana. You can also have very good mincemeat there. Then we can try some kidneys at Ananias.'

'To whet our appetite. But we'll have to eat seriously after that.'

'My stomach's about the size of a stuffed onion.'

'That's your problem.'

Carvalho paid superficial attention during their quick prowl around the bar-cum-restaurants of Argüelles. In order to select a restaurant for the ceremony of eating, Carmela referred to some notes she kept in her bag. Casa Ricardo? Know almost nothing about it. In fact, I consider I have already eaten and drunk. Carvalho was relentless until he sat before a plate of blood-sausage followed by tripe in the shade of a carafe of Noblejas wine.

'I don't understand how you can fit all that in. After what you've eaten already. Three sausages are enough to fill a whole gullet. Where do you put them?'

'I do it in order to forget.'

'You'll say that to anything.'

Can a man be wrong if he acts according to his conscience? Despite the sweet taste of the tripe, Carvalho concluded that the question deserved some thought. His eyes returned to the equestrian form of an aggressive businessman, who was browbeating three shocked provincial representatives with the weight of the evidence.

'You say to me, if I reduce the staff, you'll be on the street with unemployment benefit that will sooner or later come to an end. And what will you do then? You've told me what you think, and now I have to consider it in the light of my knowledge.'

'It's just that . . .'

'Let me finish. I weigh it in my mind. Brrmm, brrmm, brrmm. My conscience starts to turn the thing round and round. I know all about it or, okay, maybe I don't but I can imagine it. And my conscience tells me: cut down on the staff, because if you don't, Macario, it'll all be over and you'll be forced to close down. I ask you: which is worse? Bad for a few and good for many, or vice versa?'

'Seen like that, of course . . .'

'Bad for a few. And my conscience tells me a lot more. There's a process of natural selection: the strong survive, the weak go under. How many bread manufacturers have shut down? None. How many textile manufacturers? A hell of a lot. Bread is needed every day. Textiles are only needed now and then, and it's sometimes cheaper to import them.'

'With respect, Señor Macario, the point is that Catalonia is collapsing.'

'Of course!' Macario agreed, as if all the effort of his reasoning had been leading to this conclusion.

'The old guy's a bit ridiculous, eh?' Carmela whispered.

Carvalho was still turned towards the group, and Macario realised that he had aroused the interest of an attentive diner.

'We've reached the hour of truth,' he said, raising his voice. 'If it's necessary to join the Common Market, then so be it. But we're not all going to join, of course not.'

'Of course not.'

'Of course not.'

'Of course not. Only those who reach the gates in good competitive condition will be able to join. What do you manufacture? Watches. We don't need any: we buy them from the Swiss and Japanese. Naturally. If the Swiss and Japanese make the best watches, why should we make our own?'

He beamed a complicit smile at Carvalho, and the detective was so overwhelmed by the objective facts that he smiled in return.

'Or lounge suites,' Carvalho said aloud.

Macario weighed the pros and cons of this outside intervention and decided to take it in.

'Or lounge suites. What would we do with our own?'

'Maybe they could ... ' the Valencian representative still resisted.

'No suites.'

'That's right,' Carvalho confirmed from his table.

'Take another example, however: blood-sausages. Why should blood-sausages not be well made and sent to conquer Europe? I've said it before. You have to get off the beaten track.'

Carvalho decided to break off his familiarities with Macario and turned back to face Carmela. She was bewildered.

'Why, you're a right old yob! You can just sit chatting with that guy, as cool as a cucumber!'

'I quite like after-dinner philosophers. In every human being there's something of the *ABC* Sunday columnist, and after-dinner chat helps to bring out the repressed creativity. Shall I ask him whether our fritters have a future in the Common Market?'

'If you do, I'll walk out. This will end in hospital.'

'You've got to help people with their digestion.'

Rather bemused by the stranger's sudden loss of interest, Macario was now talking politics in a lower voice.

'We can't go on like this – we must recover a sense of authority. All politicans are the same.'

51

Carmela stood up first and walked ahead of Carvalho. The detective leant towards Macario's table and wished him a good meal. Macario could not quite bring himself to stand up or offer him a drink, for Carvalho was no longer paying him the slightest attention.

He had seen the murder-room on television, but in reality it seemed much more spacious, full of corners and alternative paths from *a* to *b*. The presidium table, measuring no more than sixty centimetres, stood on a small platform. The murderer must have moved and struck with a precision that seemed impossible in pitch darkness.

'With the skill and precision of an expert. It's the work of a commando, someone specially trained to use a knife in just that way.'

Santos and Mir had called together the central committee members living in Madrid, as well as the stewarding force present on the day of the murder. Carvalho asked them to sit or stand in the places that they had occupied the previous Saturday.

'Do the older members always sit in front?'

'Yes. It's a question of hearing. They don't trust microphones – what can you do? But it's also a question of communist education. You can't read the papers in the front rows, as some of them do at the back.'

Mir had got his answer in first. But that did not deter Santos Pacheco.

'That was just a joke about the papers. They also sit in front as a mark of their trust, of their historical proximity to the leadership. You can undersand them. Things aren't so simple.'

'If you say so. But some take a nap at the back and even start snoring.'

'Don't make a mountain out of a mole hill.'

'Ask them if they'd like to add anything to their police statements.'

Santos turned to the central committee members, who were spread about like sad-eyed schoolchildren.

'This gentleman is an expert in such matters – I mean in criminal investigation.' He hesitated, as if the criminal did not sound strong enough. 'Well, he's here to help us, and anything you can remember that doesn't appear in your police statement would be very useful to him and to us.'

No one said anything. They all looked at one another across the distances imposed by the missing members scattered throughout Spain.

'Let him ask us questions,' said the voice of a typical jumping-jack from the rear of the room. 'Surely he knows what he wants to know; we don't. I, for one, feel empty after making the statement.'

The others nodded. Carvalho took two steps forward and swallowed the irony flickering in his smile as he thought how, in very different circumstances, he had once dreamt of addressing the central committee.

'The loss of electricity lasted three minutes – precisely the length of time required for the hotel staff to put in a new fuse. Even if he'd had five minutes, the murderer would have had to move at record speed: leave wherever he was, reach the platform, guess the position of the heart, plunge the knife in and return to his starting point. Did anyone hear a noise? Or even notice a movement of air as someone passed? Either the murderer managed to slip into the room somehow, or he got up from the tables. And since he had so little time, he must have run very hurriedly in the space between the tables.'

'There was a lot of larking around when the lights went out,' said one of the old men in the front row. 'Garrido himself was cracking jokes, and there was a lot of bustle apart from the usual laughter and chattering. I doubt whether anyone could have spotted any movement in the room.'

'But if the murderer was sitting at one of these tables, his immediate neighbour or others around him must have noticed when he got up or moved.'

The jumping-jack intervened again.

'Sense perception is predetermined. That is, if the goal of perception had been to capture such a movement, it would have done so. But we all had our minds, first on the darkness, and then on what Garrido was saying.'

'Comrade, you take for granted that the murderer was one of us.' This was the half-question, half-complaint of a little man more furrowed than the land he must have spent much of his life cultivating.

'I'm nobody's comrade. Let's get that straight to begin with.'

'It's true,' Santos came in. 'I thought it was already clear. The gentleman is a professional hired by the Party. That doesn't mean we should not fully co-operate with him.'

'My dear gentleman hired by the Party . . . ' The others laughed as the little man stopped, sarcasm oozing through every wrinkle in his skin. 'I'll repeat what I said. You take it for granted that the murderer was here among us, that he was one of us.'

'Prepare yourselves for the worst, my friend.'

Carvalho went to the door and opened it. Two stewards were standing just outside.

'Were you here?'

'A little further away – here.' They moved back a few steps.

'But as soon as the lights went, we moved instinctively to the door to see whether they had also gone off inside.'

'Did you open the door?'

'Yes. We saw it was dark and closed the door again. Then my mate asked the people at the bottom of the stairs to find out what was happening.'

'You're sure you closed it again?'

'Quite sure.'

'It would be more normal to leave the door of a dark room open . . . '

'Mir had ordered us to keep the door closed. So that it would be hard for anyone to go in or out. He always said the same thing.'

'Why make it hard for people to go out?'

'Because someone would always take the chance to go for a smoke. It wasn't allowed in the room.'

Carvalho closed the door and faced the central committee again.

'Unless the stewards are lying, no one came from outside. If they are lying, then they are assuming direct responsibility for the crime – after all, they could just have said they didn't remember whether the door was closed or not. Now, it has to be established whether you were the only ones there. Was everyone present a member of the central committee?'

'Yes, I can vouch for that,' Santos said. 'We take a list; that is, I personally take a list of those who attend, and of those who only come for part of the time, leaving later for justifiable reasons usually connected with political work. Once the TV men had left, everyone there was a central committee member.'

'Could someone have come in with the TV men and stayed behind?' asked a woman in her fifties who looked as if she was the mother of twelve children.

'Impossible,' Mir asserted. 'Four came in and four went out. And after they left, I shut the door and went to my place.'

'The mystery of the closed room,' said the jumping-jack, as if announcing a film.

'You said it. No doubt you realise that the mystery of the closed room only exists if we believe that people can pass through walls. And I'm sure you're the least inclined to believe in such things.'

'We've got everything. There are plenty of Christians who are for the socialism you can find around here.'

They contained their laughter, feeling that they were violating the period of mourning.

'We cannot accept that the murderer was one of us. That's what they want. They want to demoralise us. They want to sow mistrust in our ranks. Has the place been properly checked? Is there no other possible exit?'

'There's an emergency exit that can be easily opened from inside, but in fact it is locked from outside. The most it adds is that the murderer could have escaped; but it was apparently not in his interest to escape, because he would have identified himself in some way.'

'It can't be accepted,' said the man of furrowed brow.

'Aranda,' said the jumping-jack, quick as a flash, 'don't be irrational. I'm tempted to think the same as you. But facts are facts. And facts are more stubborn than ideas.'

'It can't be accepted. And I blame you for calling in a professional to solve the case. It's a political case, and it must have a political solution; amongst ourselves, for the whole Party.'

'We can get an investigator who'll say you're right and prove that the murderer is the devil or the Holy Ghost. He'd save the Party, but dialectical materialism would have gone out of the window.'

'Words, just words! There are a lot of great talkers around here,' replied the man of furrowed brow.

'These folders,' Santos said, 'contain transcripts of all the tape-recordings, plus a reconstruction of Garrido's movements from the time he left home to the time he arrived at the hotel and went upstairs. Everything. If necessary, we'll reconvene the whole central committee, but there's a plenum already scheduled for next weekend to elect a provisional general secretary until the Party congress. Can you wait a few days?'

'I can.'

'Maybe you brought away a negative impression from the meeting. We have a special kind of shyness. We don't like our business being aired – it's as if we were still protecting it from repression, as if we still had an underground complex. Besides, we're under obvious social and political attack. It's no longer a question of that crude Francoite anti-communism which even liberal democrats reacted against. There's now a gut anti-communism in our society, animated by people looking for accomplices with their repressive past or afraid of the Party's progressive proposals.'

'Don't keep on. I don't vote.'

'I just wanted . . . '

'This file is enough for me, but I do need to move freely around the city. That girl, Carmela, is very nice, but I already know how to walk on my own.'

'She's at your disposal, not the other way round. Go however you like, but take care. There have been troop movements through Villaverde and San Cristobal de los Angeles. They are tactical manoeuvres designed to make people think twice. No one will say anything about them, but they always happen in times of crisis. The extremists are off the leash. They are hitting out at random and have already attacked two Party centres, in Aluche and Malasaña.'

'What did the police get out of Cerdán's interrogation?'

'The police are looking for an Oswald. Cerdán still has some influence in the Party, particularly among intellectuals and leaders of the trade-union movement. But one would have to be appallingly ignorant of the Party to think that he could lead an internal conspiracy against Garrido.'

'I'd like to speak to Cerdán.'

'That's up to you. His number is in the book.'

'You don't get on well with him?'

'He was a valuable comrade, but he knew too much.'

'When did you realise that he knew too much: before or after he left the Party?'

'A long time before, although perhaps you won't believe me.'

'Who does he hang around with now?'

'Ecologists, radicals, feminists . . . ' Santos opened his arms to indicate anything potentially too broad or alien to himself.

'Cerdán? Are we talking about the same person?'

'Presumably.'

'One personal question. You organised paramilitary squads in the partisan days. I assume you had special training.'

'War was our only special training – the civil war and the Second World War. Only a very small number of Party cadres received higher military education, in theoretical questions, and that was in exceptional cases before the war. Lister, for instance, when he had to leave Spain and take refuge in the USSR.'

'That stab was the work of an expert. The knife should really be stuck in and pulled upwards. But the table and the height of the platform were between the killer and Garrido. What about the weapon?'

'It was shown in all the papers. A Czechoslovak dagger made for special operations. It's used by Czech parachutists, for example.'

'An expert's knife, with a wide, serrated blade. One that will open a way into the chest.'

Santos's eyes quivered, as if the knife were hurting him. Carvalho turned and waved goodbye.

'If you want to see Cerdán,' Santos said, already behind him, 'he'll be at the Antonio Machado bookshop at eight this evening. He's bringing out a book.'

'Are you watching his movements?'

'I just read El País.'

'Am I invited to the funeral? Or aren't there any personal invitations?'

'It'll be at ten tomorrow morning.'

Carvalho found Carmela nervously pacing the pavement and looking again at her watch almost before it had recorded any passing of time.

'At last. I'm in a real jam. I just rang my bloody husband, and he can't fetch the kid from the nursery. I've got to go myself. Do you mind if we stop by the nursery? I'll drop him off at my sister's and then stay with you.'

'I've decided to free myself from you. Santos gave his permission.'

'And what will they say?'

'Are they higher up than Santos?'

'It's a different question. I'll let them know. But you'll be followed.'

'Where is the Antonio Machado bookshop?'

'You want a book? Or is it for the Cerdán thing?'

'I can see everyone in the Party is glued to Cerdán.'

'He's in fashion. He's been arrested, questioned . . . '

'What do you think of him?'

'I think he's a pain in the arse. But I'll go to Machado's. There's going to be a demonstration. Here.' She gave him a telephone number. 'In case I don't make it. I'll be looking after my kid this evening. If you need anything. Do you know where Machado's is? Okay, I'll write down the address. It's very near the Santa Barbara Pub. You don't know that either? Where on earth are you from? They don't teach you anything in Barcelona.'

Carvalho was alone in Madrid, on the flower-lined precinct that runs around the Hotel Continental block. He caught sight of the new ministry buildings in the middle distance and went to look for La Castellana avenue. He hoped to escape as soon as possible from a district exactly like any modern hotel and office district in any city in the world. He struck out down La Castellana with no other purpose than to assert his freedom and to check whether he was being followed. One of the young men from the airport reception committee tried to adjust his pace to that of Carvalho.

Carvalho stopped. 'Look, kid, I'm going to have some prawns and then visit the Antonio Machado bookshop. If you like, you can come and protect me at the bookshop. I don't think anything will happen while I'm eating prawns. You can take a couple of hours off to have a drink or buy yourself a lemonade.'

'I'm not a kid. My name is Julio and I prefer to collect stamps.

'I'm a philatelist. Mir will shit all over us if we lose you.'

'If I want to, I can shake you off anyway. Much better to come to an agreement.'

'You do what you like. We were told to follow you and that's what we'll do. If you give us the slip, we'll let them know.'

Carvalho walked forward two steps and resolutely stopped a taxi. Through the rear window he could see the young man gesticulating as he ran along the street and asked his driver companion for help.

'Go into this ministry. Through the side-gate. Stop. Here's the fare.'

He placed two hundred pesetas in the hands of the astonished taxi-driver. He jumped down, greeted an attendant and prepared to climb the stairs.

'Where are you off to?'

'Don Ricardo de la Cierva is expecting me.'

'Don Ricardo is not at this ministry. Didn't you see at the gate that this is the Ministry of Trade?'

Not a trace of his pursuers outside. The Madrid air smelt of grilled prawns.

'It's no accident that just as the end-of-the-millennium psychosis was getting underway, a book like Orwell's *1984* came into fashion and people again grew interested in the other two coherent projects of twentieth-century utopian literature: Huxley's *Brave New World* and Zamyatin's *We*. It is not that the end of the century confirms the utopian premonitions of those three writers. But in an age of crisis, the most critical sectors of a culture experience as a nightmare the collapse of all existing models. And when no model is or can be endorsed, the only solutions are utopianism or cynicism, sometimes masked by pragmatism masked by a cult of historical efficacy masked by the virtue of prudence.

'I would not wish to be sarcastic in the presence of the lifeless body of a man who deserved all my respect and now deserves it only because others believe in him as the spokesman of the revolutionary project. In the presence of Fernando Garrido's lifeless body, however, I wonder what has become of the *revolutionary prudence* he so much invoked in recent times to conceal that he had lost all possibility of imprudence. I was not sure whether to go ahead with this gathering, which was planned before the murder, or to cancel it and add my voice to the grief that every revolutionary must feel, even if he does not consider Fernando Garrido to have been a revolutionary. I, too, do not think he was a revolutionary, and yet I hope you will believe me when I say that I am sad, as a person can be sad only when he has lost something that affects his own identity. If I finally agreed to come, it's because the murder itself is an apparent endorsement of the negative utopia.

'Under the weight of a nightmare, the critics of reality can react by wagering on either a positive or a negative utopia. A wager on positive utopia would mean to obey Lenin's behest, formulated at a time when crisis was looming over the Russian and European socialist movement and when, for want of a model that was not a failure, Lenin adopted Liebknecht's proposal: study, agitate, organise in order to grasp a reality that cannot be apprehended by a mechanistic politics progressively devalued through the dead-end of its own logic and its refusal to join a dialectical struggle with reality. A wager on negative utopia, on the other hand, would precisely mean to see Garrido's murder as proof that Huxley's brave new world is nigh, or that Orwell's Oceania or Zamyatin's dehumanised cosmos is in sight. Such worlds are nothing other than the world system of domination, which devours its own children and integrates them into the fatalistic rules of the game of survival and equilibrium. From this perspective, the hot line does not even unify the world. It ties it up.

'Garrido's murder is an unforeseen event that will not unearth the trail of the *sans-culottes* nor bring the tanks onto the street. It is a pound of flesh offered to the logic of the system; and to question this fact is to question the system, to endanger functions like the one we are holding now, to jeopardise the situation in which the central committee can meet legally, or people over twenty-five can attend university courses, or Vázquez Montalbán can win the Planeta Prize.* Neither Orwell, Huxley nor Zamyatin could have fore-

* Planeta Prize: a major literary prize awarded to Montalbán in 1979 for his novel *Los Mares del Sur*.

60

seen that the structure necessary for the terrible world of their prophecies might be created through implicit and explicit agreement between the two antagonistic systems. Zamyatin was a narodnik, a Russian populist who believed in a peasant revolution and the implantation of an asiatic mode of production, as against the NEP system of state-capitalist accumulation started by Lenin and forged into shape by Stalin. Huxley used to poke fun at the excesses that Russian communism could produce when it was experienced not on the spot, but through the heated palaver of young inter-war English communists at a loose end between two boat-races. In fact, Huxley's work is a kind of joke designed to alert the supposedly liberal British conscience at a minimal, liberal level.

'As for Orwell, Deutscher put it well in *Heretics and Renegades*:
Although his satire is more recognisably aimed at Soviet
Russia than Zamyatin's, Orwell saw elements of Oceania in
the England of his own days as well, not to speak of the
United States. Indeed, the society of *1984* embodies all that
he hated and disliked in his own surroundings: the
drabness and monotony of the English industrial suburb,
the "filthy and grimy and smelly" ugliness of which he tried
to match in his naturalistic, repetitive, and oppressive style;
the food-rationing and the government controls which he
knew in wartime Britain . . . '

He looked up from the written notes, which he had consulted only for the quotation, and met Carvalho's gaze. Behind larger and sadder glasses than he had worn twenty-five years earlier, his eyes tried to remember and did remember. A yellow mask now covered his features, drooping like deflated tyre-tubes beneath the sharp-pointed dictatorship of a capillary bed of nails. He turned his eyes back to the collective, which approached from the horizon to form a border of faces raised on its preacher's feet.

'Naive utopians. They thought it was possible to build utopias to escape from their nightmares; and then they merely cast into the bondage of their fears all those who followed the logical sequence of the next twenty, forty or a hundred years. They did not realise that fears and nightmares change, that no imagination can forget about what happens to us. What utopia could we build today over this lifeless body of Fernando Garrido, whose name I do not take in vain, whose name I do not invoke without pain? The landscape is dark and indistinct. But precisely because the night is so black, it may prove a little easier to find one's bearings with the modest help of a pocket astronomy.

'In presenting the first issue of the review *Hasta Luego*, I expressed a certain perplexity at the new contradictions of recent reality. The contradictions have sharpened, but I am less perplexed about the task which has to be set, if the dark night of a civilisation in crisis is to issue in a juster humanity on a habitable planet, rather than a massive herd of half-wits on a noisy dunghill of chemical, pharmaceutical and radioactive waste. In my view, the nineteenth-century fusion of science and the workers' movement cannot be achieved through agitated, irrational flights of fancy, but only in a house of the left where the calm of reason prevails.

'So much time has passed that the two old allies, science and the workers' movement, may have difficulty in recognising each other. A number of different movements may in fact be involved: ecology, for instance, which is the bearer of the self-critical science of the late twentieth century; or feminism, so long as it merges its emancipatory potential with that of other forces of freedom; or why not the classical revolutionary organisations? So long as they understand that their capacity to work for a free and just humanity has to be purified and confirmed through self-criticism of the old knowledge of society that informed them at their birth. At the same time, however, they must not renounce their revolutionary inspiration or lose themselves in the pitiful social-democratic army which, having completed its services in restoring capitalism after the war, is now on the eve of collapse. The revolutionary organisations must recognise that it is they themselves – those who live by their hands – which have been exceedingly confused by the rich, the "uncreators" of the Earth. It is a pity that Fernando Garrido is not among us to take up this call, this programme of hope or positive utopia. I am sorry to say it, but he died in the ranks of the pitiful social-democratic army, in the ranks of the "uncreators" of the Earth, although he is saved for History by the memory that is left of him.'

Someone next to Carvalho said 'amen'. It was the jumping-jack from the central committee meeting. But his 'amen' was buried by the earnest yet muffled applause that one expects at a first-rate funeral or the last speech of a besieged city. Cerdán was encircled by young people ready to leave everything and follow him. They

62

were not congratulating him. They were asking for a bibliography and some illumination of reality. Carvalho thought he recognised one of the faces from the Hotel Continental. He surprised Carmela as she was putting a book in her bag, and Julio as he was slapping Cerdán on the back. The master was tired, or at least his eyes were. For he stroked them with his hands, as if to stimulate them into further contemplating the reality of the noisy dunghill of chemical, pharmaceutical and radioactive waste.

'He called us half-wits,' the jumping-jack laughed. 'We haven't been introduced. I'm Paco Leveder, and you must be Sherlock Holmes.'

'In person.'

'Did you notice? He called us half-wits. Cerdán has always been like that. All his life he's been giving people marks according to how well they understand his own lesson. Some years ago he gave me nine out of ten. But now I'm suspended. You want to meet him? Follow me.'

Cerdán saw Paco Leveder approaching with Carvalho and put on his glasses so as not to be at a disadvantage.

'Sixto, how delightful you are, still preaching the end of the world! Keep at it; one day you're bound to be right.'

Cerdán did not reply but offered his hand to Carvalho.

'After twenty years and more!'

'Ah! you two know each other? I feel cheated.'

'You have the heart of a professor of political law, Paco.'

'I've read the insults you aim at us in that libel of yours. You accuse us of being the organic intellectuals of a capitulatory leadership. That's going too far, Sixto. We've known each other for years, and no one's a patch on you as a political commissar. You even had to be asked about the political adjectives in our leaflets.'

Cerdán seemed more glued to the mute discourse in Carvalho's eyes than to Leveder's provocative talk.

'How's your life been?'

'I'm one of the half-wits who live on the noisy dunghill of chemical, pharmaceutical and radioactive waste.'

'There are two kinds of half-wit: those who are moved by the spectacle, and those who never give it a thought.'

'I never do.'

'Come on, Sixto, stop picking a row. The *señor* is not part of this war. We've come to ask for your blessing and then we'll be off.'

Cerdán began to get irritated. Nearby some pallid young people, their arms bent forever by the premature carrying of books, were pecking away at the crumbs of his knowledge.

'We'll meet later.'

'Yes, let's meet.'

'Me too?'

'If there's no other way.'

Leveder steered Carvalho to what remained of the austere cocktail, in true harmony with the time of crisis. The cubes of potato tortilla disappeared to the insistent rhythm of chopsticks that seemed driven by half the population of China.

'It's the same old Cerdán,' someone said.

'Even more pessimistic, though,' another added.

'But he's obviously distressed by the Garrido business.'

'Why shouldn't he be?'

'I sometimes say to myself: let that guy do the thinking and the rest of us can plant cabbages.'

'Did you hear?' Carvalho asked.

Leveder was mockingly concerned.

'It's not the first time I've heard that. Cerdán produces that kind of impression. He's a verbal seducer. He has mastered the magic of words and summons them from a realm whose keys are and always will be in his pocket. He's a great shaman, a medicine-man of the real and spiritual worlds. At first I adored him: I was one of Fu-Manchu's thugs. Then I hated him. Now I find him amusing. Every culture deserves a Savonarola, and Cerdán is the Savonarola of Spanish communism. Still, he does go too far, damn it. He spends the day in tears at the wailing wall, and now he's taken it into his head to work for the salvation of cabbages. You can't breathe in Madrid, I agree, but this dunghill business is much too strong. And then he starts calling us half-wits – not as a figure of speech, but as a real description. He has the gift of keeping people guessing for their mark. I remember we all used to hover around so that he would look at us and assess our worth. If Cerdán didn't look at you – crash! something had to be wrong with your IQ. Sitting on his right one day, I was filled with illusions when I heard him say: "This young man has a great analytic talent." In his view, there were people with analytic talent and people with synthetic talent. Years later he remarked to me: "So-and-so has a great analytic talent, while what's-his-name has a great synthetic talent." As far as I was concerned, both of them were complete idiots.'

The little hair remaining on Leveder's tall frame was almost red in colour, and his short beard was like a garland that highlighted the length of his face. He swallowed three chinchones in two minutes.

'The ulcer's got to be hit. Let's see if we're going to dine with Cerdán. He has an interest, after all. He'd like to worm something out of me about the Garrido affair. I'll give him a rough time, though. He must also have an interest in talking with you. Do you know each other well?'

'Too well.'

'That's bad. When you know Cerdán too well, you become immune to any religious argument. I'm working on an unpublishable essay in which I compare Cerdán's positions with those of Bernard-Henry Lévy in God's Testament. You know who I'm talking about.'

'I've never had the pleasure.'

'A French philosopher, the most *chic* at the present moment. Cerdán is very small fry in comparison.'

'I'm just a humble, uncultured private detective, but don't say so to Cerdán. I'd like to hear him talk.'

'You could always arrest him. Do you have the power to arrest people? Look, here comes the prettiest girl in the western communist bureaucracy.'

Carmela approached and pretended not to know Carvalho. Leveder introduced them, while Carmela presented Julio. Leveder lent an ear to the wage demands being formulated by Julio and Carmela. At the meeting of Party full-timers, no one had paid any attention to what any business takes into account.

'On the pretext of militant activity, we're actually being exploited.'

'You people from the leadership ought to take our side, because the old ones still think like in the forties, when you had to pay to be shot, damn it.'

'For example, we get a fortnight's marriage leave. But what if you just have a lover all your life or part of your life? No holiday? Is there a bonus for legal matrimony? What kind of communist morality is that?'

'With the number of liaisons you have, Carmela, you'd always be on holiday.'

'In fact, you're just like them. And rather than stand up to Santos or Mir or Poncela, you're quite capable of ignoring us altogether.'

'I stand up to them all the time.'

'But on serious, ideological questions. Not for us bloody rank and file.'

'The mere foot soldiers.'

Leveder was on his tenth chinchon. Carvalho concluded that it worked like an internal starch, heightening his stiffness from time to time.

'I invite you to dinner. All of you. We'll all dine with Cerdán and explain the problems of actually existing communists, not of his test-tube constructions. Cerdán!'

Cerdán allowed himself to be promptly drawn by Leveder's call, so that he should no longer be the centre of attention in the room. Leveder introduced him to Julio and Carmela, describing them as members of the bloody rank and file, and as half-witted survivors of the noisy dunghill.

'Cerdán, we invite you to dinner at Gades, and in return you can explain whether the number of five-year assignments is built into KGB widows' pensions.'

Leveder did not conceal his wish to be heard, while Cerdán was equally anxious to leave the bookshop and bring the conversation to an end. Leveder was now starting his thirteenth chinchon amid speculation about why the KGB should recruit such contradictory figures as Sixto Cerdán and Paco Leveder. Cerdán held Leveder by the arm and led him out, ahead of Carvalho, Carmela and Julio. A girl whose face was half-covered by wavy hair complained that Cerdán had left them with an unclear book-list.

'Come and eat with us,' Carvalho suggested, without taking his eyes off the birth of a soft crevice at the top of her low-necked jumper.

'I wouldn't like to disturb you.'

'You wouldn't be disturbing us. We always like to see new faces.'

'I know Leveder. I've been to his classes as an unregistered student.'

'Well, then, you're almost one of the family,' Julio said, taking her by the arm.

'I need six coffees and these two fingers,' Leveder told the Gades head-waiter as soon as he came to greet them. He then went off to the washroom, all the time keeping his eyes on the two fingers that were to be of such mysterious service to him. Cerdán smiled in search of Carvalho's complicity and got ready to complete the guest's book-list 'before we start to eat, drink and all that'. Carvalho took advantage of the cultural interlude to scrutinise the newcomer at his leisure. Her hair was between red and chestnut in colour, her eyes light-brown, and her lips more sensual than fleshy. A dark gulf appeared between her breasts at the top of a green woollen jumper, while her Germanic bone structure had been softened by three or four Latin American generations, possibly including some Indian element as witnessed by her almond-shaped eyes.

'I'm no ignoramus, you know,' Julio was joking with Carmela. 'I'm doing a slang translation of Lenin. Just say something to me and I'll translate it.'

'I don't know any Lenin. I'm a bloody rank-and-filer.'

'You must know something.'

'All right, explain the dictatorship of the proletariat in slang.'

'Power, man, is the crucial factor. All power to the people. But that's easy . . . Please be so kind as to say something by Lenin that I can translate into a language I understand.'

'Something by Lenin?' Cerdán searched his memory so hard that it seemed to creak. 'Well, one of the April theses: an open break with the provisional government, pointing towards the transfer of all governmental power to the soviets.'

Cerdán returned to his bibliography as Carmela laughed uncontrollably at Julio's simultaneous translation.

'Bourgeois democracy sucks. We gotta get it together at the grass-roots. Street credibility . . . '

Cerdán was consulted.

'What the hell's that?'

'It's the language of my tribe: the jive-Leninists.'

The Latin American girl laughed, and Cerdán felt he had the aesthetic duty to puff up his flabby cheeks in case the muscular movement produced a laugh.

'What work of Lenin's would you advise me to translate?'

'Come on, don't keep calling me *usted*. You could translate *What Is To Be Done*.'

'I've already got the title: *Getting Our Act Together*.'

Leveder suddenly appeared in his chair. The vomiting had made him feel lighter and able to control the situation.

'Here I am. Ask me anything you like.'

Cerdán told him to be quiet so that he could continue with the book-list.

'Are you supervising a thesis?'

The book-list reached its end.

'Fine,' the girl said happily, putting her notebook in her bag.

Cerdán did not even look at the menu.

'Anything at all. Spaghetti, I suppose.'

'Espaghetti alla maricona arrabiata,' Leveder ordered.

'We haven't any of that.'

'I order it in every restaurant and no one ever has it. You've got a nerve if you think I'll tell you who killed Garrido.'

'If you think I'll put up with your mental incontinence,' Cerdán snapped back, 'then you're sadly mistaken. You're old enough to control your sphincters. As Pavese said, every man over forty is responsible for his face.'

The others were not sure whether it was said in earnest or in jest and decided to wait for Leveder's reply.

'You've convinced me,' he said, and Carmela had to turn away so that Cerdán should not see her laughing.

Cerdán gave up Leveder as lost and turned to Carvalho.

'How long it's been! What have you been doing with your life? University? Publishing?'

'Import-export of capers and dried figs,' Leveder cut in.

No one seemed to hear him. Carvalho talked vaguely of business matters, while Cerdán was looking for the exact point at which their conversation had been interrupted twenty or twenty-five years earlier. He must have found it, for he looked hard at Carvalho and wanted to ask him something that could not be asked.

'Was everything okay?'

'A couple of years and then out on the street.'

'Mine was a very rough time.'

'It was written so.'

Cerdán passed over Carvalho's light irony and turned to face Leveder.

'I must tell you that your evening homily struck me as a pile of horseshit,' Leveder said.

'If you don't cut it out, I'll have to get up and leave.'

'It was the speech of a vulture, preying like that on Garrido's human carrion-meat and political carrion-meat in general. Cheers! Cheers!'

No one responded to the toast: all their eyes preferred to roam the packed restaurant. Each one remained on their island. Even Julio withdrew into himself, while Carmela looked in her bag for something she could not find. Leveder surprised them again by asking Cerdán whether his work on *Socialism and Bureaucracy* was very far advanced. From that moment, the two opened themselves up on the problems of education, on translations, on the need for time to reflect, travel or do nothing. It was a conversation between designers of the mind about the worth of various cloths or the inevitability of the return to the mini-skirt. They easily passed on to Garrido. How is Luisa? Carvalho suddenly discovered there had been a Luisa in Garrido's life, just as there must be one in Cerdán's. A Luisa. Children. Domestic questions. Everyday mental strains, never entirely stifled by big alibis.

'The last time I saw him was at an unsuccessful meeting to organise a march to Torrejón against American bases. As usual, Garrido wanted to present an air of agreement. "Together, but not mixed into one. Each with their own slogans." It was not possible. We had a very frank discussion. "I envy you," he said. "You act as if history had only just begun." That's a big part of the drama of the traditional workers' parties. They develop a privileged inner logic that cuts them off from reality.'

Leveder did not put up any resistance. He had rather a gloomy ideology that evening and was not worried that Cerdán should fall into monolgue. He merely shook his head or went to the spaghetti with the delicacy of a well-trained table companion. Carmela and Julio listened with fascination to Cerdán, as if it was the first time they had sat in the stalls at the theatre of intelligence. Even Carvalho felt captivated by the litany of sad truths that came from Cerdán's lips. Like someone fleeing from his own dream, Carvalho blinked heavily and made for the bar. He was thirsty for a draught beer.

'My name is Gladys and I very much agree with what you didn't say. The others talked and you kept silent.'

'Argentinian? Chilean? Uruguayan?'

'Why not Colombian, Peruvian or Costa Rican?'

'Everyone has their own taste in exiles.'

She laughed, throwing her head back in the manner of Rita Hayworth in *Lollipop* and revealing a young snake's neck hardly touched by little rings. She gently rested her hand on Carvalho's shoulder as if to regain her composure.

'The truth is that I'm lost. Back home, I was quite used to all this tomfoolery. We spent years and years getting worked up about the transition to socialism or whatever. In the meantime the soldiers were sharpening their bayonets. I'm Chilean. And don't get the idea I just looked on from a distance. I was in the front line, in the Freedom Express that criss-crossed the country with its message of culture and communism. But the others had the air force.'

She sadly turned a glass that had become sad in turn, the icecubes as if frozen by her brooding eyes. Carvalho leant back with his elbows on the bar and looked at the dining-room where Leveder, Cerdán and Carmela were still tuning the instruments of an impossible orchestra.

'Do you want an aspirin?'

The Chilean woman opened her eyes so as to feign more than the expected degree of surprise.

'An aspirin?'

'I have a friend – or, rather, had a friend – who used to pick girls up like that. He'd go up to one and say: "Do you want an aspirin, señorita?"'

'And did it work?'

'Always.'

'For you too?'

'You tell me.'

'Shall we drop these people? Are you interested in their speeches about History?'

'I've had enough history for today. Since I arrived in this town, I seem to have been living in a book written by a sociologist or some such prick.'

'You can't stand sociologists?'

'Among others.'

'I'm one myself.'

'I'll try to forget it.'

Carvalho began to move towards the door. Gladys followed, asking him to stop.

'Aren't you going to say goodbye? What kind of person are you?'

'They don't need us.'

But when he looked back, he saw Carmela's huge black eyes filled with malice. He paid no attention and this time pushed Gladys out of the door.

'I invite you to walk in the old part of town.'

'Madrid's full of old parts.'

'Around the Plaza Mayor.'

Carvalho shrugged. He stopped a taxi that seemed drunk on diesel oil, blacked and spluttering. The driver had to lower his scarf in order to speak.

'I've just had a tooth out,' he grumbled, 'and I'm still groggy.'

Gladys laughed into her coat.

'Why are you laughing?'

'At the aspirin.'

Carvalho put a hand on her shoulder as if to stop her laughing.

'He'll think we're laughing at him.'

'Señor, I'm not laughing at you. It's just that something very funny happened to us.'

'You can laugh at the mayor of Madrid for all I care. That's what democracy is all about.'

He dropped them opposite the Arco de Cuchilleros. They went into the Plaza Mayor as into an inner sanctum. The sound of clapping and harsh guitar-playing rose from cellars packed with winter tourists. They were almost alone in the lamp-lit square, with no other witness than the equestrian statue of King Felipe IV.

'We're like a couple of American tourists walking in a Rome square in some fifties film.'

'I was very little then.'

'I wasn't.'

Their shoulders touched as they walked. The deep warmth of a perfumed woman emanated from her ivory-like woollen coat. The curls of her lightly permed hair fell on her shoulders; and whenever she spoke, she had to toss them aside like soap-bubbles or snowdrops brighter than the yellowish street lighting. The balconies and windows seemed to enclose their own memories rather than to open on a time that did not belong to them. Carvalho remembered his own walks as a young, impecunious conspirator, or his rendezvous beneath the arches, usually next to the doorway of a municipal bureau that doubled as a tourist office with Entrambasaguas's *Madrid Cooking* on display.

'I'd like to check on something over there.'

The book was there just like in the late fifties, and it seemed as unchanged as his companions in that chorus of Madrid sub-culture.

'Do you want some literature for visiting the town?'

'I was just reminiscing. Years ago, I often used to pass this window and had to read the titles of books that were of no interest to me. Now that one does interest me.'

'The cookery book?'

'Yes.'

'You too, Brutus?'

'What do you mean?'

'All the left in this city is into cooking. They invite each other round to try out their dishes. And the little blokes do it all on their own. You'd think they were nuts. They say they are regaining their sense of identity. They've even stopped getting divorced in order to spend time in the kitchen.'

'Do you know a lot of people?'

'Yes. I have to do something. Things haven't been easy. The left here has given us quite genuine solidarity but very little money.'

Some drunken foreigners flowed into the square singing *Que viva España!* Gladys and Carvalho felt driven from the square without anyone having said anything. They went into Calle Mayor and strayed down the little streets leading to the Opera and the Plaza de Oriente. They could hear their own footsteps between the neat grilles that seemed to be drawn on the white façades and the dark brown cornices and shutters.

'Silence is golden after so much chatter.'

Carvalho agreed and put an arm round her shoulder. She tossed her head back as if to catch the arm in the nape of her neck.

'Why did you pick me? You could have gone off with Cerdán or Leveder or anyone else.'

'I've seen a lot of Leveder, and I'd only go with Cerdán to a seminar on some spiritual concoction. You were quiet, and I like quiet men.'

'I'm always hoping to meet a woman who likes quiet men. That's why I keep quiet all the time.'

'You're certainly a sly one.'

'Anyway I'm in a new city, and new cities always hold a promise of adventure.'

'I know that for you
I am one more adventure
And once the night is over
You will forget me in a trice.'

'Los Panchos.'

'I didn't learn it from Los Panchos. How old you are !'

Standing in her own light, Gladys presented a near-classic profile that was marred only by an excessively pointed nose. Carvalho ran a finger along her brow, her nose, her lips and her chin. Then he returned to her warm, moist lips. Gladys opened them gently to catch his finger, sucking it and then biting it between her teeth.

'Not so fast, stranger!'

She had run a few metres ahead before turning to see Carvalho's reaction. He caught up again and they left the Opera for the Plaza de Oriente. Carvalho could not believe that shouts of 'Franco, Franco, Franco' had ever contaminated that urban prodigy of historical reverie protected by the papier-mâché palace wall, with its glimpse of fields in the distance.

'It's the most anti-fascist place in the world. The demonstrations must have been with sunshades. It ought to be compulsory to come here with a sunshade.'

They sat on a bench and she explained how she had come from Chile with the help of the Spanish embassy. She worked as a consultant for a Barcelona publishing-house and was just passing through Madrid.

'Which publisher?'

'Bruguera.'

Gladys accompanied him to the entrance of his hotel. She read an invitation to come up in Carvalho's eyes.

'Not today. Can I see you tomorrow?'

'I'll have a very hectic day.'

'So will I. Let's say eleven in the evening. At Oliver's'.


He picked up his things from the hotel reception. He idled about the room with no desire for work, taking apart the memories shared with Cerdán that had just sprung from a forgotten trunk. A conversation on the passage from quantity to quality in connection with one of Sartre's books. He would mercilessly hunt it down in his bookcase and consign it to the flames. As soon as he returned to Barcelona. Preparations for peaceful twenty-four-hour national strikes. A work on schematism, dogmatism and Caesarism that Cerdán advised him not to show the leadership. Whole days, nights and early mornings spent questioning life and History beneath the tall pine-trees of the villa where Cerdán's parents spent their summer. I'm reading Jung. He's not a Marxist. He's a disciple of Freud, stated Cerdán with a certain lack of confidence. Then Cerdán as a constant example of the alternative to Carvalho's progressive loss of willpower in a prison full of injured sparrows and mongoloid homosexuals, real or fake epileptics, introverted escapists like Wild West gunmen beaten once and for all. And far off, in another prison under an assuredly darker sky, the exemplary Cerdán with his seminars for the working class behind bars, his gymnastics, his David Ricardo, his Party work.

'Are you doing Party work?' asked the young spiritual guides who managed to get through the communications net; especially Gabardinetti, that Hollywood swordman's stand-in who ended his days picking up Swedish girls in Australia or Australians in Sweden. At that time, behind half a kilometre of bars, he was shocked that Carvalho no longer practised, that he wasted his time following the swifts on their westward flight or listening to the story of Juanillo who stabbed women's cunts. Are you doing Party work? Get stuffed, Gabardinetti. The peaceful twenty-four-hour national strike won't happen in this prison and I won't preach it to the little old man who used to dip his prick in condensed milk and give it to the kids to suck, nor to the man who killed his son-in-law for knocking his daughter about with a sleeveboard. A sleeveboard? Are you sure, old man? Get stuffed, Gabardinetti, you ought to follow Cerdán's example – he set up a translator's cell in Toledo. In Toledo? No, Burgos. You're a communist wherever you happen to be, said Gabardinetti, before setting off on holiday to Lloret del Mar; Comrade Carvalho's faith is slackening, he doesn't give political reports, he hasn't said anything about whether Squinty fucks a cow or a sow each time he goes to the prison farm. The cow and the sow will get over it in twenty-four hours on the day when the peaceful twenty-four-hour national strike is proclaimed. How young and stupid we all were, Gabardinetti, Cerdán! How the basic gestures have remained the same since then!

From the ecstasy of the ceiling to the white bulge of the folder. Plans. Names. Statements. A list of the personal effects found on Fernando Garrido. Gold watch with an inscription by Kim Il-Sung, a packet of light tobacco, a wallet with three thousand pesetas, an identity card, a Party card, a postcard from Oriana Fallaci, a handkerchief, a latch key, an agenda, shreds of light tobacco, a lighter, a diary. When the Lafargues committed suicide, Lenin wrote: 'If someone no longer has the strength to work in the Party, he must have the courage to look reality in the face and to die like the Lafargues.' Santos Pacheco, old Indian Chief, white man kill Black Eagle.

Carvalho drew a diagram of the room, allocating people to the places indicated to him. Names, ages, distances. He paced the room at various speeds. At the speed of hatred. Of resentment. The transcript of the tape-recording:

'Let's get it over quickly, because you know I can't keep going without a smoke.'

'Ha! Ha! Ha!'

'Ah, just what we needed. A short-circuit.'

'The fuse has blown, you ignoramus.'

'Those Workers Commission people are always on strike.'

'Ha! Ha! Ha!'

'Steward! Someone should go and have a look.'

75

*The sound of an earthquake nearby.*
*Sighs of relief.*
*A sudden silence that becomes deeper and deeper.*
Fernando! Fernando! (*Santos's voice*)
*Tower of Babel.*

Santos Pacheco had foreseen that Carvalho would be puzzled: 'Don't be surprised that the tape continued after the lights went out. The main recorder was out of use, but there's a small battery one on standby, at least during the political report and the ensuing discussion.'

José Martialay Martín, construction worker, leader of Movimiento Obrero: 'It was a normal meeting, with no dominating theme. Garrido was the same as usual. I was too. I didn't realise anything until the lights went on, even though I was sitting on Fernando's right.'

Prudencia Solchaga Rozas, a miner from Almadén: 'It seems now that everything lasted a long time, but in fact it was only a few seconds. Garrido was smoking, and that was all the light there was. Now I remember that even that light soon disappeared. It must have been when Fernando fell on the table. I couldn't see anything and I heard nothing special. People were talking and making jokes about the situation. Who could have guessed what was happening?'

The light emitted by Fernando Garrido appeared in seven of the statements. 'Let's get it over quickly, because you know I can't keep going without a smoke.' Either Garrido had violated his own code, or seven members of the central committee had auto-suggested a cigarette between his lips. It was now six in the morning, too early to get Santos Pacheco out of bed and ask him whether Garrido had been smoking at the meeting.

Luis de la Mata Requeséns, a dentist from Requena (Valencia): 'There was another doctor in the room who was more suitable for what had happened: Comrade Valdivieso from La Paz, a hospital specialist in cardiovascular surgery. But the diagnosis took no more than a couple of seconds. A gaping stab wound, clear and straight to the heart. Death was instantaneous. No doubt the work of an expert, particularly because the room was dark and because it is hard to stab someone in front when he is sitting at a table. The assassin must have the eyes of a cat. Some people can move easier than others in the dark, but it's no more than a minimal difference.'

Ezequiel Hernández Amado, a priest: 'My first thought was to give him absolution. I did this in a very low voice, not because I was afraid of any comrade's reaction – my self-proclaimed atheist comrades accept that I and many others have the faith – but because absolution is an intimate ceremony between three beings: the priest, the sinner and God. I said these words *ego te absolvo a peccatis tuis* in the firm belief that Fernando Garrido had few sins to be forgiven. I am convinced that a man who has dedicated his whole life to the struggle for human dignity has a boundless credit in heaven. Maybe my professional bias played tricks on me, and maybe prayer and absolution stopped me concentrating on other things. No two individuals are alike, and there has to be some of everything in the Lord's garden.'

Carvalho sifted through his notes, converting them into a series of questions. Then he picked out a number of the questions. He tried to sleep, if only for half-an-hour. But he saw people in the street when he went to draw the curtains. Was that the smell of fritters, the click-clack of cups of coffee on saucers? He took a shower.

Toy-like silhouettes on the flat roofs of the Carrera de San Jerónimo, Fernaflor, Marqués de Cubas, Plaza de Canovas. All the police in Spain seemed to be circling or massing at the Madrid crossroads, forming a brown, festoon-like cordon around the zone of popular homage. A real armed enclosure sketched out a trapezium with its base in the Paseo del Prado, its sides in Atocha and Alcalá streets, and its top in Espoz and Mina streets and the Puerta del Sol. A jeep stood at every major intersection, and each little square had its barred police-van crammed with brown figures, guns at the ready. A helicopter flew overhead like a bird of ill omen. Garrido was shouldered from the Cortes by members of the executive committee of the Communist Party of Spain. As they appeared, the applause was held in check by an imperative 'ssh!' rising from the depths of the crowd.

'Long live the Communist Party of Spain!' a woman shouted in broken voice. A fiery *viva* licked the walls and caused the tin-police

77

silhouettes to shimmer on the rooftops.

There was a silence for the historic photo as the Party, family and state representatives took their places. Santos stood at the front of the Party delegation, his head bowed to cover the burning tears. The state officials were the head of government representing the King, the commander of the military First Region, the chairman of the Cortes, three ministers and the presiding judge of the Constitutional Court. The general secretaries of the Communist parties of Italy, Portugal, France, Japan and Romania carried their respective national flags, alongside delegations from every country with more than five communists on the electoral register. Then there were the general secretaries of the Socialist parties of Italy, France, Portugal and Greece, as well as representatives of the Sandinist Front and the Mexican PRI. Behind them came a slow, red moraine. Red flags against the arduously blue sky of a November morning; red kerchiefs in hands and jacket pockets. Red, too, seemed the fists that rose and fell with the power of hammers and the precision of mechanical pistons. A bitter-sweet woman's voice started up:

'Arise, ye starvelings from your slumbers!
Arise, ye prisoners of want!'

She was joined by the whole of the long, broad mop of red hair that followed the coffin. At the Plaza de Cánovas, the singing began to recede to the back of the mass procession, for the Madrid City Band greeted the front section with the strains of the Royal March, playing it slowly as if at the funeral of a pale young tubercular prince. After the early display of tolerance, the communist baritones were now shouting more than singing the *Internationale*, the march divided between tactical respect for the royal anthem and the emotional compulsion of the *Internationale*. Tierno Galván, the mayor of Madrid, resolved the dispute by mounting the rostrum and slowly delivering a short funeral oration.

'At the burial of a man who was not religious, there can be no better oration than to mark our respect for his heroism in denying himself the comfort of resurrection. Life and History are as one in Fernando Garrido. Ever since he was born, he believed that each man's hopes can only be realised through collective emancipation, and he became a revolutionary because he believed in man. There can be no closer or more ethical identity than that which exists between socialism and humanism. Socialism has left ethics to the philosophers and devoted itself to the working class, just as Pro-

78

metheus stole fire from the gods in order to give it to men. You all know the story of Fernando Garrido's life, particularly those of you who are aware of your own history and of the role played in it by the anti-fascist struggle for freedom. I salute our old friend, our old companion of those times of despair in which he never gave way to despair. He was a strong man, the son of a strong people and social class. I was never able to call him "comrade", but I always knew that we were comrades and that tactics and strategies could never separate us. He looked to a future, already not so far away, in which communists and socialists would be forced to build socialism with freedom and to guarantee freedom with socialism. He put you communists on the path of that truth. He showed to us socialists the end of a still long road. Someone once said that the final struggle will be between communists and ex-communists. I say to you that there will be no such final struggle, for examples like Fernando Garrido give the *Internationale* its full meaning as the song of spirit and unity.'

Once again, applause nearly perverted the meaning of the ceremony, but shushes and sobs drowned it out. Santos climbed the rostrum and stood looking at the crowd. 'Comrades!' he began and immediately fell silent, as if he had just discovered that Garrido was dead and felt his anguish harden into a ball of nothingness in his throat. 'Comrades!' he repeated, his voice stifling from grief. He lowered his head and raised his fist, so that a forest of fists gripped the noble compass of the square under the serene yet puzzled gaze of the distant statues showing through the Prado museum gates. Santos made way for the last speaker.

Rafael Alberti went up to the platform with slow legs but a swift body, the oblique majesty of his face preserved in the syrup of a bewitching poet's long white hair.

'Fernando Garrido shudders
Loneliness shudders water
Shudders with rage the soil
That has to save Spain
The soil of the working class
With clenched fists as a flag
A red red red red flag
Like the blood and the mist
That has plunged the olive-tree
Into grief and shaken the harvest

With the disorder of evening
In the very midst of morning
A disorder of shadow bitten
By the blue of black hounds of death
Fascism does not go out to fight
It kills by stealth it kills by blows
And is born again from its foggy air

'Fernando Garrido was
The guide of coexistence
Between river and water
Fire and flame voice and tool

'They'll come from future skies
Archangels or planets
To behold the beauty
Of this world constructed
With your earthly words
Fernando Garrido death
To death long live life
Death to death! Long live life!'

'Death to death!' the crowd repeated, while the slogan 'The real terrorists are you, the fascists' grew until it took over the square. The various groups of representatives mingled with one another. Santos embraced ministers and foreign delegates, and gave a martial handshake to the Madrid army commander. The stewarding force cleared a path for the cars that were to bear Garrido's remains to the civil cemetery.

'They'll let *you* through. Tell Santos I have to speak to him today if possible.'

Carmela advanced, greeting some and rebuking others. She came back just as people were moving *en masse* to the Party's hired coaches and cars that were to take them to the cemetery.

'He says he normally passes by the university campus every evening. Six o'clock at the entrance to the faculty of philosophy and literature. I'm just telling you what he said. Don't stand there gaping.'

He couldn't stay surprised for long. An explosion swept the air like a wave on the ocean, and bodies were carried away in a frantic rush to escape anywhere and nowhere. Another explosion echoed out from Atocha Station. Carvalho pulled Carmela along as he ran towards the Hotel Ritz doorway. They turned to watch how the crowd, briefly transformed into a disorderly mob, was stubbornly regrouping in a dense pack of raised fists. It was singing the *Internationale*.

Ambulances could be heard in the distance speeding to the Puerta del Sol, where one bomb had exploded, and to Atocha Station, where it was reported by word of mouth that another explosion had killed two people and injured twelve.

'No, I'm not going to the cemetery. I don't interfere in private family matters.'

'Shall we fix up to eat somewhere?'

'Do you know where you can eat cocido in Madrid?'

'Not really, but I'll find out after the funeral is over. Shall we say two o'clock?'

'Right. At my hotel.'

He had to avoid the pockets of demonstrators in order to leave the area encircled by the security forces and reach the normal traffic. He hailed a taxi and asked for Calle Profesor Waksman.

'Let's hope we get there before the end of the league cup final. There's one hell of a jam up there. It's just not possible.'

The cars seemed to be driven by paralytics or gripped by a strange force rising from the rain-darkened tarmac. The driver knew all there was to know about the recent outrages. A small bomb in the Puerta del Sol passport office and a huge one at Atocha.

'Do you follow me, mister? Am I making myself clear? One small bomb and one monster. Right? It can't be, it just can't be. Even bombs are signed.'

They reached Calle Waksman with the rain hard on their heels. Carvalho just had time to locate the doorway before the first drops of cold autumn rain fell on his back.

'Señor Jaime Siurell.'

The porter did not even look up as he pointed out the floor, all the time scratching his balls with a hand lazily placed inside his uniform. The apartment was opened by an old lady straight from the society column of a stylish American magazine.

'Tell him I'm an old friend from the States. I'd like to speak with him about James Wonderful.'

She did not return. The cream-coloured double door, with rims of gilded bronze, opened to reveal a wheelchair pushed by the large hands of James Wonderful. His flabby face muscles seemed under the control of oceanic eyes, wide open behind the lenses of his spectacles. His lower lip drooled down to the tip of his chin, perfectly in accord with a body that was crumbling right from the head to a pair of feet more flung than rested on the footboard of the wheelchair. Nothing remained of the physical hardiness of that fifty-year-old gymnast he had known twenty years before.

'Carvalho!' The word struggled from a lower lip tortuously attached to the muscles of a mouth that seemed to despise it.

Carvalho thought he could detect a smile and an emotional mist in the eyes of James Wonderful, assistant chief executive in the Second Republic,* instructor of CIA agents, regional chief for Latin America at the time when Carvalho was assigned to 'the area of presidential surveillance'. The old exile, who had survived such great physical and ideological collapse, was now a hemiplegic suffering from an obscure disease. He stretched out his hands for Carvalho to shake.

'How we hated each other!'

'Well enough.'

An attempted smile intensified the breaks in the geometry of his face. He put his hands back on the wheels and, inviting Carvalho to follow, skilfully manoeuvred the chair inside the flat. They entered a spacious living-room, full of Philippine cane furniture, flower-carpets and bright indoor vegetation. Carvalho abandoned himself to the depths of an over-large sofa, remaining below the water-line of Wonderful's sunken face, whose speech-muscles moved like stiff pieces of a precarious machine.

'I haven't heard anything about you for twenty years.'

'There hasn't been much to hear.'

'I live cut off from everyone and everything. Ten years ago, I took my pension so that I could write my memoirs. Are you still in the

---

* Spain's Second Republic lasted from 1931 until Franco's victory in 1939.

Company?'

'You know very well I'm not.'

'Yes, it's true. I asked for the sake of asking. I guess you haven't just come here to pay me a visit. Galicians never waste time. You are Galician, aren't you?'

'A cross-breed.'

'There is such a thing as genetic inheritance, particularly in survival cells. Help yourself to whatever you fancy. I can't drink anything. You can see I'm a wreck. At least I look one. But the whole of history and the whole of the world is inside my head. How did you find me?'

'Five years ago I bumped into Olson in Barcelona. We talked about old times, about you. He gave me your address.'

'Olson. He was here not so long ago. Now he's a farmer. He grows avocados in Malaga, I think. A fitting destiny. After fifty you're no longer fit for this work. What are you doing?'

'Private detective.'

'You live in Madrid?'

'No.'

'Are you here on business?'

'Yes.'

'Have I got anything to do with it?'

'Maybe.'

'So, what makes you think I can help? Can you force me to help you?'

'No.'

'I've never been a generous type. Why should I help you?'

'Out of vanity, perhaps. To show me that you're still well informed.'

'I'm an invalid. What could I possibly know? What are you mixed up in?'

'Guess.'

'It's not hard. Fernando Garrido.' Carvalho nodded with his eyes shut, but he still followed Wonderful's expression and caught the glimmer of interest flowing from his eyes. 'This business is over my head. I won't deny that I hear a few things, but I deduce more than I know. I have a very good knowledge of the method and mechanics. So, even at a distance I can sometimes have almost perfect vision about what has happened.'

'That's why I've come to you.'

'I don't know anything about this case. I'm as surprised as everyone else.'

'Surprised?'

'Yes. The word already gives you some information.'

'Was it an unexpected assassination for the Company?'

'I'm just speaking for myself. Something big had already been in the air, but Garrido wasn't the one who fitted exactly.'

'Who, then?'

'Martialay.'

'The Company?'

'Who knows. Maybe not directly. Not like before. Now everything's much more sophisticated.'

'Why Martialay?'

'The Party's not worried, but they are at trade-union headquarters. The union elections are coming up. But it was hard to rig a scandal to get rid of Martialay. What can you dig up on a man who does gymnastics in his track-suit at six in the morning?'

'Why the change of victim?'

'I don't know. Nor do I know who it was. There must be very few people in the know. Have you got a family?'

'No.'

'Pity. It comes in useful sooner or later. Who will help you get out of bed and sit in your wheelchair?'

'Why did they swap Garrido for Martialay?'

'Don't abuse a friendship we never had. You were right. You got me to speak out of vanity, but I've already said enough. Seriously, though, I can't tell you anything. Where do you live?'

'Barcelona.'

'Could you do me a favour? The municipal periodicals library has complete sets of the pre-war press. Could you send me some photocopies of *L'Opinió*? I've realised that I don't know everything I should in order to finish my memoirs. The title is *I'll Never Reach Ithaca*. Do you like it?'

'If it wasn't the Company, who else?'

'Or maybe *I'll Never Return to Ithaca* would be a better idea. What do you think? Sometimes I regret not having gone back to Barcelona, but I find Madrid attractive and I'm afraid of returning to a city that was never right for me.'

'What will be the next stage?'

Wonderful dropped his alert composure and became just an

aged, autistic hemiplegic, cut off from the forced conversation with Carvalho. He no longer looked at his visitor, nor at anything identifiable outside himself. Carvalho stood up and got ready to leave. Wonderful did not react until the detective was standing in the door.

'I don't think anything will come of it immediately. This crime was a long-term investment. I don't know, but that's the feeling I get. They won't even lose the union elections. Such blows are to be feared the most. Be careful. I'd like someone to survive who has been through those years with me. Every death removes part of our own image. Has that occurred to you?'

'What photocopies would you like?'

'Forget it. It doesn't matter. I haven't written a line and I never will.'

'They've got cocido at the Gran Tasca today', announced Carmela. 'Thanks to you, I'm learning quite a few things. They already treat me like a weirdo in the Party. "Do you know where they serve cocido?" Today it was the Cuatro Caminos branch secretary who told me. I was skilfully interrogating the *Mundo Obrero* lot, and then this comrade comes up with a brilliant observation. "Today's the day for cocido at the Gran Tasca." So let's go before they run out. Is that how you go through life, picking out restaurants? Am I acceptable as an eating companion, or do you prefer that alley-cat from last night? What an exit, pal. Better than Belmondo in *A bout de souffle*. Even Cerdán realised, and the talk turned to the lady's legs.'

'What did Cerdán think of the lady's legs?'

'Leveder brought it up. He really is frivolous, part of the frivolous faction. But Cerdán introduced an analytic note by disagreeing about the ideal proportions.'

'What?'

'He ended up saying, almost in German, that she had a big arse. But he sounded like Lukács, Adorno or one of those characters.'

'How did the meeting end?'

'I'll swap information if you tell me how yours wound up.'

'In bed, but each in our own.'

'That's a new idea, is it?'

'And each in our own house.'

'Even more interesting. A tele-linkup.'

Carvalho spoke about the similar origin of pot au feu as an excellent cocido came into view. The chickpea, he said, marks the style of the Spanish pot au feu, and it is nearly always the dried vegetable that gives it its particular nuance. In Yucatán, for example, cocido is made with lentils, while in Brazil it is based on black beans. In the chickpea cocido of the peoples of Spain, the Madrid version is characterised by the use of chorizo sausage, while its Catalan counterpart relies on blood sausage and little meatballs.

'You Catalans really are smart. Why didn't that ever occur to us?'

'What do you think of Martialay?'

'Heroic. One of the hero sector. I mean, one of those who spent all their life in jail, plus some borrowed time.'

'He's tough?'

'Tough as nails. But what's he got to do with cocido?'

'Would the trade union significantly alter its line if Martialay were no longer leader?'

'No. At least, not for a long time.'

'Who will replace Garrido?'

'I'm sure Santos will for the moment, and then we'll see if the congress is brought forward or not. It's due for next summer. If Santos is the man, he'll carry out the same politics as Garrido. If it's not him, we could be in for a real bust-up. The only ones who could win are Martialay, Cansinos or Sepúlveda.'

'Leveder?'

'What! It's a miracle he's even hanging on. He goes his own way too much. He used to drive Garrido mad by abstaining all the time. He's too flash, too much of a playboy.'

'We've already dealt with Martialay. What about the others? Cansinos?'

'A workaholic. He talks a lot about the popular movement and has really come into his own since the municipal election agreement with the Socialists. He's too hard for the softies, and too soft for the hards. He may scrape in by the middle road.'

'Sepúlveda.'

'He's an engineer. Let's say, one of the few survivors from the sixties intake of intellectuals. I think he's holding up well, because when he doesn't want anyone to understand him, no one ever does. He gets going on the scientific-technological revolution, and in the end you can't tell whether he believes in it or not.'

'And the rest?'

'They've puffed themselves up too much. Burnt out in petty struggles.'

'Who do you go for?'

'Santos is my man. He looks like a Roman senator, and that means a lot to me. He's a guy who's never screwed anyone or even tricked them. He's capable of doing anything for the Party. He was fascinated by Garrido.'

'Is he ambitious?'

'No. It's hard for an ambitious man to get on in a Party that will be in opposition until the year 2000. Don't you think so?'

'Ambition can adjust to any terrain. There are even ambitious road-sweepers'.

'Santos is very special. Just think: a married man who still keeps his underground flat. From time to time, he leaves his family and goes to spend a few days in that flat from the hard years. He lives like a monk. No one has ever discovered a hobby or vice in his life. His career in the Party has no ups and downs. He has never taken any big or false steps. Everyone else on the executive has been through a difficult moment, when they were over-critical or made some gross blunder. But not Santos. Sometimes he seems like an extra-terrestrial, so firmly are his feet planted on the ground. You could imagine him in a museum. That's what I think at times. He's just like the model. That's what militants must have been like before. Before what? Before all this crap we have nowadays.'

'Was Garrido in danger of losing his job?'

'No. The guy could be very trying, because he always ran things his own way and was used to clockwork underground activity. But he had historical reflexes, and that was much appreciated in a party that tends to take things at a gentle pace. He managed to make himself irreplaceable.'

'How has the rank and file responded to the assassination?'

'There was an immediate call to stay calm; not to open ourselves up to provocation. If this had happened three years ago, there would have been an armed confrontation. But the country has grown used to people dying. Terrorism has produced a general insensitivity to death. Hey! You're not drinking, and they said you soaked it up like a sponge.'

'I'd like to be on a level with Santos when I meet him.'

'Well, I've drunk a little and I feel fine.'

The wine had put some flourish into her delicate cheeks and softened eyes that were decidedly friendly towards Carvalho.

'Why are you a member?'

'Come on! What a question!' She looked puzzled and shook her head, as if the answer had been stored in some recess of the brain. 'At some point I opted for one particular thing, and I haven't had good enough reason to change my mind. I guess it's because I still believe in the Party as the political vanguard of the working class, and in the working class as the rising social force that gives a progressive meaning to History. Isn't that what used to be said? But look, don't act like such a saboteur. If you go round asking the membership that little question, you'll soon land me in trouble. It's like asking what a table is.'

'I'd like to see what everyday life is like in a Party branch. In your area, for example.'

'No sooner said than done. This evening, if you like. There's a meeting.'

'I can't this evening.'

'Big-arse?'

Carvalho pinched her cheek. She gently kicked him from under the table.

Santos stood out against the horizon, with its massed form of the faculty of philosophy and literature. He seemed absorbed in reflection, his hands clasped behind his back and his eyes lost on an imperceptible molecule of the countryside tinged mauve by the setting sun. As Santos waited and Carvalho drew closer, two men suddenly stepped in between.

'Santos,' Carvalho said, and the daydreamer turned towards the group.

88

'Let him through.'

The two walked together in silence. Then Santos felt that he ought to justify himself. He passed by the university complex every evening. In 1936 he had been on the point of completing his course, and despite the struggles and the years of hardship, the university city had stuck in his memory as a fascinating paradise.

'It was the promised city. Virtually all the faculties were in the course of construction. An arcadia of learning. We were very naive – particularly those of us who had come from the bottom or near the bottom. It had cost us such a lot to reach university. I worked nights in my uncle's bindery. I was like a character from one of Baroja's novels: maybe Manuel in *The Struggle for Life*. But the war prevented me from ending up a good bourgeois. This view helps me to relax. At this time of year, there's almost no one here in the early evening, apart from the occasional jogger. They make me depressed. They put on such a face of agony. Instead of running so much, they could eat and smoke less.'

'I wanted to see you. It has to be accepted that the murderer is one of you.'

'A hundred and thirty candidates.'

'No. Twenty or so. Only twenty had the time to make themselves mobile, kill Garrido and return to their place. Personally, I'd reduce the number to six. Look at this diagram.' Santos stopped and took his glasses from his top jacket pocket. 'Only the first two rows of the area perpendicular to the chairman's table. That's where the murderer came from.'

'You deduce that from the time involved?'

'And from the path the killer must have taken in order to hit Garrido where he did. Don't forget that you were all in complete darkness, so that the light from Garrido's cigarette must have served as a beacon.'

'I'm sorry to spoil your theory, but Garrido wasn't smoking.'

'Seven of the statements say he was.'

'He wasn't smoking. The question was raised moments before the meeting began. He was a heavy smoker and made a move to light a cigarette. We joked with him about the formal ban on smoking in a closed room. Besides, he joked about it himself when the meeting began. He said we should get it over straight away, because he couldn't take not smoking.'

'Sure. So that statements . . . '

'Hallucination or an obsessive fixation with the fact that he was a smoker. It's hard even for me to imagine him without a cigarette in his mouth. A journalist once wrote that he seemed to take cigarettes ready lit from his jacket pocket.'

'A lighted cigarette would also solve how the murderer found his bearing.'

'The problem remains, as I said, because Garrido wasn't smoking. Ask Helena or Martialay. They'll confirm it. Or ask Mir. There's also the tape-recording, in which he jokes about not smoking.'

'How is it possible that seven statements refer to him as smoking, even though no one was specifically asked about it? One even says that as soon as the light of the cigarette disappeared . . . '

'Light and the cigarette. Nobody saw one on the table. Nor on Garrido's clothing when we lifted him up. He wasn't smoking. Get the idea out of your head.'

'How did the murderer get his bearings? How could he strike such an accurate blow?'

Santos shrugged his shoulders. Carvalho thought he could detect a certain relief in Santos's movements, as if the false scent had covered an awkward truth.

'In any case, I'm sticking to these twenty names, and especially the six I've underlined.'

Santos put his glasses back on less readily than before. When he looked up from the sheet of paper, he had a sceptical smile on his face.

'Packed in those twenty names are a hundred years in Franco's jails and another century of militant activity in worse conditions than anyone can imagine. For God's sake! And these six names. Do you know who they are?'

'No. But you do.'

'They'd have to be the most cynical, two-faced people in the world. It's incredible, and I don't believe it.'

'You're a materialist, and that includes being a rationalist.'

'I'm a communist.' He had raised his voice and stopped in a rigid posture, seemingly prepared for a fight to the finish. But he gradually became less tense. A leaden weariness gripped his features and spread to a frame that seemed to shrink with the collapse of its essential pillars. 'Take no notice. What do you want to know?'

'More details about twenty names, and especially these six.'

'You'll have them tomorrow morning.'

He quickened his pace, as if to shake off Carvalho's company. Carvalho suddenly grasped him by the arm and forced him to stop.

'I didn't get into this out of curiosity, my friend. You're the one who called me in. If you like, I'll drop it now and you can hunt the killer yourself with the complete works of Lenin or Muza the Moor.'

'Please excuse my irrationality. Try to understand. I'm the least able to accept that a comrade could have killed Fernando. They've pinned a bloody legend on us that doesn't fit what we're really like. During the war, it was a question of life or death. Then there was the guerrilla struggle. But every attempt to prove that bloody legend has been a complete failure. Do you know the libels written by Semprún and Arrabal against the Party?'

'I don't even read such things.'

'When they want to mention concrete names, they always stick to one event that occurred in 1940.'

'Don't tell me the story of your life. I'm not interested.'

'It's our ethical heritage that is at stake. That heritage is the great historical force of communists. The day we lose it, we'll be as vulnerable as any prophet, as implausible as any prophet. In today's world, people hate prophets who demand a constant tension with reality.'

'Please. Don't tell me the story of your life. Presumably when a plumber or an electrician calls on you, you don't explain to him how the world was created. Just think of me as a plumber, nothing else.'

'Don't you realise that Fernando's murder is an attempt to kill a party with more than forty years of struggle behind it?'

Carvalho shrugged and turned around, so that now Santos was following him. They quickly resumed a normal pace, and Santos finally broke the silence with a neutral, forceful voice.

'You'll have what you asked for at ten o'clock precisely. If need be, I'll call together the twenty, the six, or as many as necessary.'

'All I need at the moment is a very detailed report, including personal information. Resources from work or accumulated wealth. Private life.'

'I'm sorry to disappoint you, but our files don't contain such material. You'd better ask Fonseca.'

'I was already thinking of that.'

He walked with a thirst for the last beauties of a landscape that would keep growing darker until night heaped black cotton fibres on the mountains in the distance. Something more than cotton. A fine air returned to give the air a definitely autumnal quality, adding touches of urgency to the beckoning lights of the Plaza de la Moncloa. A waterproofed jogger passed alongside, with the useless stride of a horse fleeing the knacker's yard. He was unsure whether he should surrender to the fear of water or to the necessity of walking under such benevolent rain. He decided to set off in search of the Puerta de Hierro and San Antonio de la Florida. As people raced along the streets, he enjoyed feeling the secret complicity of rain. A half-buried memory called out to him – a cider-filled hallway glowing with the reflected sunlight of youth. Just as he was becoming a saturated sponge, he reached the hallway (recovered, who knows, from another life) of the cider-bar Casa Mingo, a refuge for people fleeing the rain and for Asturians of every kind. Nothing had changed of his life or dream, and anyway he had not lived or dreamed enough reliably to compare reality and desire. He delivered himself up to the penetratingly cool cider, which was stingily dashed out in glasses little used to such a controlled stream. Wet inside and out, he soaked up the apple-froth with chorizos cooked in cider and pasties too full of onions to conceal the paucity of meat. Had he been here before? No doubt.

A fragment of conspiratorial activity stuck in his brain like a cigarette-end sticks to the lips. It was a Sunday, twenty-five years ago, and the enormous hall was teeming with omelette-filled masses unaware that, in a corner, he was seeking to overthrow the dictatorship verse by verse, sentence by brilliant sentence. Ortega must be recuperated – he vaguely remembered the words of his companion, now some kind of vice-president in some upper or lower chamber. He had doubtless been referring to Ortega y Gasset. Ortega has failed to make the leap from subject to object, said that little moustache, the moustache of an Ortegan socialist specialised in stopping punches from the shock groups of the university Falange. What a stupid prick! Here is a product of Iberia *se non è vero è ben trovato*. The civil guard, the prick, San Fermin, balls, cunt, pimp, son of a whore. But Ortega y Gasset had stopped half-way between subject and object, at the *y* separating Ortega and Gasset. Ortega or Gasset, which shall we end up as?

'More chorizo.'

'Did you like it?'

'There's nothing like chorizo.'

'And it's Asturian too.'

'Do you swear it's Asturian?'

'The chorizo and me are both Asturian.'

Spain and me are like that, *señora*. He took paper napkins and drew diagrams of the central committee meeting-room. But instead of communists, he sketched footballers in theoretical forward positions facing terrified defenders and hopelessly defeated goalkeepers.

'Can I make a long-distance call?'

'No. But there's a kiosk a few metres from here.'

It was raining. Too heavily, as if to balance his wish to speak with Charo and Biscuter. He'd left his town for two days and he already felt half a world and half a life away, as if Madrid thrust a past and a geography upon him. No. They didn't have hake in cider. A woman in cider. He needed a woman in cider. A Celtic woman, with fair complexion slightly sullied by a lack of Aryanness and blue eyes more concrete and distrustful than Viking blue. Gladys was not the type, but she was the only possibility around. Unless he spent the evening trying his luck beneath tables with the long-wedded calves of faded Celtic women, accompanied by sauce-lipped men who wiped their plates with a huge slice of bread. He decided to run the shortest possible distance between the two psychological points of attraction. He swapped the cider for brandy until he felt at ease between the four cardinal points of his body. With his depression drowned in cider, a brandy-induced euphoria fixed his mind on two or three faceless *décolletages*. Driven away by combative male eyes, as shiny as their lips were greasy, Carvalho spared them their life and their female and returned to the rain that had been waiting with deceptive gentleness. He could not find a taxi until he was nearly at North Station. He asked to be driven to his hotel, so that he could take a hot bath and phone Biscuter.

'Boss, I was beginning to get worried.'

'That's bad. You shouldn't get worried so quickly. Any news?'

'I've rung Charo two or three times. She was very angry, boss, because she doesn't even know which hotel you're at.'

'I'm at the Hotel Opera.'

'How about that, boss. They've got an Opera there?'

'It looks like a cheap chocolate-box.'

'Will you call her?'

'It's a bad time. I'd get her just when she was hardest at work.'

I'd get her just when she was faking an orgasm with one of her regular customers. 'Tell her I'll ring if this business lasts much longer. Tell her tomorrow, at meal-time.'

'We've eaten together, boss. I made a finger-licking moussaka and invited her round. Did I do wrong? She was very sad and spent the whole meal talking about you.'

'Did she eat or not?'

'Like a horse.'

'What's it like in the Ramblas?'

'Wet. It's been raining all day. Is there going to be war, boss?'

'What war?'

'That's what people are saying here. Another eighteenth of July. The Garrido thing was a signal. What are people doing there?'

'Eating chorizo in cider.'

'Isn't that just great!'

He hung up and filled the bath with hot water. As he was getting in, he discovered that the rain had driven the cold into his body. But now the hot water drove it out again and he began to feel comfortable. Closing his eyes, he could see a dark room in which a single bright point, right at the end, shone so faintly that it did not show up Garrido's face. The intensity of its glow varied with the man's breathing. And so, since the light of a cigarette is essentially intermittent, it should have been much more apparent to the others, creating an area of relative visibility around the smoker's face. A fixed glow. But how? Garrido himself giving signals to his assassin? Here I am. Here is my heart waiting for your knife. Someone is sitting next to him. Helena Subirats? Santos Pacheco? What is clear is that Garrido must have given out a signal, creating the beacon that guided his killer's steps. A ring. Maybe a ring. But no metal or precious stone could project its gleam without the intervention of light.

'Fonseca. I'm sorry to call you at this hour.'

'Don't worry. I'm your faithful servant.'

'I've read and reread the list of personal effects found on Garrido's body. It carries the seal of your department. Did nothing go
unnoticed?'

'The list mentions everything that was on the body when it was
handed over to us.'

'Some witnesses insist that Garrido was smoking, and that could
have been the killer's guiding light. But Santos swears and swears
again that Garrido was not smoking at that moment.'

'If he says so . . . '

'How do you explain the precision of the killer's path?'

'Training. A lot of training.'

'Where? Did someone from the central committee hire the Hotel
Continental meeting-room for rehearsals?'

'That wouldn't have been necessary. It's enough to reproduce a
similar set-up. Garrido always sat in the same place. The distances
could have been calculated to perfection.'

'That doesn't seem a good enough explanation.'

'It's a question of taste or inclination.'

Oliver's belonged to the neo-classical style. It didn't matter which
one – perhaps a spin-off from the decorative modernism that
sprang up in the second half of the sixties through the hardening of
camp sensibilities. Just as the Renaissance tried to imitate Greek
and Roman art more than a thousand years after its effective extinction, so the neo-modernists retrieved the last imaginative fling of
pre-monopoly capitalism forty or fifty years after its decay. A soothing effect resulted from the use of colours, forms and volumes
determined by high ceilings for an uneroded space. The inevitably
sadistic contribution of the decorator had been to condemn bodies
to something like the theoretical crouching position of people opening their bowels. Seats for pre-Arabs or post-Japanese, or feather

weight abdomens conditioned to hard-boiled egg sandwiches.

When Carvalho sat down, he felt that he was about to be interrogated by someone much better placed than himself, and this expectation shaped the way in which all those present looked at one another. They were inescapably forced to keep a look-out for the one who would play the role of grand inquisitor. This unpleasant sensation of being badly seated for the game of life sometimes disguised itself as curiosity for the faces, names and epithets that were seeking room in the inquisitor's harem, or in the basement where much of Madrid's cultured and distinguished homosexual world is known to collect. In the heterosexual room were ex-actresses of the ex-theatre, ex-actors in the post-May '68 intellectual ex-life, whose verbal radicalism was continually renewed and suitably dented by an improper sideways fall into an intervocalic position.

Inheritors of Segovian sausage-factories, converted to the negation of the negation of the negation of a radical, abrasive, dodecaphonic, paradigmatic Bakuninsm seven miles from anywhere and seven leagues from before and after the discovery that fathers do not bring new-born babies from Paris and cannot save them from the degree zero of development or from death, were explaining their latest *nouvelle cuisine* discoveries, the discovery of a seventies conspiracy, it being false that 1970 was a good year for Rioja, no need to go further than 1971 Muga, crucial for survival despite the communist betrayal and the fact that a close friend of mine at the Sorbonne, a Cambodian himself who translated Saint-John Perse into Cambodian, became a head-shrinker in Cambodia, where the fuck could he be now?

Princes of the baroque ended every night at Oliver's, beginning their elegant oration the same morning over coffee and rolls, their lungs full without oxygen or anything, still reading Gongora with a fat woman sitting on their lungs. Starlets without distinction of sex or status talked about semi-theatrical, semi-physiological performances, all the eyes in their body sketched with a small tube; then they would drop the conversation to finish it a few hours later at Boccaccio's, with depressed male and female nipples because there is massive unemployment and people don't give a fuck, which comes to the same thing. Fugitive editors or ex-editors of *Mundo Obrero*, former concrete poets, five thousand Andalusian novelists and a theosophist from Alcoy, a sensitive forty-year-old with bad nerves and a nurse with a cunt at half-mast, expelled CP members

96

and those who expelled them, the general secretaries of all the left-wing pilgrimages to Santiago de Compostella, Umbral's last discovery and Cejador's next-to-last one, black-market salesmen of *El País* articles, a girl from Seville who goes to bed late and alone, the empty chair of someone who hasn't shown up, survivors of the 1963 purge and triplet great-grandchildren of Sitting Bull, people who come to see if they are noticed, others who know the secret of the Planeta Prize-winner or Kennedy's assassination, an ETA terrorist disguised as a kid from the North, the nun who converted Borges to Kropotkinism and now displays blue-blooded stigmata on the palms of her hands.

'This is unbearable. We should have stayed at Malasaña's. There's more atmosphere there. This is like an old crock's garage.'

Gladys interpreted what she heard to Carvalho. For his part, he was fascinated by her pearly teeth that seemed miraculously artificial.

'The census is over. I've had my fill of prodigies.'

'I haven't yet described those in the north corner.'

She is wearing a mohair sweater, whose V-neck separates the hemispheres of her breasts. Carvalho has a premonition of equatorial heat in the dark humidity of her flesh. Like a moist finger, his eyes travel from the birth of the spheres down to the south of a vegetative body.

'I'm sure there's more atmosphere at Malasaña's, but the people are less erotic – they're basically as healthy as bonny little babies. At least no one here is running away from crow's feet or the spread of carbon 14.'

'Are you improvising, or reciting your secret verse?'

'Am I boring you?'

'No. But I've had enough. Can't we talk in private?'

'Just talk? You'll be sorry after. I'm not what I seem. I'm a cold, calculating woman who'll lead you to ruin.'

'Lead on.'

'You asked for it.'

As she rose, she passed her forearm over her buttocks and thighs – a gesture Carvalho had not seen since an Eleanor Parker flim of the fifties.

'What are you staring at?'

The coolness of the street was soothing to his skin.

'Who leads, you or me?' she asked.

'I'm just passing through town.'

'I haven't any fixed abode either. I live outside town, in a flat some friends lent me.'

'Let's get a taxi.'

'No so fast, stranger. I've got a car. It's also borrowed. Like everything I have.'

'I was quietly standing against the bar, resting from a dialectical punch-up, when you came looking for me.'

'Don't act the simpleton. Why were you looking at me?'

'There was nothing better to look at.'

'That girl wasn't bad.'

'What girl?'

'The brunette who was with you.'

'She wasn't with me. I think she knocks around with the other guy, the one who was translating Lenin into slang.'

'Well, you must have met in another life, because you were looking at each other like first cousins.'

Later, Carvalho kissed her near-red hair as she was driving, while she flashed back a series of smiles occasionally lit up by the headlights of an oncoming car. Now and again, Gladys caught Carvalho's hand with her lips and left a string of little kisses. The car's route was unknown to Carvalho, although he guessed they were going along the Coruña road to a residential suburb. Then they passed through motionless streets forming the darkened web of an elegant district. The car stopped and they kissed, Carvalho's tongue on the edge of the abyss, hers lightly perched on the railings. Gladys's tongue limbered up on the way of crossed kisses that marked their advance onto a crackling gravel path, just before the old glass door which she rather clumsily unlocked.

'No. Not there. They may come back any minute. Come to my room.'

Carvalho saw a cracked porcelain wash-basin, a shiny coat-hanger and a firmly locked window. He could not take in much else, because Gladys switched off the main light and put on a tiny bed-side lamp. The bed promised to be a soft homeland, and the two bodies immediately fell upon it.

She did not let herself be undressed. As she pulled the mohair sweater over her head, two breasts leapt out with two raspberries on the end. Gladys put her hands under her breasts, as if to feel their weight or to prevent them falling. Her hands served as a plate for Carvalho's sucking lips and then moved to stop his hands on their journey down her spine to the anal abyss.

'Gently.'

It struck Carvalho she had spoken with the voice of a whore, or a mother of six children weighed down by shopping, cooking and varicose veins. But her soft smile had nothing in common with the tone of her voice, nor did the small lips that pecked at Carvalho's lips, chin and chest-hair, leaving two bite-marks on his nipples that showed an unsettling presence of the canine teeth. Carvalho's hands had clutched her buttocks, separating them to spread the secret and the aroma of the enclosed grooves.

'Gently,' Gladys repeated, with a restless voice but cold eyes staring at those of Carvalho. Using the tips of his fingers, the man raised the moist down that marked the trail from her anus to a small vulva stretched to acquire greater proportions.

'Gently.'

There was already greater harmony between look and voice. Carvalho let himself roll back with Gladys on top and lifted her to see her hair, breasts and soft look of surprise. Without giving her time to recover, he placed her on his penis and penetrated her. They looked at each other without moving or speaking, but Gladys's eyes searched for explanations that Carvalho was not disposed to give. Gladys shut her eyes, lifted her head, rested her palms on Carvalho's belly and began to move up and down in a perfect gymnastic rhythm assisted by regular panting. Carvalho toured the geography of the dark-brown, painted-timber ceiling and the geography of Gladys's face, sublime, ecstatic when she leant her head back, and conquered, exhausted when she dropped it towards the man's skewering body. The arrival of orgasm was announced by a few sighs, a controlled moan, and the weakness of bent arms deserted by the brain. Finally, Gladys's body closed on his like a lid, and an oily dampness lubricated their sexual parts.

'What are you doing?' Carvalho had taken her strongly by the arms, forcing her onto all fours on the bed. 'What are you doing, stupid. Don't think you're going to have me in the arse.'

Carvalho helped his favourite son to find the entrance to the limp vagina, and then he grasped the woman's hips and buttocks and forced them to gyrate. Gladys's face had disappeared beneath the dome of her head, shaken by the to-and-fro movement of a body stretched to meet the tenacious rod. But her brain was still working like that of a computer programmer, and from time to time it sent order to her hands to strike freedom blows against the inordinate pressure of Carvalho's talons on her hips and buttocks. Crushed against the sheets, Gladys's face emitted a howl to the west: she slid forward, leaving Carvalho's purple member in the lurch, mocked by the squelching separation of flesh. He fell by her side, not in search of company but in order to protect the withdrawal of his penis to its original position. Carvlho's eyes were an inch or two from Gladys's open eye, full of smiling neutrality.

'You were starved.'

'Are you always so domineering in bed?'

'Me, domineering? You did what you wanted. At least you didn't try to bugger me. I can't stand that.'

She dropped the tone of post-operative analysis and lightly stroked the tip of Carvalho's nose.

'Are you thirsty? Shall I make something? Will you let yourself be surprised?'

'Yes, surprise me.'

As Gladys jumped out of bed, all her orbs visually jingled like bells.

'Did you have a lot for supper?'

'A rustic meal.'

'A bajativo would be good for you. Do you know what that is?'

'It sounds distinctly bad.'

'It's a kind of tonic liqueur.'

'It's my night tonight. I don't need aphrodisiacs.'

'Don't be silly. I didn't mean it like that.'

She left the room wearing only her mohair sweater. Carvalho let himself relax, uncertain whether to continue along the path of drowsiness or to get up and see what Gladys was making. He rose and tried to open the window. It was bolted.

'What are you doing?'

Gladys was standing in the door, an amphibious animal with angora wool and red-haired sexual parts, carrying a glass of green potion in each hand.

'They're bolted.'

'The house is empty most of the year and there are a lot of burglaries in the neighbourhood. I didn't want to touch anything. I only really come here to sleep.'

Cavalho took her by the waist and put his member between her legs.

'Again? You'll knock the drink over.'

She pulled herself free and held out one glass while raising the other to her lips.

'What's this?' Carvalho sniffed the contents.

'It's a very fine liqueur: peppermint, cognac, coffee cream and ice.'

'Must be good for the ovaries.'

'What an ass you are !'

'No, really, peppermint is very good for the ovaries.'

Gladys was sitting on the bed, her shoulders propped against the headrest. She lifted the glass to her small lips and her eyes filled with delight.

'It's excellent, drink some.'

Carvalho left his glass on the little table and put Gladys's beside it. He asked her for a deep kiss. At first she replied in the same vein, but then she softened and started tickling her tongue against the roof of his mouth. He picked the glass which she had been holding and knocked back half its contents.

'Tastes like a purgative. It's not bad though.'

'What an ass you are! You really are an ass tonight.'

Gladys lifted the other glass to her lips and left it against her faultless teeth.

'You'e not drinking?'

'I've already had some,' she replied.

Carvalho stretched out his hands to lift the lower part of her mohair sweater, but his arm did not support the action of his fingers. A tingling sensation crept over his eyes and muscles, so that

Gladys's anxious face already seemed full of ants.

'What's the matter?' the anxious face inquired, but he could no longer see or hear anything.

He woke with the feeling that he was being watched. By the light of the small opaque lamp, he rediscovered the space of the room and the two or three objects he had had time to register: the shiny clothes-hanger, the cracked porcelain wash-basin. He shot out his right arm in search of Gladys's body and found a strident, glass-shattering scream which pierced his chest like an ultrasonic alarm. He turned his head. Seated on a mattress, desperately attempting to cover the flesh sticking through the slits of her blouse, a terrified teenager with sunken eyes continued to scream while looking at Carvalho as at some vermin. He sat up and tried to cover her mouth. But he stopped when the door sprang open and two huge, breathless men flooded into the room as if they were a hundred. One of them began to spit out flash-lights at such a rate that Carvalho was forced to close his eyes. The scream had changed into hysterical weeping.

'He tried to rape me! He hit me!'

Feeling punches on his stomach, Carvalho lashed out and kicked one of the bodies. But the other one fell on him and pounded his head with more punches. He desperately squeezed a bit of face with both hands, feeling the distortions of a cheek, an ear and an eyelid trying to close protectively over an eye. Now that the flashes had stopped, he tried to use his restored eyesight to stand up and confront the situation. He saw himself, a naked, ridiculous observer of his own limp member, and an unknown, weeping girl draped in a sheet who was now and again hurling snotty accusations from a corner of the room. There were three of them. The photographer smiled as he kept watch over his camera. The other two were drawing closer, a pistol in one of the four hands.

'You're a filthy swine. She's under age.'

The gun's orifice fitted Carvalho's navel like a nozzle.

'Get down on all fours.'

The one who spoke tried to hide his strong Latin American accent, producing the kind of Spanish found in dubbed Puerto Rican films.

'What have you done with Gladys?'

'Who's Gladys? This is my sister and she's called Alicia. What did this pig do to you, Alicia?'

'It was horrible.'

'Have the photos come out all right?'

The photographer nodded.

'Take her out.'

The photgrapher took the girl by the arm. She had stopped crying and was smoothing the creased sheet into a blue terylene peplos. She let herself be taken from the room, glancing neutrally at Carvalho with the indifference of a life-companion.

'Can I get dressed?'

'We prefer you naked. We're going to stick a bottle up your arse and then cut your balls off so that you can't use them anymore. That's how degenerates like you have to be treated. What's your favourite bottle? Is coca-cola all right?'

He had wrinkled his nose and forehead as he spoke, as if it would help to make him sound more aggressive. The other man said nothing, his blue eyes watching Carvalho with a technological neutrality buttressed by his firm grip on the Beretta.

'Where did you find her? That little slut, I mean.'

'You'll be sorry you said that. She's my little sister.'

'Well, there are sluts in the best of families.'

Carried away by his role, he made as if to pounce on Carvalho in defence of his honour. His companions held him back with his free hand.

'Drop it. He's provoking you.'

The man with blue eyes and fair hair had an accent suggestive of Central Europe. Czech? German? Soviet? The Latin American looked like a well-preserved ex-boxer. Even his bald patch had kept him in trim against the scandal of decay. He drew out a long black cudgel and forced Carvalho to jump by hitting him on the legs. Finally, he delivered an accurate blow to the back of the knee, so that the detective fell to the ground on his knees.

'Don't move!'

He held Carvalho in his sights, while the other man handcuffed his wrists behind him.

'Put something on him.'

'I'll put a shirt on him. But let his balls hang down – it'll be easier to cut them off.'

They pulled him on his back and tied his ankles to one foot of the bed. Then they switched off the light and went out. His eyes had been flayed by so much shock that the darkness had a soothing effect on them. He surprised himself humming an old Catherine Sauvage song:

Braves gens

Ecoutez la triste ritournelle

Des amants qui ont vécu dans l'Histoire

Parce qu'ils ont aimé des femmes infidèles

Qui les ont trompés ignominieusement.

He laughed and repeated the last line with delight. There must be a lot at stake for them to bring up a submarine like Gladys. Soon the pain in his arms dulled his good spirits and forced him to wriggle on his back in order to stop the piercing pins and needles in his arm muscles. At the same time, all the danger in the world seemed to be poised over his cold, damp penis. Resting on his shoulder-blades, he finally managed to relieve the pain in his arms, but could not find a position that would equalise the muscular tension. Whenever he took the pressure off his arms, his neck started to hurt. The door opened. A rectangle of light poured onto his legs as far as the waist, leaving his neck and face in darkness. It was the Latin American.

'Do you like the position? You can stay like that for a week. No, you wouldn't be able to stand it. A few hours from now, you'll be as limp as a fig. You can stay there in your own piss and shit.'

He put his foot on Carvalho's genitals.

'I'll leave them as flat as two dried figs.'

He was obsessed with figs.

'Maybe we could talk and clear things up.'

'We'll decide when to talk and clear things up.'

'Forget it.'

The Central European filled the space of the door. The other man briefly increased the pressure of his foot on Carvalho's genitals and then pulled away with a murmur of disgust.

'You should leave him to me.'

He dived into a dark corner of the room and watched the scene unfold between Carvalho and the Central European.

'It's very uncomfortable talking from here.'

'I assure you all your discomforts are precisely calculated and can easily be increased.'

'What do you want?'

'Just think it over.'

He stepped back and ceased to be a powerful shadow standing in his own light. The other man moved across the room and, without saying a word, locked the door behind them. As soon as the sound of the key faded away, pain re-entered Carvalho's consciousness as if it had been awaiting the result of an unsuccessful interview.

He had bitten his lips so much that they were bloody and painful. His bones seemed like iron spikes boring into his flesh, and attempts to ease the pain by breathing deeply had gradually become gasping efforts to stifle the sound of his own suffering. But when the door opened once again, he could still piece together a priest-like face by the light of the overhead lamp. When they untied him and his legs dropped to the ground, he felt as if they were pinned by thousands of tiny needles in direct communication with every nerve centre. His legs failed when they stood him up, and the two men helped him into a long, bare corridor, like the walk to the scaffold. He was then taken into a living-room which housed millions of pesetas of distinction. The Central European sat beside a desk framed by the most ivory-like tusks in the world, while the Latin American helped Carvalho onto a spineless pouffe where he was swallowed by thousands of polyurethane pellets cross at having to make way for him.

'Take the handcuffs off and keep the gun at the back of his neck. You must not move, Señor Carvalho. It's a very noisy seat, and my colleague can get flustered at the slightest noise.'

The Central European was drawing or writing on a sheet of paper. Carvalho felt another's presence just behind him as he held his newly freed wrists and rubbed his arms after their long journey through pain and impotence. The photographer's footsteps could be heard approaching from the floor above. He passed in front of Carvalho without glancing at him. In his hand was a wad of photographs, which he deposited on the desk for the man with blue eyes and fair hair. Only then did the head look up. His eyes listlessly pecked at the photos, moving to Carvalho and back in apparent search of a point of reference.

'Very nice pictures. They'll look beautiful when they're published. Show them to him.'

Carvalho saw himself pouncing on a poor half-naked girl, whose panic-distorted features were further evidence against him. Fifteen or twenty photos. The attempt to shut her up. The surprise at their sudden entry. The flagrant nudity. The attempt to conceal it. The photographer returned the pictures to the desk and left the way he had come.

'Very nice. Very nice. Would you like them to be published?'

'If you left the selection to me I wouldn't care. My parents wouldn't scold me. I'm an orphan. I haven't got a wife or children.'

'But you do have clients. And your present client cannot risk a scandal. After the leader's assassination, all they need is for the private detective to be mixed up in the corruption of a minor.'

He could be Central European. But he could also be merely an aggressive executive turned out by some business school, where the language is desexed by polyglottal references.

'Blackmail, eh?'

'That depends.'

'You've wasted too much time trying to blackmail one of the few men in the country that has nothing to hide.'

'Nothing to hide?'

'Nothing, not even the most horrible of things. I couldn't give a shit about the others, my friend, and you look as if you believe me.'

'I'll cut your balls off with a razor-blade,' a voice said behind his back. Carvalho remembered that he was still naked from the waist down, a victim of the voracious pelleted pouffe.

'Your buddy must be the latest model. I've never met this kind of castrating gorilla before. He's absolutely obsessed.'

The castrating gorilla caught him by the hair and forced his head back. Then he slowly dribbled onto Carvalho's lips, in a heavy, mercury-like stream. The detective wiped it off with the back of his hand, holding down the retching that rose in concentric circles from his stomach. The blue eyes had grown smaller, as if to assess his capacity for cleaning away the saliva.

'Don't speak unless you're asked to. Just answer our questions. Maybe you don't care about these pictures, but they will certainly swell the file. Santos will be interested in them. What guidelines have you been given? Which path did they tell you to follow in your investigation?'

'Which company are you from? Is it the CIA or the KGB? Or something quite different?'

'We're from the Society for the Protection of Baby Whales. You've already met Fonseca. What did you agree? What's the state of the official investigation?'

'I just talked about old times with Fonseca.'

'Please. You're not in the best position for being witty. The way things are at the moment, your death wouldn't merit half-an-hour of police time, or half a thought from your Party people.'

'I'm not in any party.'

'Okay, but you'd better play ball. All we want is simple information that won't compromise anyone. Who are you going to pin the murder on?'

'Who do you advise?'

'That's a good question.'

'Excellent,' added the man obsessed with testicles.

'This game is being played for high stakes, and you're just the little ball in the roulette wheel. You'll drop in the number and colour chosen by the croupier. We want to know what number and colour you've been given.'

'For the moment, it's up to me to find one.'

'Don't play the fool or take me for one. There are dozens of people watching you and one other. You could do with some help.'

'What, you people?'

'It depends on whether you co-operate. We need to be kept periodically informed on the course of your investigation. Particularly now that the little ball is about to drop into one of the holes.'

'You seem to know everything. You tell me which hole it will drop into.'

'I know very little. I know what I have to do with you – what I should say and ask. But that's all. Everyone has their own task in this game. I'm just playing a role.'

'Doesn't the business of the photographs strike you as rather grotesque?'

'Did you find it grotesque to be doubled up for three hours? Would you find it grotesque to spend another three or another hundred like that? Who's to stop us? Don't get stuck on details. Think of the whole.'

'May I have my trousers back?'

'My colleague is the trousers expert. Ask him.'

The man obsessed wth castration was watching Carvalho with a look of boredom. He did not quite understand that he had been given his cue. He prepared to make some impact, screwing up his nose and face and hardening his voice.

'Out of the question. Let him think it over for a bit. Then we'll see.'

He pulled Carvalho by his shirt towards one of the doors. The other man began to walk back through the room.

'Think it over a little more,' he said without turning to Carvalho. 'You'll be hearing from us again soon.'

They left him in the bedroom he had shared with Gladys and the rape victim. After checking that the door was locked and the window bolted from outside, he threw himself onto the bed. The static time in the room took most of the edge off the pain, and his heavy eyelids soon separated him from the physical darkness and opened the gates of sleep. Seated on a barber's chair, he looked in a mirror and saw the smiling head of a hanged man.

He was awakened by the sound of the opened door banging in a cold persistent wind. When he put his feet on the floor, he immediately found his empty trousers. He put them on with the urgency of a drug-addict, as if recovering part of his skin, and then finished dressing. With help from a spontaneous opening of the door, he slipped into the corridor and tiptoed along it with his back against the wall. He stopped by the living-room door to listen to the sounds of the house. They were all caused by the vigorous wind, which rubbed like sandpaper against the outside walls and tried to scalp the sighing trees in the garden. One man lost in a living-room of more than a hundred metres. It was his own image that fell on him in the manner of an obvious truth. He looked through the house as if he were a Robinson Crusoe on some desert island. He had been with Gladys and the rape victim in the servant's room. The house was a family residence whose only interest lay in the imagination used to differentiate the eight bathrooms and in the money spent on decorating its five hundred square metres of living space. Family photographs. The diploma of an agronomic engineer: Leandro Sánchez Reatain. A photo signed by Franco. Another by Juan Carlos. In the cellar, heaps of Rioja bottles without any criteria of selection. Carvalho deduced that a wholesaler had collected all the worst vintages since the Moroccan revolt of 1921. A larder full of supermarket ham and sausages. In a huge refrigerator, which could have held a thousand tins of peaches in syrup, Carvalho found ten that had escaped the voracious appetite of a syrupy family. He also nibbled with relish at a chorizo of no identifiable origin. Not a trace of the two thugs, the photographer, the rape victim or Gladys. He thought of ringing Carmela but did not know where she might be. It was seven in the morning.

He went into the garden and discovered a whole landscape of gardens, slate-roofed mansions, and television aerials seemingly capable of beaming to the moon assorted scenes of fifth-dynasty barbecues around spits of enriched iron and bronzed bronze. He could date this residential suburb from the youthfulness of most of its trees. It was to the north of Madrid, although he did not know the exact distance from the Coruña road. He walked along the edge of a swimming-pool covered with blue plastic. The bumpy seats of a swing were bathed in moonlight. He sat on one and silently began to swing himself backwards and forwards under a well-oiled frame. Forwards to a hollow-eyed moon, backwards to the diamond sparkle of the sumptuous gravel. A headstrong toad darted under the swing to the pool, vanishing into the paralytic waters beneath the plastic cover. Carvalho went up to the skies made impotently dark by the powerful moon. At Lerida prison, he had transformed the same sky into an imaginary escape-route to the reality sealed off by four cornerstones. A comrade had sent him a postcard reproduction of a magic Klee canvas, in which the moon was a red ball playing on the roofs of a cubic city. It was the moon of Lerida. The moon of Madrid twenty and more years later. As he finally brought himself to a standstill, he felt that his body had been penetrated by an excessive cold which combined the night-dew of Lerida and the dew now sparkling on the gravel of a villa turned Cheka head-quarters. What the hell are you doing here? What the hell would you do anywhere else?

'Do you know the worst torture for a prisoner? Not to be allowed to see the sky.'


Dawn was breaking. The three runaway brothers had been given rare permission to exercise with the four political prisoners from Lerida prison-farm. The brothers had tried to escape twelve times and had each accumulated a hundred and fifty years of sentences. They had claimed responsibility for crimes in every part of Spain, so that they would continually be moved and given a chance to break free. Two of them never said a word. The other accepted cigarettes and almost drank the sky.

'I won't speak loud in case those bastards hear and put it straight in their book. Have you people been in Burgos? It's full of your comrades.'

'Do you know someone called Cerdán?'

'Cerdán. Rings a bell. A young guy, like you lot. It's something else there. All the reds in Spain, if you'll excuse me. I say "reds" with respect. I respect the reds. I'd like to see Khrushchev come here on a motor-bike and drive all those swine into the sea. Me and my old brother escaped from Burgos in the dust-cart. Six kilo-metres smelling of rubbish. And then they wouldn't let us wash all the time in solidarity.'

A praying mantis had attached itself to potatoes recently peeled by the huge abortion of a cook who was putting his meat out to dry by the light of the waxing moon.

'That's the slimiest animal there is. It kills the male after fucking it.'

The escapist knew all the animals that slipped into and out of prisons. He used toothpicks and fishing thread to make splints for wounded sparrows.

'There really ought to be a swing in this yard.'

That was absolutely right. A swing would have allowed them to go up and up, over the white cubic architecture of that country prison and ever closer to the red Klee moon-ball. Two weeks later, the runaway brothers were taken to Puerto de Santa María prison. They went into the middle of the rounded building and cast a final look of wearied disdain at the short-sighted chief warder, who used to write alexandrines in his spare time.

Carvalho clapped his hands to shake off the dust left on them by the chains of the swing. The crunch of gravel accompanied him to the over-decorated iron gate. He walked into a tidy, almost useless dawn street, typical of a choice residential suburb. He made for the first turning and passed uniform constructions in search of an exit from the labyrinth. The noise of traffic was louder to the west, and so he went in that direction until he met the Coruña road and the first strings of headlighted car-drivers. He crawled up a slope, appearing on the highway like a child of morning and the road. It took him some time to find the customary gesture of a hitch-hiker. As the cars passed, they splashed him with hurried indifference. He walked a few metres and back, repeating the gesture in the face of blind headlights. A family Chrysler stopped. The driver was a plump man with white whiskers. He was wearing a waistcoat.

'A breakdown?'

'No. A party that went on too long.'

'Parties are never too long if you're having a good time.'

'The girl I went with had gone to sleep.'

'Women only think of themselves.'

He was barely touching the wheel, as if it made him sick.

'Do you know the name of the place you picked me up at?'

'Las Rozas. It's a very posh area. I own the little hotel higher up.'

'That is also a very nice part, but quite different. It's called the Almendro Heights, a development I'm doing up with some of my pals. Do you know how much our patch cost us fifteen years back? Twenty-five pesetas. No kidding. What's left is now going for a hundred and fifty or two hundred. It depends.'

'On what?'

'On how much sun it gets.'

The sun was establishing itself over the city roof-tops.

'One day I'll sell the lot and never be seen again. Can you imagine their faces?'

'Whose?'

'My wife's, for example. Look here, they'll say, your husband

111

sold me this house. Where is my husband? At the other end.'

'Of the world?'

'Of whatever. But at the other end. Are you Basque? Good. Because I'd like to go to the other end, but only if there aren't any Basques. They thought they had more guts than anyone else. It's all because of that beret. It flattens their brains. True. I love my wife and kids, but they eat me up. Where are you from?'

'Barcelona.'

'Shake!'

He shook his hand.

'That's another story. They're smarter than anyone. More money and more education. And they don't set off bombs like Basques. That's another story: it's Europe.'

'About time too!'

At first he had the Hollywood-type suspicion that it was the wrong room. He stepped back. But the blue files open on the bed, and the inviting smile of the stout man hunched in the little hotel armchair, confirmed that he had made no mistake and that he ought to enter without taking his eyes off the hand stuck in an over-size jacket.

'I've spent the whole night here waiting for you.'

'We hadn't arranged to meet.'

'You're the man of the moment. You have an appointment with everybody.'

His head was raised towards the ceiling and one hand gripped the arm of the chair to control the seismic laughter of his body.

'I don't hold grudges. I had a few winks in the chair, but then I couldn't resist making some room on the bed. No, I didn't move your files. That's how they were.'

'Are you Russian, American, German, Czech? Your accent seems Central European, and I've had my fill of Central Europeans this morning.'

'What is a Central European? Who are we Central Europeans?

We're crossroaders, people of the road. Even I don't know what I am. Shall I order breakfast for two?'

'What about my reputation?'

This time he used his free hand to hold down the epicentre of laughter, the third fold of heaped flesh lying precisely over his flies.

'Did you lose the other hand at the siege of Stalingrad?'

He piled up more roars of laughter, but without taking out the invisible hand.

'You're very funny, the funniest detective I've ever met. Yes, sir, that's a good start. If we have some breakfast, our humour will get even better. I'd like to eat here.'

It was an instruction. Carvalho lifted the telephone and ordered breakfast for two.

'I don't think I'll have anything. Hotel breakfasts fill me with horror.'

'I'll eat them both, then. It's the ritual that's important. The sound of cups, pouring milk, a butter-knife on the toast. It calms the mind.'

'Your comrades aren't as friendly as you.'

'What comrades?'

'I spent the night with two gentlemen who were very skilful at interrogating me.'

'You see! You have an appointment with everybody. They got there ahead of me, curse them. What time was the meeting?'

'Two in the morning.'

'I was here long before that,' he sighed with relief. 'In fact I was first, but you didn't keep my appointment. I'll point it out.'

'Who to?'

'Señor Carvalho, I have nothing to do with your morning rendez-vous. Let's say it wasn't people from my company. I work for a serious company, and we don't get in each other's way. Everyone has a clearly defined area. What did they want?'

'The same as you.'

'I haven't asked anything yet. I've come to offer you something.'

'What?'

'Protection. I know you already have an escort of noble and loyal communists. I also know that the Spanish police can protect you. But this is too complicated a game, Señor Carvalho. Please describe your companions from last night.'

Carvalho described them.

'I know the Latin American. He's a dangerous type: a recent convert who wants to get on. I don't know the other one. They must have brought him in specially. Everything's become too complicated, Señor Carvalho. At times, even I had to stop and say to myself: right, who are you with and who are you against? Have you read Le Carré's novels? I always get confused with Le Carré. Does Smiley really work for the Intelligence Service? He never knows the origin of what he finds or where it will end. Imagine that Smiley one day discovers he is working for the KGB. What would be his first concern? To find out whether the five-year postings count towards his pension. I'd like to retire soon. I've got thirty-five years service behind me.'

'Serving whom?'

'Humanity.'

'Where will you retire to?'

'To a little house that's already awaiting me by the sea. I won't tell you which sea.'

'How can you protect me?'

'That depends on the interest we have in protecting you, on what you give in return.'

'You want to know from time to time how my investigation is going.'

'Exactly.'

'And above all, you want me to tell you the name of the murderer I propose to my client.'

'Very clever.'

'I suspect that both you and my recent interrogators already know who did it, but that you'd like time to take a position on the official murderer.'

'It's a very unusual murder. Obviously it's damaging to the Communist Party of Spain and the Workers' Commissions. But who stands to gain? International monopoly capitalism? Moscow and its strategy for Southern Europe? Well, both of them benefit. Have you noticed?'

'And the whole world. Sounds like an *El País* editorial.'

'But that doesn't mean that either of them is behind the crime. International politics is full of outsiders: every petty ruler starts by setting up his own secret service and goes on to develop the atom bomb. That's the only way they can win respect. It's not like before. When I first started, only the big powers were in a position to make such efforts. Working then was a pleasure. Now the market is full of bungling amateurs. For example, Gadafy is doing the unspeakable, subcontracting agents from other secret services. That's right. So you can find yourself working in the same cause as agents of either side. It's not serious.'

A waitress divided her shifty look between the two men and left the trolley exactly in the middle.

'My nephew isn't hungry, but I'll eat it all.'

The girl wished him a good meal and left the room.

'Your reputation is safe. I'm very thoughtful with my partners.'

'How many are there on my tail? After you, who else is going to ask me the same thing?'

'I doubt whether anyone else will dare to approach you so directly. But a lot of people seem to be following the case at a distance, and an outsider may step in at any moment. We have an interest in protecting you. The jams you get nowadays are such rubbish. It'll be very simple for you. The window of this room looks onto the street. When you have something to communicate, lean out and move an object up and down. Any object you like.'

'What if it's night-time?'

'Just the same. We follow you day and night.'

'Last night also?'

'Also. I didn't care that my rivals were one jump ahead. I wanted to have a good stretch in this room looking at your files. Have you worked out the distance from the other tables to Garrido's or the length of time during which the lights were out? That narrows the suspects to the first three rows, and still more to those seated at right angles to Garrido. Strange that the criminal could find his way round in the dark. Has that struck you?'

'Tell me the name you're interested in.'

'I don't even know the murderer I'm interested in. I don't control the whole game. But I'm an old hand and all I'll tell you is objective facts. Won't you even have some coffee?' He poured a cup out for Carvalho. 'I suppose that now you'll get in touch with Fonseca and tell him about your two meetings.'

'As soon as you leave.'

'Go ahead. Don't mind me.'

'I'd like to have a shower and then ring on my own.'

'Individualism is the ruin of the Spanish.'

He stood up with the help of both hands.

'Thank you very much for being so amicable. Your colleagues weren't quite the same.'

'They're young and rearing to go. Experience is an important quality. I don't need to resort to violence. But watch out, Señor Carvalho. If necessary, I'll put a bullet between your eyes without losing a minute's sleep.'

He seemed to turn his back on Carvalho as he went out, but one of his eyes stayed on the detective until the door was between them.

'Las Rozas. Leandro Sánchez Reatain. We'll soon find out who that gentleman is.'

Fonseca passed the sheet of paper to Sánchez 'Dillinger' Ariño, who took it with great interest and sped from the room like a motor-launch. Fonseca noted with satisfaction the diligent attitude of his assistant.

'You see? There's real concern to get to the bottom of the matter. Did they do you any harm? The savages!'

Carvalho held his stare to see whether there was a glint of irony in his watery eyes. But Fonseca did seem about to cry at the thought of Carvalho's sufferings.

'Apart from anything else, it was a violation of our sovereignty.'

Pilar nodded her head over the typewriter. Fonseca dialled a number.

'The minister, please.'

'Minister, we've just suffered a violent attack on our sovereignty.'

He related what had happened to Carvalho.

'The minister is at your service,' said Fonseca, tapping the microphone with his hand.

'Thank you very much.'

'He's deeply grateful. We'll work together till the end. Of course, minister. The good name of this office and of Spain stands higher than anything else.'

He put down the receiver and stood up with a flurry of abstract indignation.

116

'I can't stand any foreigner laying his hands on a Spaniard. I can't bear it.' He sobbed and covered his face with his hands. 'They'll end up pissing in our shops and shitting on our tombs.'

'Can you tell from the leads I gave you which secret service they belong to?'

'What are you asking, my boy? In Madrid there are regular agents from twenty-four intelligence services and international organisations. You say one was fat, very fat? Did he hold his mouth like this?'

'No, he held it like that.'

'You're sure?'

'Sure.'

'Then it's not the one I was thinking of.'

Sánchez Ariñó came in and handed him a note.

'Good God! Good God!'

Carvalho jumped up in alarm, but Fonseca looked at him with a relaxed, witty smile.

'Well, how about that! It turns out that the house exists but not the owner. Sánchez Reatain died four months ago in a road accident and the house is up for sale.'

'Some of the food in the fridge had been bought recently, and the swing in the garden had been oiled not long before.'

'Did you have a swing on it?'

'Yes.'

Fonseca and his assistant looked at each other.

'You had a swing,' Fonseca repeated, as if trying to convince himself.

'Strange. The house is still owned by the Sánchez Reatain family and hasn't been let to anyone. Very strange.'

'Is it possible to talk to the family?'

'No point. It's split up. The wife is at a brother's house in Switzerland and the sons are studying abroad. They even discharged the servants and hired the services of an agency to clean it once a week.'

'Which agency?'

'Which agency?'

'Dillinger' left the room once again, assuming a fastidious responsibility for the question.

'An interesting quesion. Which agency? That must have been where the contact was made. You're a fine professional. It's obvious that you've had some education. I won't offer you a job here because even I don't know how long I'll last. What times these are, when the greatest loyalty is rewarded with disloyalty!'

'I'd like access to the confidential files on every member of the PCE central committee.'

'If you've got a week to kill, I don't see any obstacle. But they won't tell you anything you don't already know. They merely chart their criminal career until the Party was made legal. I'd have to consult my superiors.'

'I'd like to see reports not about criminal activity, as you call it, but about their private life. What they say on the phone, for example.'

'There's a lot of myth about this phone-tapping business. Ours is a poor country, and we have neither the technology not the staff to keep listening in on every red in the country. If you can be more specific and tell me which five or six you're interested in, it might be easier to put together. But not dozens. Don't ask for the impossible. You can't tell me that you haven't got a list of candidates.'

'I'll swap it for yours.'

'We'll study the offer.'

For the moment, Fonseca's eyes were content to study Carvalho.

'I have got a suspect – or rather, two. But one above all.'

'Who?'

'I'll be frank and then leave it to you to name your favourites. My suspects are Martialay and Marcos Ordóñez. Martialay and Garrido were on very bad terms. Garrido, as you know, was very euro and liberal on the outside, but he couldn't stand losing control of any power centre such as was happening with the trade-union movement. As for Marcos Ordóñez, the story's as long as your arm. You know who I'm talking about?'

'No.'

'Cut the jokes.'

'I'm not joking.'

'Marcos Ordóñez is one of the historic figures from before the war. He was thick as thieves with Garrido until the struggle for the succession back in the late forties. Against Garrido, Ordóñez supported a guy who's now dead, called Galdón. When Garrido won, Ordóñez was marginalised to such an extent that he had to go to work in a factory in Czechoslovakia. Has no one really ever told you the stories of people like that? You've only heard a part: how heroically they resisted the torturers of that butcher Franco, and so on.

118

Yes, I know all that. But there was a lot of shit flying around in exile, particularly among the leadership. A lot of jealousy, both big and small. A lot of battles between influential Party families. Let's go back to Marcos Ordóñez. After the Twentieth Congress of the CPSU, Garrido needed all possible support to force through destalinisation in the Party, and so he started drawing people back to confront the Stalinist conspiracy. Ordóñez was one of those reintegrated, but only on terms of complete political prostration. Just think. He was one of the first and he only reached the executive committee in 1973 or thereabouts, more or less at the end of his life. He's a very sick man, deeply marked by the moral suffering to which he was subjected. Try to understand. Put yourself in his shoes.'

'I can see you have a high opinion of Marcos Ordóñez.'

'Why do you say that?'

'His fate obviously makes you sad.'

'Well, you can't have a heart of stone. It's true, I've studied these people so much that I'm not indifferent to them. It's only because of my Catholic principles that I've been able to resist their enormous seductive power and avoid becoming a communist.'

Miss Pilar let out the first series of short guffaws. But after a little stern hesitation, Fonseca followed with roars of laughter that brought him to the verge of suffocation.

'The Urbana Matritense,' Dillinger said from the door.

'The Urbana Matritense,' Fonseca repeated softly, casting ocular rays of expectation towards the listless Dilinger. 'What's that?'

'The company that does house-cleaning. Nothing out of the ordinary. It's a family firm with more than fifty years of tradition.'

'You can stuff your tradition. Investigate, investigate, investigate!'

Fonseca rigidly tapped Dillinger on the lapel. Carvalho passed alongside them, muttering something in the way of goodbye.

'You're off already? I promise to keep you right up to date with what I find out.'

Carvalho indicated his agreement.

'But next time I won't let you off so lightly. I did all the talking.'

'We swapped roles for once.'

Santos was waiting alone at the corner of a long committee table. He showed Carvalho the obsessive blue files piled up behind him. He stood up to walk around the table while Carvalho was sounding the innards of the twenty files.

'You can go if you like. I've got a couple of hours' work.'

'I'll stay if you don't mind.'

Carvalho put his hand in his pocket and drew out a note-pad and a plan of the Hotel Continental conference-room. Imagining the pad as the platform table, he placed each file in such a way as to represent the position of the central committee member whose photograph and political history were contained inside it.

'Good work.'

'I did it alone. I didn't want anyone to stick their nose into it.'

As if he were waiting for the result of an examination, Santos continued to walk up and down, with an occasional glance at Carvalho's activity. The detective read each biography, took notes, put the file to one side, and left the photograph at the relevant point around the note-pad. He considered each picture in turn, scrutinising the eyes in the blow-ups of banal passport photos. Finally, he separated out six photos and six dossiers and put them at the other end of the table.

'Are those the suspects?' Santos stopped with a sceptical smile on his lips.

'The main ones, yes.'

'Juan Sepúlveda Civit, Marcos Ordóñez Laguardia, Juan Antonio Lecumberri Aranaz, Félix Esparza Julve, Jorge Leveder Sánchez-Espeso, Roberto Escapá Azancot. A fine selection. I congratulate you.'

'I've borne in mind their position in the room. And I've eliminated women and old men since they wouldn't have been able to deliver such a knife wound. These six names do not exhaust every possibility. If I get nowhere with them, I'll continue until we've

120

covered all twenty.'

'I suppose you've read the life-history of these people. I also notice that you've selected one veteran, Marcos Ordóñez. Was he physically capable of doing it?'

'Theoretically, no. But he may have had the psychological capacity. According to my information, he'd piled up a number of grievances against Garrido.'

'Have they been telling you about the purge in the fifties? But Ordóñez was rehabilitated and promoted to high Party posts.'

'Still, Ordóñez's exile in Czechoslovakia seems to have lost him even his family. His own wife wrote a letter to the Party leadership disowning her husband and accusing him of Titoism. Was it a very serious thing to be a Titoist?'

'Very serious until 1954.'

'What happened in '54?'

'The new leadership team in the USSR revised its position on Yugoslavia. It was the beginning of destalinisation.'

'Did the Ordóñez couple get together again?'

'No. She went to Spain for underground work and was arrested in '58. She was only released about 1965 – quite a long spell.'

'What does she do now?'

'She died in Bucharest two years ago. She was a sheer physical wreck, and so we sent her to a Romanian sanatorium.'

'Were there any children?'

'They stayed with the mother and vanished after she was picked up. They have nothing to do with the Party nowadays. One's a tailor in Barcelona, I think, and the other has a restaurant in Melbourne.'

'Do they keep in touch with the father?'

'Only just.'

'A fine political history, to the greater honour and glory of militant discipline.'

'We were fighting a military dictatorship and were not too concerned about nuances. We were tough, not only with others but also with ourselves. I never saw my children grow up: they're strangers to me. Our children grew up thanks to the tenacity of our wives, who lived like widows from one trial to another, one prison to the next. Some fared a lot worse than Ordóñez. At least things could be put right in his case.'

'Juan Sepúlveda Civit. Industrial engineer. Forty-two years old. Member of the People's Liberation Front who joined the Communist Party in 1965. Responsible for the liberal professions for nearly ten years until regionalisation. What does regionalisation mean?'

'When the Party began to grow, it switched from occupational to regional organisation. One of the aims was to check the corporatist deviations that were beginning to appear.'

'Sepúlveda Civit. Court-martialled with El Felipe in 1962. Public Order Court in 1967. Sacked from Perkins, Pegaso. Married with two children. I see his dues are four thousand pesetas a month. That's a lot of money.'

'It's one per cent of his income.'

'Four hundred thousand a month. Not bad.'

'He's very highly thought of as an engineer. The Party turns to him when it has financial problems: elections, special expenditure.'

'According to my information, he may be one of Garrido's legatees. It says here that he clashed with Garrido about the decisions of the last congress. He identified with "Leninist" against "euro-communist" positions.'

'That may be a little exaggerated. That tendency could be seen in him, and it would anyway be logical in his case. Sepúlveda is a great militant. But he cannot shake off a social and cultural conditioning which sometimes drives him into maximalist positions. Intellectuals are usually more radical than workers; it's a way of affirming themselves. We have to be as wary of arrogant intellectual know-alls as we are of humble intellectuals with an inferiority complex in relation to the working class.'

'You've studied the problem a lot.'

'It's my job. I'm a bureaucrat, don't forget.'

'Married with two children. His wife is not a member, but she helps on occasions and gave him active assistance during the election campaign. Her name is Lamadrid Raistegnac. Sounds very familiar.'

'Her father belongs to twenty administrative councils. He's a papal count or something.'

'You have very good connections. Let's continue. Juan Antonio Lecumberri Arranaz. Comes from ETA (military wing). Well, I'm damned! Now we're getting somewhere. A recent recruit: 1973. A violent past – tried as an ETA man in 1967, wounded in a clash with the *guardia civil*. Economist. Currently a member of the Party finance committee. Exempt. I suppose that means he's a full-timer.'

'He helps to collect Party finances and is also one of those responsible for organisation. He's rather a difficult lad. He's recently seemed weighed down by political work and on the point of requesting a leave of absence. He got married three years ago, and his wife doesn't understand the vow of poverty he forces on her. He could earn a very good living indeed. It's understandable. But that doesn't strike me as reason enough to kill Garrido.'

'Félix Esparza Julve. Forty years old. Already a member of the Communist Youth in Burgos in 1953. The son of exiles. A commission agent. Married. Three children. A Party full-timer in the early sixties in Paris and Asturias.'

'We sent him into Asturias to reorganise the Party after the round-ups of '62 and '63. I was a friend of his father, one of the bravest comrades who went into exile in 1939. We smuggled him into Spain in 1944 to make contact with the Valencia guerrillas. He was arrested and reduced to a pitiful state, dying of TB in San Miguel de los Reyes prison. I've been a kind of godparent to Félix. I call him Julvito. For reasons connected with Party work, I've spent more time living with him than with my own children. I'd put my head on the chopping-block for him.'

'But not for the others? What should we deduce from that?'

'The others deserve all my trust, and right now I really would prefer a supernatural explanation that would free everyone from blame. I feel ashamed to have helped you compile these dossiers, and to be haggling with you over the honour of my comrades.'

'There's one assassin in a party of two hundred thousand members. That's not a bad average.'

'No, that's the wrong way to look at it. There's an assassin in a central committee of little over a hundred members, in which the herioc history of the Party is distilled. That's the problem, the insoluble problem.'

'Paco Leveder Sánchez-Espeso. I see that you've given a very frivolous account of him. Why do you call him "a professional oppositionist"?'

'He's mad about aesthetics and always adopts the most beautiful posture. But he's been a very hard-fighting militant, both at university and on the intellectual front. He spent three or four years in prison and always stood up for the Party when he had to. He's on the central committee because he's all the rage among intellectuals.'

'You say here: voted against Garrido.'

'The present central committee was elected at the last congress.

123

In turn, it elected the general secretary and the executive committee. Garrido was elected almost unanimously. The almost was Leveder. He raised his solitary arm when asked if anyone was against.'

'You didn't send him to Siberia?'

'It must be accepted that the days of unanimity are over in this party.'

'Did he justify voting against Garrido.'

'Yes. He asked to speak and gave his motivation. He said he was voting against as a matter of basic Party education, to teach the charismatic leaders that they are not gods. I think his explanation disturbed Garrido more than the actual negative vote. He erupted, in the way he used to erupt with a charge of repressed inner violence that clung to his words. They weren't on good terms with each other after that. They joked a lot in order to cover it up, but there was a basic antipathy between them.'

'So Leveder is your prime suspect?'

'Absolutely not. He's a frivolous type and an aesthete. Do people kill out of frivolity or aestheticism? Maybe in books or films, but not in real life.'

'Leveder is separated and has a daughter. Separated from a member of the PCE-Internacional. He's a sociology lecturer at the Faculty of Information Sciences. I see that you describe him as anarchistic.'

'He calls himself a liberal-Marxist, but I think he's a democratist: an anarchist involved as a communist for reasons of historical efficacy.'

'Roberto Escapá Azancot, a farmer from La Mancha. Elected mayor of his village at the last municipal elections. Thiry-five years of age. Married. Four children. Member of the Party since 1970. Very little information.'

'He's a reliable, hard-working comrade, but without much of a history. One of the great Party workers who can keep a whole region going on his own. Worth his weight in gold. I may have forgotten to mention that he plays the flageolet and has helped to revive it throughout La Mancha.'

'Did Garrido like the flageolet?'

'He never gave an opinion one way or the other.'

Marcos Ordóñez: the face of an old frog, wise and weary. Lecumberri, that of a Basque in whom the seeds of rebellion have been sown. Esparza Julve, the smiling look of a salesman in the backroom of a shop. Irony as a method of knowledge in Leveder's smile. The agricultural solidity of La Mancha cheese in Escapá Azancot's expression. And raised above them all, Sepúlveda's ministerial head of press conferences and programmatic speeches, an important head.

'If you don't need me.'

'No, I don't need you.'

'Have you given these names to Fonseca?'

'No.'

'Will you?'

'No.'

'Why not?'

'I don't want to rush things or put anyone in danger. I don't want to manufacture an Oswald.'

'Thanks for the trust you've shown in me.'

When Santos Pacheco left, Carvalho put his feet on the table and leant back on the hind legs of the chair. He suppressed the temptation to lift the nearby telephone and call the six under investigation. He gathered together the files and photographs. Then he looked out of the balcony windows at the tree-lined street with the name of a river. Julio and his companion were propped against the car they used to follow him. A white van could be seen a few metres further down the road. Carvalho looked at it absentmindedly until his mind settled on the inscription: Urbana Matritense. Carvalho could feel the pistol in his shoulder-holster. He picked up the files, left the room, grunted nonchalantly in response to Mir, and went straight up to a girl who was tapping away at her machine.

'Give me a large bag that can hold all these files.'

He sealed the bag with sellotape and stressed that it should be given to Santos. He went into the street. Julio and his friend were still there, but not the van.

'A van has just gone off.'

'Yes. Just now.'

'I'll get in with you.'

'We're not supposed to. But okay, let's go.'

Carvalho folded and refolded the notes he had taken on the six men and put them in his top jacket pocket.

'Make as if you're going to Party headquarters.'

'Okay, man, to Castelló. It's so little known.'

The van followed in an obvious way, even drawing alongside at one point.

'Keep next to the van.'

'He lowered his window and smiled to the Latin American, who was sitting beside the driver. Carvalho took out his pistol and aimed it at the face of the man obsessed with castration. His twitching face suddenly pulled back, and the van darted off to the left.

'Step on it.'

Through the rear window he could see the van trying to move back into a position of pursuit.

'Our friend's a playful sort. As if there weren't enough trouble already.'

Julio also had a gun in his hand and was looking anxiously at Carvalho.

'It's an old story. Those bastards in the van spend the night knocking my balls around.'

Julio swapped the gun for a biro and took down the van's licence number.

'There's no point. They've got connections. I don't know who exactly, but they want to show me they've got some.'

The van drew alongside again. The man next to the driver lowered his window and held out a sheet of paper in the wind. Carvalho stretched out and snatched the paper and the man's hand.

'Accelerate!'

He heard the man cry out as his arm broke against the rim of the open window. With the sheet of paper in his hand, Carvalho looked back to see the van losing speed and other cars filling the gap between them: *five this evening at the Princess VIP-lounge.*

126

'What a stupid idea! That guy won't forget you in a hurry.'

'He's an American fucker who got what was coming to him. Now drop me by a market.'

'What kind?'

'A food market.'

'Ah! A supermarket?'

'No, a market.'

'There's a small one in Diego de León.'

He told them to inform Carmela that he wanted to see her mid-afternoon.

'Can you two suggest a place?'

'She often goes to La Manuela, in Malasaña.'

'Okay. At six o'clock.'

At the entrance to the market a man was playing *Los estudiantes navarros* on a Spanish lute. Some newspaper lying by his feet had collected a precious rainfall of one- and five-peseta pieces. Carvalho passed through the little market with the close interest of someone visiting a tiny Romanesque church. Madrid markets provide a lesson in polychromic symmetry, with their plumed onion, metallic tuna-heads, glassy, finely dressed trouts, scraps of humanised cardboard boxes, oily Toro pastry, chorizos from Candelario, individually polished green beans from La Granja, porcelain chickpeas. He bought some cooked tripe, capipota, frozen peas, the first fresh artichokes of the year, a head of garlic, almonds, pine kernels, a chunk of meaty tuna fish, a tin of anchovies, oil, onions and tomatoes. Eventually he found himself with his hands full at the gates of the market, on a day when it was not good to be there with his hands full. This obvious fact struck him as he stood by the lute-player, now strumming the popular Basque tune *Maite, Maitechu mia*. The musician looked like any railwayman on strike, with strong cubic arms and dangling legs. Suspicious and sarcastic, he watched Carvalho put the bags on the ground and drop a five-peseta piece on the newspaper. His eyes filled with gravity and he played more slowly and precisely. The music was drowned by the roar of traffic as Carvalho walked up the narrow pavement wondering what to do with the bags. He stopped a taxi.

'Go to the Hotel Opera and tell the receptionist to take these bags up to room three hundred and eleven.'

'What's in them?'

'Supper for two.'

The driver eyed the contents.

'It's not that I don't trust you, but anything can happen.'

He smiled at the sight of the tip.

'I'll go like the wind. Have a good meal.'

Carvalho went into a telephone box without a telephone, then into another with its cords snapped and its pieces scattered about. In the end, he managed to phone from a bar after he had consumed a portion of live shellfish and half a bottle of chilled white Rioja.

'Haven't you got any Ruedas?'

'No. Only Valdepeñas or Rioja.'

Madrid's wine life is fully programmed in advance. That was his last banal thought before he shut the cubicle door and began to arrange meetings with the six men on the list. He rang the central committee and asked them to find the comrade from La Mancha for the next day.

'It's a bad day for me. I'm preparing classes for tomorrow. I'm surrounded by hungry students who think only of studying. Tomorrow too. Maybe we could eat together. Any old thing.'

'I never eat any old thing. Be my guest at Lhardy's.'

'Have you won the pools?'

'The Party's paying.'

Leveder knew his way around the menu but he made expiatory efforts to forget. Suppressing his impulse to help Carvalho, he sat back and somewhat uneasily waited for him to choose. His eyes reacted approvingly, but he himself ordered oxtail soup and fresh grilled salmon.

'I've got an ulcer. Otherwise I'd be living it up with you.'

Carvalho had ordered Iranian caviar and Madrid-style tripe.

'Well chosen,' Leveder said with a convincing expression. 'The best caviar is Iranian and the best tripe is here at Lhardy's. When you return to Barcelona, you can take a portion of jellied tripe. They sell it in the shop downstairs. Will you be going soon?'

'As soon as I'm through. I'm not staying for the fun of it.'

The Lhardy atmosphere surrounded the meal like an English private club decorated by a French interior designer of neo-classical inspiration from the late nineteenth century. It was an ideal atmosphere for steaming-hot dishes, but perhaps not very suitable for cold ones.

'An excellent place to talk about the Party.'

Leveder winked and lifted a glass of mineral water to his lips.

'Wonderful mineral water. Seventy-two vintage. It was a great year for the water. But keep clear of 1973: it rained little and the water tastes of the bottom of a well. Don't you butter your toast?'

'It seems idiotic when the caviar is so sweet.'

Carvalho poured another glass of ice-cold vodka and let Leveder rack his brain for the purpose of the meeting. Leveder returned to Lhardy's, to Carvalho, and even leant over to ask:

'Have you got me down as the prime suspect?'

'As a conversation partner.'

'Did the old guard denounce me? They don't actually dislike me, but we speak two different languages. I never use expressions like "objective conditions", "resituate", "social structure", "it is necessary to obtain the optimun conditions", "the working class is paying the price of the crisis", and so on. Do you understand me? It's not that I don't believe in the reality behind all such language, but I have to struggle to find synonyms. In every tribe there is nothing as alarming as violations of the linguistic code. Maybe that's why I'm under suspicion. Besides, I voted against Garrido – as I'm sure you know. But I didn't kill him. I have a great historical appetite and I'd certainly like to be Napoleon or the Virgin Mary. But I haven't quite got the necessary determination, especially if it's a question of tyrannicide.'

'Was Garrido a tyrant?'

'A scientific tyrant, like all the general secretaries of Communist Parties. They exercise their tyranny not by divine appointment but with a mandate from the executive committee, which itself has a mandate from a central committee mandated by the Party. And the Party in turn has a mandate from History. You will have recognised that I am a Trotskyist. So why don't you ask what a Trotskyist like me is doing in a party like this? Go on, ask me.'

'Take it as asked.'

'Avoiding the temptation of joining a Trotskyist party. As Che said, if you have to make mistakes, it's preferable to make them with

129

the working class. I've always preferred to be where the objective vanguard of the real working class has been. And so, I've turned my back on a lot of people: on my brother, who is president of the Coria pigeon-shooters and owns half the region, and on my wife, who belongs to some Marxist grouplet. She's been through all the tiny Communist Parties, because she has a great capacity for affection. She likes all the sweet little left-wing parties. Before we got married, I used to give her little chairs or coffee-pots to make her happy. The present that excited her most was an Italian coffee-pot that only made enough for two people. It was the same in politics. She joined the cause of anyone who put together a tuppeny-ha'penny left-wing Marxist party. Now I think she's a Marxist-Leninist Anabaptist or something like that. Señor Carvalho, I like to make mistakes on a grand scale. As I sit before you, I assume responsibility for all Stalin's crimes and all the bad Soviet harvests since the liquidation of the kulaks and small private farmers. What I don't take responsibility for are all the little idiots like my wife or Cerdán, who go around setting up trashy market-stalls or cobbling together Cerdán's type of snivelling Marxism. It's obscene. They go around showing their sores and saying: "We've been betrayed." Shit! they should have it all stuffed up their arse.'

Leveder was really and truly indignant.

'From everything I've said, you will conclude that I did not kill Garrido. At bottom, I had a great affection for the old man, even though I was losing my historical respect for him. Given his age and position, he should have set off a real reform of the Party. He should have carried destalinisation to is ultimate conclusion, arriving at an identification of rank and file and leadership without which any project for a mass party is no more than a swindle. He should have used his authority from the days of underground activity to launch an internal cultural revolution. I repeat, *cultural*, because every Communist Party has an internal culture, an awareness of its identity conditioned by its evolution as an organic intellectual. Do you follow me? Do you think such an internal culture can be the same in a party influenced by Gramsci and Togliatti and a party influenced by Thorez and Marchais which drummed out Nizan, Lefebvre and Garaudy, to take them in chronological order?'

'For you, then, Garrido was in the way.'

'Yes, because he was alone. He'd been ditching valuable people who could have helped in the struggle. And when the time came to join battle, he was surrounded by people who were neither alone nor willing to help him put the Party right. Besides, he didn't trust those who didn't say amen after his speeches. The die was cast. We might have gone on till the year two thousand in that dead-end situation, neither fish nor fowl, neither one thing nor the other. Now at least it will be necessary to make a decision.'

'Who is your candidate?'

'Anyone except Santos.'

'Why's that?'

'Because he's a nice old chap who would practise necrophilia with the Fernando Garrido of his heart. I prefer a climber who has some sense of reality.'

'Who's a climber?'

'Everyone and no one. In such a party, a climber is always a relative concept. The absolute climbers are in parties that can win here and now.'

'Is anyone enough of a climber to have killed in order to take over?'

'No. That's a stupid way of posing things. This was not a murder directed at Garrido but at the Party. Who would wish to murder a party in order to take it over?'

'Still, the murderer is one of you.'

'The murderer is a traitor. You don't have to be an eagle or a private eye to see that.'

Carvalho put his sketch of the Hotel Continental murder-room on the tablecloth, a few millimetres from a sorbet Marc de Champagne. He drew a circle in front of the presidium.

'If the time available is taken into account, then the murderer must have come from this circle. Look at the names written here and tell me who is the traitor.'

Leveder stared at Carvalho and then glued his eyes to the sheet of paper, examining rather than reading each name. He flopped against the back of his chair and let out a sigh. Tears seemed to be in his eyes.

'Are you paying for the meal?'

'Yes.'

'Then please excuse me.'

He stood up and went in search of the stairs to the street.

'I'm meeting the parliamentary commission at five o'clock. At six I must go to San Cristobal and try to convince some comrades that the Polish working class is not paid by the CIA. At eight there's an Executive meeting to finalise the last details for the next meeting of the central committee – the one that will elect a provisional general secretary and convoke an emergency congress. With a lot of luck, I hope to be home by four in the morning. Don't be surprised if I tell you I haven't much time.'

Sepúlveda Civit still smelt of deodorant mixed with face lotion. Smart appearance, muscular frame, efficiency, an upright sense of existence already noticeable in the rare Cortes speeches that Garrido's leading role had allowed him to make. He could have continued his day's schedule. At seven I'll get up for a spot of jogging. At eight I'll have breakfast with the kids and take them to school – the only way I can ever see them. At nine I must report to my engineer's office at Entrecanales y Tavora, but by eleven I should be at the town hall, where I'm an adviser on transport matters. At one I have to discuss with the Entrecanales y Tavora management the possibility of a tunnel at Salardú that won't cause the Pyrenees to collapse. At two Carvalho recalled a song from his adolescence: the moon comes out at one, the sun comes out at two, the train comes out at three, the cat comes out at four, San Francisco at five, his wife at six, he puts it in her at seven, it's coming out of her at eight, the baby comes out at nine, it's all starting again at ten. Sepúlveda Civit could not guess the silent song echoing in Carvalho's head, but he did guess that the detective did not take his time problems seriously. He looked at his digital watch, which responded as if to a signal by emitting an astral melody vaguely reminiscent of the Last Post. He raised his eyes critically towards Carvalho. You see? The music warns me, hounds me, and you just sit there without saying a word.

'Were you saying something?'

'I'm sorry. I usually have trouble with my digestion.'

'You should do as I do. I hardly eat anything. Just a roll with vegetables and very occasionally some meat, a cup of milk, a fruit juice, coffee, and that's that. Then I catch up in the evening – when there isn't a meeting, of course. The problem is that there's always a meeting. You've got to have an arse of iron to be active in politics. That's what they call Berlinguer: iron-arse.'

Carvalho placed before him the same sketch of the conference room that he had shown Leveder.

'You were sitting here,' he said, pointing to the circle.

Sepúlveda looked painstakingly at the diagram.

'Right. And I'll jump on to what you were about to say. The man with the knife must have come from that area. Look.'

He opened a drawer and took out a plan exactly like Carvalho's. The desks were shaded differently according to their distance from the presiding table.

'I got one of my assistants to calculate the time it would have taken to move from each spot and back. It's not so simple, because there are also age factors involved. I even expressed it in a mathematical formula. Here.'

'That's very useful.'

'I'll explain it to you if you like.'

'My last contact with maths was when I failed my exam at fourteen. After that I did arts.'

'Can you be a private detective without any maths?'

'I assure you I'm very good at arithmetic.'

Not a trace of a smile on this executive of the pasteurised revolution.

'Let's see if your maths and my arithmetic have led to the same conclusions.'

'I can see that they have, from the way you've drawn the circle,' Sepúlveda replied. 'But I can demonstrate that someone sitting on the side would have had time to approach, kill and return before the lights went back on. The problem is still the same. One of orientation. Those at right-angles to the table could have found their way more easily.'

'Found their way? But the room was in darkness.'

'That's the crux, and I've worked it out. Garrido was smoking. The murderer found his way by the faint glow of the cigarette.'

'More than three – no, more than four will swear that they made Garrido put his cigarette out before he entered the room. Even if

133

he didn't, the murderer could not have relied on such a chance factor. He'd have assumed that Garrido would respect the formal ban on smoking. Anyway, it's very hard to aim such a precise blow by such a weak light.'

'Training makes everything possible, and the blow was obviously struck by an expert.'

'An expert who trained by the light of a fag-end?'

'You must solve the problem of the signal – that's my advice. Solve that and you've solved the case All the rest is a waste of time, even these interviews with well-placed suspects.'

'Do you accept that you are a well-placed suspect?'

'I do. It's an objective fact, and we Marxists believe in objective facts. If there was no guiding signal, the only possibility is that the murderer had cat's eyes capable of orienting him in pitch darkness.'

'Another method is to work from the testament.'

'Which testament are you talking about?'

'Who gains from the will? That's usually the first question in detective stories.'

'I'm sorry to contradict you, but this isn't a detective story. It's a political story, and the murderer tried not only to destroy a man but also to discredit his testament.'

'That's what eveyone keeps telling me.'

'It's enough to be a rationlist. You don't even need to apply dialectical materialism.'

He had spoken with a certain Madrid accent, stressing the syllables, separating them with short puffs of air, much as the Chinese do. Someone had once told him that the people of Madrid speak like the Chinese.

'Let's get back to the testament, just in case. Sometimes the classic answers allow us to ask the true questions. Who stood to gain from the testament?'

'You're looking for a political dauphin, eh? Don't be so naive. This is a different ball-game. And don't look at me. I've never been a dauphin. We intellectual workers carry great weight in the Party, for we bring concrete knowledge and a capacity for theorisation. But we're still mistrusted. Don't forget that although intellectuals set the communist movement in motion, they never trusted their own sort. Look at Lenin. And the grandaddy of them all, Marx himself, had some very harsh things to say about intellectuals. For our part, we have a definite guilt complex and we realise that the throne has to be given to someone closer to the working class by origin. Maybe by the year two thousand, when the working class will be something different, it will have disappeared in its original sense. Adam Schaff has already pointed to that possibility. But for the moment, the working class is the working class; we are still a long way from such a change in the economic formation, driven by automation, the microelectronic revolution, and so on. Do you follow?'

Why didn't you ask me if you were making yourself clear, instead of whether I follow or understand? Sepúlveda glanced at his watch again. The class was over; but Carvalho still had the strength to lift a finger.

'May I ask you a question?'

'So long as it's only one.'

'How would you have marked Garrido in order to stab him?'

The engineer had half risen, but now he fell back into his rotating chair.

'I don't know. But Garrido did have some kind of signal on him. I remember it perfectly well: a point of light. I repeat. I can perfectly recall a point of light.'

He had not been inside a bookshop since the day in Amsterdam when he had had to watch someone involved in the tattoo case. He cast a sceptical glance over the new titles displayed in the VIP bookshop on Avenida Princesa, although he did dip into one or two of them. Sooner or later he would have to bring himself up to date, so that he could buy and burn books with a full awareness of what he was doing. His period as buyer-reader had come to an end in the early seventies, when he suddenly saw himself as the slave of a culture that had cut him off from life and falsified his feelings as antibiotics can destroy the body's defences. Out of the corner of his eye, he watched the Central European night-owl draw closer; the Central European he had met that morning could not be far away. The man still had the coolness of many hours before. He stood next to Carvalho and took a red book from one of the piles on offer. *Communism in Freedom* by Robert Havemann.

'We didn't like at all what you did to our colleague.'

'You should be more choosy about the company you keep.'

'After all, you didn't come out of it too badly, while his arm's broken in two places.'

'An arm counts for a lot.'

'We'd like to know what the fat guy said to you in the hotel this morning.'

'He ate all my toast. He didn't have time to say anything. Really, if you know so much about what the other guy is doing, why don't you team up? Is he somewhere around?'

'If not him, then one of his cronies. Don't be too smart. You shouldn't feel protected by our rivals. The day when you're least expecting it, we'll squash you both in one go. Don't try to play a double game. How is the investigation going?'

Carvalho managed to hold back a sarcastic reply. A block of disgust and indignation sealed his mouth. A remote nerve-centre transmitted the order that he shoud smash the son-of-a-bitch's face in, turn it into one big bleeding shit-hole. He felt an elbow in the small of his back, but it didn't belong to the same man. Turning his head, he saw the rat-like shape of a man who continued to elbow him with the arm of a hand holding a carefully chosen book.

'Is he a friend of yours?'

'No. But he'll help you avoid doing something stupid. I tell you, you can't even move. It's very simple. All you have to do is pass us information at the right moment. Neither you nor your employers will lose out. By the way, you had a meal with Leveder and then arranged an interview with Sepúlveda. Anything interesting?'

'Routine.'

'Are they suspects?'

'They know how to talk and like to listen to themselves. My father always told me to get to know people older and wiser than myself. Could you tell your friend to lay off? They'll take us for homosexuals.'

'As I said, I don't know the gentleman, but you'd better not forget our agreement. The man with the broken arm dreams of the time when he'll have you to himself. Did you mention our meeting to Fonseca?'

136

'Yes. You've made yourselves a bad enemy. Fonseca loathes you. He's a great professional who holds the theory that we don't need to import torturers. I'd like to ask you a question. May I?'

'Go ahead.'

'Why is the fridge in that house so full of peaches and syrup?'

'I'm not in charge of the household administration.'

'Very low-grade peaches at that.'

'I'm sorry. I'll protest through the normal channels. We'll be seeing each other again.'

Carvalho turned sharply and pushed the rat-man who was digging his kidneys.

'Mind what you're touching, you pansy! This filthy pig was trying to touch me up!'

Watched by a quick-to-form circle of people, he seized the little man by the lapels.

'Good Lord! What would a fine young man like that have against pansies?' The voice gave rise to general laughter.

The rat-man let himself be shaken by Carvalho. Not a muscle in his face moved, while his cold black eyes looked daggers into Carvalho's gleaming eyes.

'Someone call the police!' said Carvalho, his face flushed and the veins on his temples wriggling like snakes.

'Come on, your highness, let him go. What airs our fine young man has!' The crowd opened for the boy with the effeminate voice. Wearing a three-cornered hat, a white silk scarf and a brown cape, he stood there twirling both his tongue and a small cane encrusted with mother-of-pearl. The rat-man profited from the distraction to spit a few words into Carvalho's face.

'You keep that up and your guts will be all over the wall.'

One of his hands was buried in his raincoat pocket, thrusting the muzzle of a revolver against Carvalho's belly. The detective pushed him away in disgust.

'Piss off, you dirty little queer!'

The rat-man straightened his coat, looked calmly at the spectators and left in no great hurry. Carvalho did not have time to watch his departure, for the boy with the three-cornered hat was trying to capture his attention with little taps of the cane on his arm.

'It's not on to be quite such a he-man. Where do you think you're living, Mr Universe? That guy touched you with respect, while you insulted him like the guttersnipe you are.'

'Get out of my sight, you scarecrow.'

'Jesus, what a nasty piece of work!'

'Okay, the party's over.'

The VIP security man gently pushed the angry defender of homosexuals.

'And you, sir, if you want to make some complaint, go to the manager instead of stirring things up.'

'What can he complain about? That his hymen was broken?' The boy with the hat was still as keyed up as a violin.

'I told you to shut your face, you little ponce.'

The security guard had been resting his palms on the young man's chest, and now, almost without a fresh movement, he pushed him back against a shelf full of cookery books. The bohemian sculpture collapsed beneath an avalanche of hefty tomes. Carvalho glimpsed his slim white calves, which descended sockless into two moccasins worn thin by the hard nocturnal pavements of Madrid. He did not have the nerve to keep his eyes on the tear-filled face that emerged from the heap of books with an old-fashioned dignity of a man in the stocks.

Movement consists not in moving but in being moved. Where are they leading me? A Gethsemane-type anguish drove him disoriented into the street. I'll wait here until they hand over the sacrificial lamb. It was him. No, him. He walked slowly towards the Moncloa, allowing sufficient time for those doomed to follow or catch him up. What are you waiting for, fatso? But he didn't appear. Carvalho went into a long-distance telephone box and called Biscuter. Is everything the same? And Charo? Tell Charo . . . No, don't tell her anything. What are the Ramblas like? How's the food in Madrid, boss? Go easy on the tripe. Think of your liver. Tripe is good for the uric acid. Biscuter wouldn't be convinced. Are you looking at the Ramblas? It's almost night, boss. Biscuter would be able to smell the harbour – that special smell of autumn evenings which rises from the Puerto de la Paz and reminds the people of

Barcelona of their maritime destiny, restoring their self-image of contemplative beings astonished to discover their feet in the Mediterranean basin. A lady has lost her daughter, boss. She got lost in Marbella or Tunis. Will you see her, boss? The woman is very upset. A contortionist can get lost anywhere. What's a contortionist, boss? Someone who can put one foot around the back of her neck and the other in a pocket. It's like one of Forges's jokes, boss.

'I've finished for today. Could we go to your place?'

'To my place? Sure. No problem. But first I've got to stop by my Party branch, pick up the kid from my aunt's house and have a bit of a fight with my husband.'

At the Café Malasaña there are twenty anarchistic ex-communists, twenty neo-liberal ex-anarchists and two waiters who look as if they play Monopoly by day and the class struggle by night. But everyone seems disguised as a runaway boy or girl from some home or other who is forced to pose for the 'Malasaña way of life'.

'It wasn't called Malasaña in my time.'

'Under Franco even the districts were called Spain. But this place has always been Malasaña, since long before *La verbana de la Paloma* was written.'

'Why has it become so fashionable?'

'Because it's old without being archaeological, and it has a lot of young progressive people who had a baby nine months after May '68.'

'May I come along while you go to your branch, pick up your kid and sort out your husband?'

'You may.'

'First I must drop by the hotel to pick up some bags. Have you got any oil at home?'

'Oil and butter. Everything necessary.'

Outside the hotel, Carmela said goodbye with a look that was at once question and answer. When he returned with the paper bags, she changed her smile into a full alpine fold.

'What's that?'

'If you don't mind, I'd like to invite you to supper at your house. I'll cook.'

'Europeans like hell! You Catalans are really Americans. Well, I'm blowed. May I know what's on the menu?'

139

'I'm still thinking it out. Depends how things go.'

'Our branch premises smell of blood-pudding with rice, because the barman is from Aragon and they're always made with rice there.'

'Some are.'

Carmela did not open her mouth once while they stuttered across rush-hour Madrid. It was full of expert traffic policemen irritated by the ubiquitous jeeps and army lorries – khaki sponges who soaked up the nocturnal darkness punctuated by a cold, gloomy light.

'Didn't you see the amber light, miss?'

'I did, but not for long. It vanished straight away.'

'Do you think we're playing hide-and-seek with the traffic lights?'

'Don't shout so. This gentleman is from Barcelona and he'll think he's in Africa.'

'We'll see if he's from Barcelona, because they're supposed to drive like in Europe. Let's see if he gives you an earful.'

The policeman did not understand Carmela's laughter and was on the point of doubling the fine he scribbled in his receipt book. Once they were out of range, she burst into uncontrollable laughter, as if telling herself a story worthy of the utmost hilarity.

'If you tell me too, we can laugh together. I thought you were in mourning.'

'It's the oil.'

'What about it?'

'I told you I had butter!'

Her continued laughter drew a veil of tears over her smokey eyes.

'Would you like to come in? It's a very together branch. Today there'll be a very heated discussion on the policy of the two blocs. For something like that, the old guard calls a full mobilisation and rolls out its tanks. They think eurocommunism is to blame for unemployment. I won't stay for the whole show, but we can listen to a bit.'

Behind the raised metal shutters, another glass door opened on a bar that would have seemed quite normal but for the wall-pictures of Marx, Lenin and Garrido, and the posters advertising the *Mundo Obrero* festival. People were moving down a corridor to the meeting-room, although a number of stragglers were still paying at the bar. Carmela went from one person to another, dropping comments here and a compliment or sarcastic remark there. A compelling joke left her unmoved, while Carvalho, standing by her side, observed the liturgy of communication between the leadership and the rank and file. The leadership was on the right, weighing in at seventy-five kilos. Young full-time cadres, strong-voiced and with a Beatles hair-style ten years behind the times; at home with syntactical constructions apart from the possibly excessive use of 'anyway . . .' or 'at the level of . . .'. The rank and file on the left: fifty or sixty people with an average of fifty, thanks to the correct balance between sixty- and forty-year-olds; mostly workers from the industrial belt; their wives fascinated by the ritual and, at the same time, in the process of emancipation through questions not always springing from woman's condition. Do you think it's right, comrade? How long must we workers go on paying for the economic crisis?

'This meeting has a special significance . . . The leadership wishes that the murder of our general secretary, comrade Fernando Garrido, should not interfere with the normal course of our activity. Every scheduled meeting will take place. It's the best answer we can give to the provocateurs.'

The thirty-year-old cadre, who already had signs of forty around his eyes, spoke with the rhetorical tone of a rehearsed speech and left the impression that he would wall up the rank and file whose dreams of storming the Winter Palace had been stolen for ever. It's not that we stand half-way between the two blocs: a communist ought to know that one bloc arose for aggression and the other for self-defence. But if that game were treated as a historical fatality, the emancipation struggle of every people in the world would be paralysed until the clash between the blocs had been resolved, and one would be drawn into one or other sphere of influence. We should not forget that we Spaniards are in the sphere of influence of the capitalist bloc, and that we must relate to this objective fact not as an inevitable reality but as a determinant of our strategy. History has shown that there is not just one model for the implantation of socialism. In our view, democratic freedoms are an instrument for reaching socialism in a context of pluralism and liberty.

'What I want most is the freedom to work and eat, instead of living like an animal.'

It was the first intervention from the base. The second was delivered by a well-built woman who seemed as resolute as God on the day of creation.

'You want to go beyond bloc politics? Fine. I agree. But how? The blocs are there, and one day the imperialists will launch an attack

141

on the socialist countries. What will we do then?'

The young cadre breathed deeply and leant back in his chair before answering the question that had been handed to him on a plate.

'We'll do what no one has ever placed in doubt. We'll fight against imperialism.'

Nudges of complicity among the rank and file. Nods of agreement. A general impression that eurocommunism has been saved. Carmela cannot understand why Carvalho initially resists when she says they have to go; why he sits tight to hear an old man, who begins his presumably involved question by recounting that he received his Party card in June 1936 at a bar on Calle Hortaleza.

'You seem to have enjoyed it.'

'For a minute I thought that twenty-four years of my life had not passed, that it was the day after I left the Party.'

'Ah! You've been part of the scene?'

'I was.'

'Well, it doesn't show.'

Carmela's boy is like all the other fair-haired children in Madrid. The head of the nursery suggests that she should have come earlier, because she's had to stay behind specially. The boy tells his mother that hens can only fly a little.

'Who told you that, sweetie?'

'The lady. That's why there's no need to keep them caged like parrots.'

The boy naturally points at Carvalho and asks: 'Who's that, mummy?' Since Carvalho does not answer, she says that he is a gentleman from Barcelona. This produces a sceptical smile on the child's face: he cannot believe there is anything else in the world but the straight line from Madrid to the sky. Carmela parks on a double-yellow line in front of a brightly lit building. The wind is blowing the blue-and-red poster: *Eurocommunism and Class Struggle.* Carmela takes the boy, goes into the building and shortly emerges

142

with a man who is now carrying the child. They exchange rather heated words, but she shrugs and walks off.

'He's completely shameless. It's the first time this month I've told him to look after the kid, and he says he can't. I certainly messed up his date. He can go and . . . '

'Don't you live together?'

'I don't know. When he doesn't have a Party meeting, he's got one as a member of some parliamentary advisory committee, or, if not, then some municipal advisory committee. And then he goes round speaking on whether the Soviet tanks should remain in Afghanistan or keep going until they reach Madrid. He's not the only one to live like that, overrun by a thousand responsibilities, but I'm sick to death of it. In the end I've got to work, function in the Party, do the shopping, keep house and be a mother – which is the least of my worries. And if you complain, some old women comrades come round and tell you a life-story that makes your hair stand on end. Fifteen years of whispering sweet nothings through the prison grille at Carabanchel or Burgos, then a kid for every period on parole, and finally, at seventy years of age, the amnesty, legalisation and sun-bathing on a park bench. I can even understand that, because it had to be done and there was nothing more to it. But now? What my husband does isn't Party work. It's just plain vice, and the wish to avoid anything other than political responsibility. So, what have you got in those bags?'

'Have you got any wine?'

'There must be some bottle or other at home.'

'With no surname or christian name?'

'You must have noticed that we don't belong to the gastronomic faction, although there are more and more who cook in order to forget.'

'Forget what?'

'That there's been a reform but no political break, for example; or that they were made monarchists overnight and sent out waving the little flag. Some people are very sensitive.'

'I'm terrified just at the thought that you might have a litre bottle of wine. Is it a litre?'

'I think so.'

'Well, stop at the first bar you can. That's the only place we can buy wine at this hour.'

Carvalho tried unsuccessfully to buy something other than Rioja or Valdepeñas, but at the fourth bar he managed to get chatting with a man from Simancas who was quite partial to Cigales. Have you people in Barcelona heard of Cigales wine? The only ones around here who ask for it are from Segovia or further north. It's no better that Rioja, but it's quite different. You said it, mister, you said it. Did you hear? It's no better than Rioja, but it's different. Look, there are some very good wines in León. No, damn it, not in León; in El Bierzo. This bloke is an El Bierzo separatist. I'm from where I am, like you and like this gentleman from Barcelona. But they're a special kind of people in Barcelona. Very special.'

'You had to tear yourself away?'

'We moved from wine to the autonomy statutes. Funny, but that often happens. One day Spain will be a federation of certified-origin wines.'

A small lift in keeping with the low-rent building had enough room for Carmela, Carvalho with his paper-bags, and a fifty-year-old woman whose powerful, crown-like head sported a silver hair-do. Afraid that the narrow lift would endanger the metallic architecture of her perm, she raised her eyebrows heavenward as if to keep a constant check on the precise arrangement of her hair. Her farewell 'good-night' was charged with sarcasm and a sense of triumph that the invaders had not even managed to graze the architraves of her capillary cathedral. She passed Carmela with a moralising look as if she were repeating the family code to herself.

'I could be your assistant.'

Carvalho went into the kitchen and filled his lungs with air that smelt of omelette. Surveying the kitchen implements, he overcame a natural dejection at the memory of the times in prison when he used to cook with ladle-measures and a metal plate.

'I see you have a healthy diet. Eggs, grilled meat, tins of asparagus. They're highly diuretic.'

'Sometimes I feel like cooking and I cook. We nearly always eat out, and in the evening the kid is over the moon with steak and

144

chips. What's the menu, then?'

'Tripe and capipota with peas and artichokes, and larded tuna.'

'It will take us till midnight.'

'Three-quarters of an hour.'

'That's what you tell every woman.'

'I wouldn't like to offend you sensitivities as an emancipated woman, but since you obviously don't have a larding device, I wonder if you could give me a darning needle.'

Carmela put on a wounded look, left the kitchen and returned with three different sets of needles.

'Don't get the wrong idea. They're my mother's. She sometimes comes to be with the kid and then starts darning my jumpers like mad.'

Carvalho bored a number of tunnels in the chunk of fish and filled them with anchovies. Having sprinkled on salt and pepper and rolled the creature in flour, he browned it in oil with a few cloves of garlic and left it over a low gas. He then stripped off the artichoke leaves until their white hearts became visible. The next step was to cut the ends, divide each artichoke into four, fry the sixteen pieces and set them aside. In the same oil, he slowly heated the tripe and capipota and then added some sautéd tomato and onion. When everything was well mixed together, he put in some peas and some stock made from Carmela's assortment of cubes. By then the tuna was already done on the other ring. Setting it aside, he worked the left-over juices into a Spanish sauce enriched with little pieces of fennel. He then took the sauce off the flame and turned back to the tripe, adding the fried artichokes and a pinch of hazel nuts, some almonds, pine kernels, garlic and toast softened in a little stock. Finally, he waited for the tuna to cool before cutting it into slices and covering it with the hot sauce on a serving-dish.

'But those are two main courses.'

'I've gone too many days without cooking. Anything left over will be very good tomorrow, particularly the tripe.'

Carmela repeated the word tripe and contented herself with a slice of larded tuna.

'Do you cook like this every day?'

'Sherlock Holmes played the violin. I cook.'

'And what were you thinking about while you were cooking?'

'Culture. You Marxists think you get enough by setting the material conditions to music, but you're as much slaves to culture as anybody else. Even the election percentages are converted into culture. In France there's a culture of twenty per cent, in Italy of thirty. Here you have a culture of nine or ten per cent.

'Did that occur to you while you were cooking the tripe or the tuna?'

'Garrido's murderer is another cultural theme. He's either a traitor or a messiah. In the whole history of the communist movement, there's only one top-level murder that was done as an emergency cleansing operation. The killing of Beria. That's what I was thinking as I worried in case the frozen peas weren't sufficiently cooked to enhance the artichokes. You're not drinking any wine?'

'It goes straight to my head.'

'Some time ago, when your language was still fresh in my mind, I may have been able to explain better. Whether you have ten or thirty per cent of the vote, you have a clear sense of being the driving force of history. You've even got your enemies to believe it, and they're as afraid of ten per cent as they are of thirty. You may not represent a quantitative danger, but you'll always be a qualitative one. They killed Garrido to transform you into a band of cold, calculating cultural assassins who need the central committee protocol to stage a sacrifice. The murderer is one of you, and at such moments he knows that he is condemned to death. Not by you, who are up to your neck in a liberal culture-graft, but by the very people who incited him to commit the crime.'

'Why doesn't he do a bunk?'

'I'll be able to answer you tomorrow. But I could almost tell you in advance. The reason is that he is trapped, completely trapped, and he has to act out his role till the end.'

'It's a pity. We'll drop one percentage point at the next elections.'

'Maybe not. You now have the chance to elect a general secretary who will fit the market. But you won't do it. Your culture stands in the way. You will be forced to choose between a historical figure who will keep the myths alive, and a true son of the apparatus, smart enough to have got this far without any serious mishap. The hour of truth will come in fifteen or twenty years, when no heroes are left from the struggle against Franco and the rank and file have become thoroughly anti-liturgical. I may not live to see it and perhaps it doesn't interest me a great deal. But it will be very interesting when no European Communist Party has any martyrs, not even a student expelled in 1974.'

146

'I can't see that coming. Just a fortnight ago one of our comrades was stabbed at Malasaña.'

Carmela was keen on the after-dinner chat and dialectical tension. She put a Joan Baez disc on the record-player and offered Carvalho an array of unfinished bottles: chinchon, cognac, cointreau. He poured himself some chinchon in a glass that had once been a nutella container and sank into a hissing plastic sofa. She listened to the music on the edge of another chair in the three-piece suite, holding her knees in her arms and only straying from her swarm of thoughts to observe Caravlho's self-communion.

'It's very late. Do any taxis pass by?'

'Stay and sleep here.'

'What about your husband and son?'

'I took the boy to my parents-in-law, and who knows where the old man is. I don't think he'll come to sleep here.'

It was a neutral conversation between the landlady of a boarding-house and an uncertain customer. Carvalho tried to peer from a distance into the low-necked jumper of his potential landlady, driver or travelling companion.

It was at the same session on the Marne in August 1956 that Garrido had talked about the comrade's arse: not in the abstract, but the flesh-and-blood woman comrade discovered in the bed of Biel Ciurena, a medical student who had turned up with a pharmacy Pasionaria. Although the rules of secret Party meetings were not written down in physiological detail, a division still existed between male and female sections in the sleeping rooms. This was an unforeseen obstacle for Roser Bertran, better known as the pharmacy Pasionaria, who was eager to show the necessary link between Marx's goal of changing History and Rimbaud's goal of changing Life. So when night came, Roser and Biel lay ostentatiously on one of the metal beds of the French Communist Party's summer-school residence. Surprised in their third tangle by a veteran who had just scraped onto the last or next-to-last boat from Alicante in 1939, Roser looked up from the theoretical, near-practical position of a woman being screwed by a Majorcan trainee psychiatrist (later a follower of Lacan). 'Could you turn the light out, comrade.' The veteran turned it out, but an hour later the couple had to present themselves before Garrido himself.

The general secretary took the drama out of the situation by offering them a cigarette, with no distinctions as to sex and with apologies for the enforced puritanism of harsh clandestine life.

'In order to get you here, we had to key up not only most of the Party organisation in Spain and France, but a major support network of the French Communist Party. You are here to clarify the situation and tasks in our country. Three, four days, a week. It would not be proper, Biel, if you responded to this organisational effort by losing yourself in contemplation of the comrade's arse.'

The arse in question leapt from the chair and supported a Pioneer-type feminist harangue, all the worthier in that, according to the not unexpected figures mentioned by Helena Subirats on the first day, women made up a precarious fifteen per cent of those attending the course. Which would be worse? That Biel should lose himself in contemplation of the woman comrade's arse, or that she, Roser Bertran, should do the same thinking about the male comrade's arse?

Although ten years would pass before the publication of Germaine Greer's *The Female Eunuch* and photos of cunts in *Schuck*, Garrido had read Kollontai at the height of adolescence and was aware of his macho indiscretion. 'It's just that women have greater powers of concentration' – such an upright excuse that even the pharmacy Pasionaria was satisfied. Not only did she leave the meeting in better cheer, but she was actually persuaded that she should not have too much trust in her greater powers of concentration, and that it would be a mark of civility to practise abstinence for the rest of the course. Those veterans of an assault on the main contradiction must not believe that the younger generation lacks self-control.


'What are you thinking about?'
'The arses of women comrades.'
'Mine, for example?'

148

'Not a concrete arse, but one that can be generalised.'

'Wonderful. It must be a very ugly arse, battered by hours and hours of meetings.'

'Either you go to few meetings, or your arse is made of excellent raw material.'

'Is that a hint?'

The comrade's arse. Look at the comrade's arse and investigate the murder of Garrido. Carvalho made an effort to swallow the political taboo sticking in his gullet.

'You communist women inhibit me. I suspect you've only got an epic sense or an ethical sense of fucking.'

'I don't know what you mean. Maybe it was like that during the siege of Stalingrad. You rather tend to live in the past.'

'Doubtless a hangover from adolescence.'

'Wasn't there free love in your time?'

'No. And now?'

'Just as little.'

Carmela sighed with an air of disenchantment.

'But there's no ethics or epics, you can rest assured.'

Carvalho managed to free himself from the noisy plastic and perched on the edge of the sofa facing Carmela. Should I put on a smile of complicity or just get on with it? The street door made a noise as it opened.

'Now's the moment when the husband enters and stabs the unfaithful wife's lover. It will be an unjust death.'

Carmela looked at the door with perplexity and indignation.

'If it's him he'll certainly get an earful.'

It wasn't him. The door was almost too small for the fat, smiling man whose pistol-waving hand forced Carvalho to stay still. He invaded the room, followed by a pale-faced man directly descended from a hitherto unknown illegitimate son of Carlos II the Possessed.

'Cool it. Don't be scared, madam. Your friend will tell you I'm a peaceful man.'

'Who is this bloke?'

'I am Pepe's uncle. Isn't that right, Pepe?'

'My uncle from America? Or from the Soviet Union?'

'Are you still at it? Never mind. What does it matter to you? Did you hear, Pérez? I haven't introduced you to my friend Pérez. His surname is a real find.'

The fat man laughed, putting away his gun but keeping an eye on

Carvalho.

'Are you just passing or do you plan to stay long?'

'Just visiting, señora. First of all, Señor Carvalho, let me congratulate you for the VIP number. You're a bit suicidal, though,
because that kid you held up to ridicule won't forget you in a hurry.
I also heard that you broke the arm of a real professional. Not a
good idea, even though he's an opponent of mine. I admit you're a
man of resources, and so I prefer to visit you on neutral ground,
rather than in the street or at your hotel. Here, in the home of this
charming lady. You have a very typical Madrid-style charm.'

'Thank you very kindly.'

'Some say that Andalusians are the nicest Spaniards. But I go
more for *madrileños*.'

'I thank you in the name of the people of Madrid.'

The pale-face man was sniffing more than examining the room.
The fat man moved his nose like a rabbit in mock imitation and sat
at the far end of the sofa where Carvalho was still perched.

'We haven't been introduced,' Carmela said, crossing her legs
and surrendering to the anatomy of the sofa.

'I'm a very ordinary man who's devoted to learning new things.
Pérez is my assistant.'

'I'm well aware of what this lady is involved in,' the fat man said,
'but it doesn't bother me if she's present during our conversation.'

'That's assuming we have a conversation. For my part, I have
nothing to say to you.'

'Don't be so rash. Of course you have a lot to say to me. In a few
hours – however many it takes – you'll be surprised at how much
you've told me. Since we last met, you've had a number of interesting meetings. Fonseca, Santos Pacheco, Leveder, Sepúlveda Civit.
I think you're beginning to get close.'

'You tell me. Both you and the guys on the pavement outside
already know the ending.'

'I give you my word of honour that I don't. Listen hard to what

I say. I do not know. They told me: Ask Señor Carvalho to give a report. I'm just following orders. Don't move, señora.'

The sharply emphatic voice had seemed unthinkable in that plump body almost overflowing the sofa yet alert to every possible movement.

'I want to have a piss.'

'Pérez, take this lady to the toilet. Examine it first and then let her go in quite freely.'

Pérez followed Carmela out of the room.

'Alone at last. But don't think that the relation of forces has improved. I'm much faster than you imagine, and you don't want Pérez to get nervous, do you? He's a real tough guy who doesn't distinguish between the sexes. A real brute. Let's get down to business and finish it as soon as possible. Which will be the winning horse? Make a prediction.'

'You overestimate me. I'm only just beginning.'

'Santos Pacheco was looking very nervous. Particularly when you met outside the university. It's understandable that he's afraid. Whatever the verdict, he'll be the loser. I put myself in his shoes. For an old communist like Santos Pacheco, it must be very, very hard to take. Don't be too smart. Don't think the whole thing will rebound on us.'

'What would you advise me to do? As one professional to another. Should I give you the information first, or the others?'

'Not a shred of doubt. Give it to me. If I could say everything, I'd easily convince you that I'm the more profitable choice.'

'We haven't discussed money.'

'There are many ways of paying someone.'

'For instance?'

'Life, peace and quiet. Does that seem too little? But let's stick to the point. You're beginning to get close. Tell me the name of your prime suspects.'

Carmela returned with Pérez behind her.

'When I'm nervous it makes me want to piss.'

They heard again the sound of the street door and then a whistled greeting.

'No!' Carmela cried out.

The fat man stood up with difficulty, and a Beretta appeared in Pérez's hand. When the steps were just outside the door, Carvalho knocked the fat man upside down on the sofa. Pérez's gun wavered between Carvalho, Carmela and the man shouting from the door.

'What's going on here?'

Carmela started to flee, but Pérez held her back with one arm. The newcomer advanced on him without hesitation.

'Leave my wife alone!'

Carvalho hurled himself on Pérez and pinned him to the wall like Christ on the cross.

'And who are you?'

Carmela's husband just had time to speak before Carvalho grabbed her by the hand and pulled her out of the room.

'Carmela, where are you going?'

'Beat it, you too!'

'But what the fuck is happening?'

Carvalho rushed onto the landing and raced down the stairs. His hand was still gripping Carmela's.

'Run, Paco, run!' she shouted with her face turned upward.

They went into the street. Carvalho took cover behind a car and forced Carmela to crouch down. Her eyes remained at the level of her jacket as he pulled out a heavy black pistol smelling of oil and confined places.

'What's happening to my Paco?'

'The kid's a bit slow.'

'I'd like to have seen you in his place. I'm going to look for him.'

'They won't do anything to him. Keep still.'

The door suddenly lit up and revealed the figures of the fat man and his assistant. They moved slowly and deliberately, conversing about a subject of moderate interest. They walked to the corner of the street, where their bodies and voices turned and disappeared. Carvalho motioned to Carmela that she should stay crouched down, while he inched forward behind the parked cars in a line parallel to the two men. When he reached the corner, he saw them get into a stationary car. He waited for its rear lights to vanish into the night and then returned to where he had left Carmela. She was no longer there. He crossed the street and climbed the stairs two by two. The door to the flat was closed.

'It's me, Pepe.'

Carmela opened the door, her eyes filled with tears.

'The brutes. Look what they've done to my Paco.'

He brushed past her and reached the living-room in two strides. The man was sprawled on a chair with a red flower of blood on his parted lips. A broken arm hung awkwardly beside a body groaning from every pore. His eyes looked critically at Carvalho and then turned to Carmela for an explanation.

'He's a friend.'

'Can he walk?'

The man nodded that he could.

'He should be taken to a clinic or an emergency centre, above all for his arm.'

Once he was sitting in the rear of the car, the man looked now at the back of Carvalho's neck and now at the back of Carmela's, all the time working out the logic of what had happened.

'Tell them it was a fight. That they tried to rob you. Make up two or three descriptions. If we told them the truth, they'd keep us all night and pass it right up to the minister of the interior.'

The car went into the ambulance tunnel. While Carmela gave the details to the admissions clerk, an attendant wheeled Paco into the inner zones of the temple.

'Relatives aren't allowed in. We'll give you a report in half-an-hour. You may go to the waiting-room.'

An automatic coffee-machine and an equally automatic device for water, cola and orangeade. Parents of motor-cyclists flattened by the night; wives of anonymous victims of stab wounds; grown-up daughters of women seized by hemiplegia very soon after a rich meal of cabbage, potatoes and a snappy little hake; a taxi-driver who has crushed an old man in Calle Arturo Soria; the thin husband of a bulky pregnant woman who has burnt her hand in bubbling oil used to fry Roman-style squid. Carvalho left the room to light a cigar and let his mind focus on the ambulances depositing their shattered victims of the night. 'When night falls and lengthens its shadows, few animals do not close their eyes and few sufferers do not feel greater pain.' Carvalho translated the lines of Ausias March into Castilian, in a determined effort to mangle the versification. An old man hobbled into view on the nocturnal horizon, clutching his lower abdomen with one hand and spurring his frail body forward with the other.

'Are you a doctor?'

'No.'

'I've walked all the way from Lavapiés. They inserted a urine-lead the other night and now I've got spasms.'

There was a few days' growth of beard on his fleshless, chick-like face topped by a beret. He nervously opened his flies to show Carvalho a bandaged penis from which a plastic tube led to a urine-filled bag resting against a scrawny thigh covered with veins and empty skin.

'You'll catch cold.'

'It hurts so much.'

Carvalho took him by the arm and helped him into the admissions office. The receptionist tossed her head in irritation.

'You again?'

'It hurts very much.'

'So you came back on foot? Come on. Go inside.'

The old man penetrated the temple. The woman continued to shake her head and said to Carvalho:

'He's waiting for a bed for a prostate operation and he just keeps turning up, sometimes at four or five in the morning. He always comes alone on foot.'

Dawn was already breaking when the taxi dropped Carvalho at the Hotel Opera. As he went up in the lift, he cocked his revolver in order to sweep aside anything that might prevent him from taking a warm shower and relaxing for a while between clean sheets. He threw open the room door and did the same at the entrance to the bathroom. He turned the lock and stood avidly under the shower for a very long time. Once in bed, he masturbated in an attempt to calm himself, then looked for a sleep-inducing pattern on the ceiling and on the cavernous sheets he pulled over his head. It was all in vain. He got up and put on his clothes. In the street he cast his eyes over a monotonous horizon of white coffee and variously shaped fritters on the bars of early-morning cafés. He eventually found one which, though not prepared to make him a ham and tomato sandwich, did not drive him away at the sound of such a ridiculous and evidently Catalan demand. They agreed to fry him some pickled pork, which inevitably had the typically Madrid taste of iguana or capon crocodile.

154

Marcos Ordóñez Laguardia was a stalwart practitioner of the old Party culture marked above all by a sense of punctuality. 'It was a bad sign if a comrade arrived five minutes late. It meant that he was certainly having problems. That trained us in a sense of punctuality.' He was replying to Carvalho's observation that the old communist had arrived at the entrance to the José Díaz Foundation just as the clock was striking nine. The other employees arrived in a broken trickle, greeted by Ordóñez's tolerant smile and an occasional remark about the comforts of a warm bed. 'I can see you're one of the pre-war people, Marcos. A man of steel. A komsomol leader, that's what you are, Marcos.' The joke came from a brunette wearing seamed stockings and a mole beside her mouth. Marcos smiled contentedly at his ever-repeated morning victory, which encouraged him to begin the day under the sign of a small yet certain success. He looked like an ageing mandarin, polite, well-groomed, with an almost Japanese kindness.

'I don't want to mislead. I heard from Santos that you wanted to see me. He wanted to prepare me for the worst. Frankness is a communist virtue. That's what I said to him.'

Who killed Garrido? No one? Everybody? No, he accepted that he was incapable of isolating a face, an arm, a motive.

'It's clear why. To discredit the Party. The mystery is how a comrade could have taken such a crime upon himself. I know why you want to question me. I've had a pretty unhappy life, but it shouldn't be exaggerated. There can be no birth without suffering. Nor History without suffering. At the very time that I was excluded from the leadership and sent to work in a factory in Czechoslovakia, thousands of Greeks were being butchered by the capitalist counter-revolution, thousands of Asians and Africans were being persecuted for their anti-imperialist ideas. How many were tortured to death? Who takes that into account? And yet, everyone points to the big and small errors – inhuman, I agree – committed by the communist movement. I could complain, but I don't. I learnt a lot, that's true. And I suffered a lot. But I knew that my suffering had a historical purpose beyond my personal fortunes.'

'Did you take that into account when you shat all over the Party and Garrido?'

'I won't deny that I sometimes shat on them, and on much else besides. At one time or another, we have all hated what we love most. Hate passes, but the love remains.'

155

'Did Garrido ever try to justify himself to you?'

'Not directly. Times were different. There was a fight against Stalinism, sometimes with Stalinist methods and while Stalin was still alive. In fact, the tendency or current of opinion to which I belonged was much more Stalinist than Garrido's. History has proved him right.'

'What did you feel when Garrido was murdered?'

A sudden paralysis transformed the old face into a mask. But the muscles slowly started to move again and the lips murmered:

'Bewilderment.'

'You were on the Madrid front during the war – not behind the lines but right at the front. You're a man who knows how to fight. Afterwards you saw battle in Catalonia.'

'I know how to wield a machete, if that's what you mean. Sure. With the right training, it's possible that I'd have had the strength to use it at least once. Even if I'm an old man suffering from arteriosclerosis who can't think as he used to. So, you may deduce that I stabbed Garrido in spite of the fact that he rehabilitated me and gave me a leadership position. Do you know what we Party leaders are called? The "Youth Front". Because, roughly speaking, we have thirty years on each leg. But don't go looking among the old ones. We belong to the old culture. We're all Bukharins. We'd all have preferred to die rather than objectively harm the Party. The young ones are different. If you ask them whether they would sacrifice themselves for the march of History, they'll tell you that the march is not to their liking. They've been through different times. I'd like to see them in a civil war or in the underground period of the forties or fifties. But no one can learn from someone else's experience.'

The speech continued with old examples of the Marxist culture of sacrifice. Do you know the Arthur London case? He only spoke out when his example was capable of helping the new communist perspective of socialism with a human face. Carvalho shut his eyes.

'Are you sleepy?'

'I hardly got any sleep.'

'You ought to get the right number of hours. You have to pay for excesses.'

Lecumberri Aranaz was boxed up in a little office of the José Díaz Foundation, operating an old-style calculator with paper rolls.

156

'The accounts never work out right. Excuse me a moment.'

Carvalho used the time to take a little nap, which soon became a short deep sleep. He awoke with saliva in the corner of his mouth, and his blinking eyes slowly returned Lecumberri's mocking gaze.

'Wouldn't you do better to have a quick lie-down?'

'Since I arrived in Madrid, I haven't been able to sleep peacefully for a single night. When I'm not being knocked around, someone threatens me with a pistol.'

'We were better off against Franco.'

It was not the Basque style of sarcasm. More like the paradoxical remark of a Mediterranean aesthete. Carvalho shrugged his shoulders.

'You've had a very interesting life. You were an ETA activist if I'm not mistaken.'

'Well, ETA wasn't the same as it is now. There was less activity. Just compare the rate of attacks then and now. It's quite different.'

He was so Basque that the only things missing were a beret on his head and a pan of stuffed peppers on the accounts table.

'What is a Basque like you doing in a town like this?'

'I sometimes wonder.'

'As an ETA activist, you must have been given special training for armed combat.'

'Rubbish! Four boring talks and a bit of target practice. But, as I say, the times were different. We were all part-time volunteers. Now they're supposed to have a training camp in the Arab Emirates or Libya. In my days, we went to the mountains in the French Basque country. Four bits of nonsense and then off to put the wind up Franco.'

'Why did you become a communist?'

'Because I thought that the historical role of ETA had come to an end. All the same, I still believe that the Communist Party has never properly understood the national question. Even now it doesn't. I also thought that if people like me joined, we could help to turn the CP in Euzkadi into a Basque party. Today I don't know what to tell you. These walls are falling on top of me.'

'Were you ever held by the police when you were in ETA?'

'Yes.'

'Tortured presumably.'

'A good assumption.'

'But you did not receive a particularly long sentence.'

157

'The Burgos people had fallen and that was enough to vent their fury. Anyway, they couldn't pin a lot on me.'

'Didn't the police give you any more trouble?'

'A few skirmishes.'

'I heard that you've asked for a leave of absence from being a Party full-timer.'

'Did they announce it on television? I didn't know I was so popular.'

'What are your reasons?'

'I'm not up to the present style of operation. A Party leader still has no private life. It used to be because of the underground conditions, and now it's because there are too few cadres for all the areas of democratic life we have to work in. There's family pressure. I'm nearly forty and I've hardly lived. I'd like to go round the world, for example, or do what I like at weekends. Go for a walk on the beaches of San Sebastian. See the kids playing in the sand. Watch them growing up. Listen to what they say. I've a career, not just the tasks of a Party activist. I'm tired. I'm not a revolutionary, only an anti-fascist. A lot of us discovered this after Franco's death, but we haven't made it clear enough to ourselves. It's not good when political activity becomes a routine. I'm dried up – no drive, no imagination. I want to go home! I'll be off as soon as we get rid of Garrido's corpse.'

A tight-lipped mouth, black shiny eyes, muscular rigidity in a small frame, words spat out with passion. They've killed my father. Fernando Garrido was more than a father to me, just like Santos. I've revered him ever since the first drop of my mother's milk. Esparza Julve, a wholesale dealer in tropical fruit: lychees, kiwis, mangoes, papayas, passion fruit, pineapples.

'How much are the Galicians?'

'A hundred pesetas for the cheapest.'

'Which Galicians are you talking about?'

'There are New Zealand kiwis and hothouse-grown Galician

158

kiwis. Buy some. Those from Australasia are the nicest. The Galician ones are coarser, although they taste very good. Perhaps a little acid, eh? Treat my crates like your mother! Or better than your mother! We had an argument, and now it's pot luck how the goods arrive. There was a time when we were together all day. When my father died in prison, I went to France and stayed in Santos's house. Well, Santos would come and go. Few people knew that he spent more time inside the country than outside, risking his life all the time. You've seen Santos: so jovial, so diplomatic, so well mannered. But has he got guts! I still go to him when I have any kind of problem. He looks as if he only understands politics, but he has a brain for any problem you care to mention. As for Fernando, I'd have done anything for him – well, anything he asked. Do you think they censured me when I decided to stop being a full-timer? No, sir. They actually tried to cheer me up, because they knew I'd done my duty even if my heart hadn't been in it towards the end. It wasn't the life for me. A thousand hours of meetings every week. I've always been a restless type, and I needed to develop things on my own initiative. Now I'm on the central committee as a representative of small businessmen, very small, but I serve the Party. Esparza, a little surety needed here. Esparza, fifty thousand pesetas over there. And Esparza keeps giving, because there are many ways of serving the Party. Some devote their whole life to it. Others all their intelligence. Still others contribute their good will or money. That's the beauty of a new, modern party, a new-model party, as Fernando put it. The party based on cells was more up my street. Why should I deny it? I don't know, it seemed more communist. But in these things, too, you either innovate or go to the wall.

'What gets me about the conservatives is that these guys present themselves as the most wonderful progressives in the world, but when you look a bit closer their ideas turn out to be as old as the hills. Whether they're Leninist or not. We'll see. What would Lenin have done in Spain in 1975? Would he have hurled himself against the bayonets? No, he was no idiot, and only idiots do idiotic things. I'm none too keen on theories. My father was a miner and I was on the way to being a farmhand when they made me a Party full-timer. Then I set up in small-time trade like I'm doing now. But although I'm no theoretician, I know how to listen and I've had the chance to hear people who know what's in the interest of the working class. A good communist is not only someone who busts his arse fighting the bourgeoisie or fills his mouth with phrases like the dictatorship of the proletariat. It's someone who has an overall vision of things and of what should be done in the interests of the working class. Would you like to try a passion fruit?'

An obscene old bollock filled with a little acidic juice.

'You have to get used to the taste. In some restaurants, they even make ice-cream with it. They don't know what to invent any more. If a peasant produced a melon that tasted of soused tuna fish, he'd make a fortune in no time.'

'You were on close terms with Garrido. Did he ever say anything that could have been interpreted as a warning of what was about to happen?'

'Garrido was a very calm and courageous man who didn't get scared about every little thing. I saw him just a moment before he went into the central committee room. A group of comrades from La Mancha were waiting to pay him their respects. He saw me among them and put his arm round my shoulder. How goes it, Julvito? I don't know why, but he always called me Julvito. Santos started it and all the old-timers followed suit. When I was a kid, I used to go on holiday in the Crimea or Romania with Santos's and Garrido's children. So many memories. So many hopes.'

'Was Garrido calm on the day of the murder?'

'As calm as we are now. I was with him on the day he left the Cortes and a group of Fuerza Nueva women called him a murderer and told him to go back to Moscow. He went up to them and said: "I'd rather be a prisoner in Spain than a free man in Moscow." The women just stood there gaping – a verse translation of the Bible would have fitted in their wide-open mouths. Calm. Courageous. We exchanged a few words on the day of the crime. I asked him about the trade-union question, complaining that the socialists were beginning to turn nasty. Quite normal, he replied; they follow their policy and we ours, but we'll meet up at the end of the day. On the day of the Last Judgement, I added, because I like a joke and I always spoke to him with complete confidence. Not that late, Julvito, not that late. Sometimes it's hard to be patient, because, just between you and me, the socialist comrades are really quite amazing. As someone put it, we've come out of prison and look what's coming out of the woodwork. Very good. I'll tell you another good one: PSOE, a hundred years of history . . . and forty years on holiday. We shouldn't be sectarian, but they sometimes make it very difficult. They don't trust us – or, rather, it's in their interest to seem as if they don't, so as to disqualify us in the eyes of the bourgeoisie. True, we played some dirty tricks in the past, but so did they, and we stood shoulder to shoulder during the civil war.

'In the end, I keep this up to be faithful to myself, but it's really time for me to take a rest. I've worked flat out for years and years and I'd like to drop it now, but Santos talked me round. Just a few more years to set an example, Julvito, so that the younger ones can be with you and discover the moral legacy of the communists. That's why I'm still on the central committee, but it's not the thing for me. I would go on working at the base, helping as best I could, but the central committee is for people with all of history in front of them, not behind them as is the case with me. I went abroad once to work with my two hands in Germany. But it was the same story: there was still the Party organisation abroad. "What shall we decide, then?" Santos used to ask, whenever he came on a visit. "You leave Spain to see the back of us, but then you make contact again." Maybe it's stronger then me – I took it in with my mother's milk. More than ever at times like these, when we have to show that the assassins won't destroy us. If the Franco regime couldn't do it, then this mafia certainly can't.'

'Was Garrido killed by the mafia?'

'No, I'm talking about the Trilateral Commission. Who else, eh? Garrido and eurocommunism weren't up their street. The image of a civilised communism, the kind there has to be, was disarming a lot of anti-communists. And that drove them wild in the Trilateral.'

'The Trilateral can kill someone without taking his life. It can start off a crushing campaign of character assassination.'

'It was them. No doubt about it. They wanted to smash an image, to rule the eurocommunist programme out of court. Just think what a setback, what a scandal. How will we stand in world opinion? That does matter, because, as Garrido used to say, we cannot live in isolation. We must take a global view of everything and everybody that goes to make up our party, and of the position it occupies in Spanish society as a whole.'

'You know it by heart.'

'When you have Garrido, he's worth taking advantage of. They tried to annihilate forty years of Spanish communism.'

He insisted that Carvalho should try a Galician kiwi and an Australasian kiwi.

161

'What do they resemble? Nowadays, you can grow tobacco at the North Pole, so long as you create the right atmospheric conditions. I started out as a partner in a firm that grew endives – you know, those white Belgian salad vegetables. It was a disaster at the time, but now they've carved out a place in the market. Everything has its time, and what forges ahead in one period often simply collapses in the next. You can see how things are. History has no heart, and no brain either.'

'Democratic Municipal Administration': a course from the fifteenth to the thirtieth of October, sponsored by the Cultural Office of the City of Madrid. 'Municipal Politics and the Means of Communication': organised by Ana Segura and Ferrán Cortes; a trip to Chinchón; a visit to the printing works of the Official State Bulletin; a round table on 'Urban Semiology'; two hundred and ten mayors, councillors responsible for cultural matters, two-tone faces, bare heads, gnarled hands, long-winded lawyers, ex-priest councillors. Escapá Azancot? I don't know if he's here. The one with the flageolet? Escapá Azancot! You are wanted at the press-office! He walked alongside with the sun in his face. a peasant economy of gestures, hard of hearing in the left ear, a head leaning in compensation like the tower of Pisa. Excuse me, but I forgot what I was going to say when I took the notes.

'Here you're known as the man with the flageolet.'

'Yes, I play it.'

'But what is it?'

'A wind instrument, like the hornpipe, only a bit shorter. It's been played in La Mancha since time immemorial, although they say it's of French origin. My grandfather used to play it, and my father and an uncle actually make them. All that was virtually abandoned until the coming of democracy. But since everyone is pulling signs of identity from under every stone, we now have our flageolet. What do you think of it?'

'Does the Party support demands related to the flageolet?'

'Well, it hasn't said no. And when someone from the leadership passes through my village, they sit right through a one-hour concert.'

'Do you take a flageolet to central committee meetings?'

'Escapá, are the ones speaking today also from your party?' someone asked.

'They couldn't possibly be from yours; you haven't got anyone who knows the first thing about anything. That guy's a socialist. They're furious because so far all the committee chairmen are communists and the mayor of Madrid is a socialist. Is what they say any use or isn't it? That's what should be asked, not whether they're hounds or greyhounds.'

'I think they paid homage to Garrido on the day of his murder.'

'A flageolet concert was scheduled for the Casa de Campo, but Fernando couldn't come. So we took our instruments and went off to the Hotel Continental. No big deal. One number and it was over, because he was late and the central committee comrades were waiting. We forced him to accept the flageolet of honour and that was that. He said he had a very bad ear and that if he played, it would sound even worse than it did.'

'What is the flageolet of honour?'

'Something to put in the buttonhole. A tiny model flageolet. We made it red so that he wouldn't protest.'

'Did Garrido put it on?'

'I put it on him myself, and then he said a few words.'

'Have you given out many such emblems?'

'None like that one. They're usually gold or silver. But we decided that Garrido's should be red.'

'You personally ordered a special model for Garrido?'

'No, not me. In fact we weren't the ones who thought of it. One day a comrade came from the central committee to report on what had been discussed. Although I'm also on the central committee, I'd sooner another comrade came to our village branch to explain how it went. So a comrade came and, as usual, the discussion went on to our flageolets. Garrido ought to hear about this. Well, we did everything demanded of us. And it would be nice if you made him an honorary associate, so that people could see the Party encouraging popular culture. So, an honorary associate. No sooner said than done. The discussion got quite lively, and the comrade went back to Madrid with a specimen he could use to order Garrido's special emblem.'

Carvalho's stomach was filled with an icy void. On the brink of solving the mystery, he tried to complicate the peasant mayor's intentions, as if he couldn't believe that the truth was so simple and easy to reach. When he asked the question that capped hours and hours of flying like a blowfly or dragonfly, a vulture or a barnyard bird, his own voice seemed quite strange to him.

'Which comrade suggested the idea and took responsibility for arranging the special emblem?'

'Esparza.'

'Esparza Julve.'

'Yes, Julvito. It was touch and go because the emblem only arrived at the moment we were to pin it on in the hall of the Hotel Continental. I'd forgotten that detail because of the business that blew up afterwards. "I'll wear it whenever I go to La Mancha," Garrido said. "That's not doing it justice," someone urged. "You ought to wear the flageolet in the capital." And that's how it rested. He walked towards the meeting-room, my colleagues from La Mancha stood discussing the ceremony, and Esparza and I followed Garrido so as not to be late for the meeting. Who would have thought that Garrido would die wearing the flageolet? I'll write an article for *Mundo Obrero*. They won't believe it back home.'

'The emblem wasn't in the list of objects found on Garrido's body.'

'It's so little. It must have gone unnoticed.'

'The man who compiled the list even wrote down the flakes of light tobacco found at the bottom of his jacket pockets.'

'Then I don't understand. Unless it fell off when we moved the body. There were a few minutes of confusion until the two doctors on the central committee said nothing could be done. What's the flageolet got to do with all this?'

'Every detail must be considered.'

'It's just that the talk is due to begin and I don't want to miss it. The course costs small fortune and I wasn't born a mayor. Do you understand? What you don't know, you have to learn.'

Carvalho left behind the hum of the course students and stopped at a crossroads only he could see. Fonseca? Santos Pacheco? Back to see Esparza? Play around with the thugs who must be waiting outside the city hall?

'To the Puerta del Sol.'

164

'But it's just round the corner.'

'I got up tired.'

'Well, it will cost you two hundred pesetas just for the pleasure of it.'

'There are dearer pleasures.'

'And then you'll say there's a crisis.'

'Drop me right outside the State Security Office.'

'Mission Impossible coming up!'

The taxi-driver did not take his eyes off him in the rear-view mirror. He bowed solemnly when he saw that the tip was in the region of thirty pesetas. Carvalho got out and took the shortest route between the pavement and the armed policeman standing on guard.

'Señor Pérez Hinestrilla de la Montesa.'

'You mean Pérez-Montesa de la Hinestrilla.'

'He wears a waistcoat.'

'That doesn't mean anything.'

Duck or turkey? It would be necessary to decide which was the defining feature: the long neck kneaded by a prominent Adam's apple; or the small head, with thick lips and scant chin, crowned by short hair displaying the diametrically opposed aspects of Prussian and punk capillary culture. Pérez-Montesa de la Hinestrilla tried to compromise.

'You will appreciate that I cannot reveal secret information unless I know the purpose for which it is required. You are asking for highly confidential reports about the members of the PCE central committee. Fine. I'll give them to you as a mark of trust, but you'll have to give me some other token in return so that I can justify myself to my superiors.'

'Do you want me to tell you the prime suspect?'

'That seems fair.'

'Do you promise he won't die a quarter of an hour after I give you his name?'

'What are you suggesting?'

165

'Is it so hard to understand?'

'You are talking to a public servant of a democratic government who has himself been a democrat for many years. I was a share-holder in the journal *Cuadernos para el Diálogo*.'*

'You seem a nice enough kid, but are you able to guarantee what I am asking? Will you take responsibility for disclosing the name of a man I may then find drilled full of holes?'

It was either anger or a violent struggle within himself. He sighed and struck a punishing blow against the back of his tall, carved-wood chair.

'Why are you putting me on the spot like this?'

It's true. Why am I facing him with a moral dilemma that could wreck his brilliant career? Who knows, he could soon be a chief executive, a government representative on some autonomous regional body, a minister at forty or forty-five. But precisely because he had the air of a weak prince, the cynical detective used a form of moral blackmail he would not have used with anyone else. Why me?

'You were a member of the Communist Party.'

'That was an adolescent prank. At most a couple of months. I didn't know what the Communist Party was. I thought it was an attempt to resurrect the FUE student union. Which university student of my age hasn't held Marxist ideas at some time in his life? For all of us, or nearly all, the experience was an effective enough vaccine. I don't owe anything to the Party.'

'It's no longer a question of parties or more or less powerful intermediaries. There are gangsters loose: real professionals of political crime who want to finish the job.'

'What's that to me? In the end he's a murderer, and we are arguing over the life of a murderer.'

Caravlho shrugged and seemed to settle with pleasure into the soft Oxford armchair. He closed his eyelids, as if trying to sleep or to imagine something. The waistcoated public servant talked in a loud voice, with himself, with Carvalho, with the past, with the future, with Humanity.

'You'll be the first to tell the Party.'

'I give you my word that the Party will know nothing of your role

* *Cuadernos para el Diálogo*: a broad opposition journal that appeared legally during the latter years of the Franco regime.

in all this.'

'I haven't played any role and I don't intend to. I must consult my superiors, or at least Superintendent Fonseca.'

Carvalho smiled with all the sorrow his face could concentrate.

'At least I must tell the minister.'

Carvalho shook his head, as if another pound of sorrow had been added to the crushing weight of incomprehension and estrangement.

'The head of government, then. Or don't you trust him either?'

'Do you think the head of government will keep a secret between him, you and me?'

'Leave me some way out. I can't take all the responsibility.'

'I'd like the head of government to promise that it will go no further than us three.'

'That's a crazy suggestion, but I'll try.'

He took a diary from his pocket and dialled three numbers on a telephone that stood majestically apart from the one connected to the switchboard.

'Extension ten . . .'

His Adam's apple was wildly agitated, determined to break all records for moving up and down a human neck.

'Hi there, president. Yes, it's me again.'

He closed his eyes with pleasure, sensing Carvalho's respect for unaffectedness in high places.

'Look. It may be possible to speed things up, and I need your permission to show some confidential reports. Everything will have to remain between you, me and him. No; that, no. Nor that. I know it's a problem, but there's no other way. Thanks for your trust.'

He opened a drawer and took a handful of tissues to mop up some imaginary perspiration. Then he made a sign for Carvalho to follow him into a side room where there was barely enough space to stand between the cupboards packed against every wall. He took a key ring from his pocket and went to work on a deep-set lock. Zinc drawers tinged with rust and old age opened up before Carvalho's eyes. The assistant chief executive selected a box, placed it under a thin arm lost in the sleeve of his jacket, and relocked the drawer and cupboard. Back in the main office, he put the box on the edge of a table facing Carvalho. The detective took it with him to the sofa and crossed his legs into an improvised desk that hid the box from view.

He opened it and looked for the file. 'Son of Emerenciano and Leonor. Father: a miner and member of the Communist Party of Spain since 1932. Mother: a back-up activist in the coalfield until her arrest in October 1934. Amnestied by the Popular Front in February 1936. Married on the Ebro front in February 1938. Exiled 1939. Birth of Félix Esparza Julve in Toulon, January 1940. Father active in the French Resistance. Mother deported with her child to the Massif Central. Domestic service for a high-ranking German officer saved her from a concentration camp. At the end of the war, the father entered Spain with the maquis. Arrested on the outskirts of Villafranca del Bierzo in 1947. Died of TB in El Dueso prison in 1951. The son studied at the PCF-funded Marcel Cachin College in Paris. Summer camps in Romania and the USSR. Member of the Spanish delegation to the Moscow Youth Festival in 1958. Agronomic studies at Humboldt University in East Germany. Rapid rise in the Party. First mission to Spain: subversive activity, the 1962 strikes in the Asturias. Arrested under a false name in Madrid, 1965. Eight months in Carabanchel. Sentence quashed. Rearrested in the break-up of the Party apparatus in Ciudad Real in 1965. Sentenced to four years in Cáceres prison. Applied for parole in 1967. Apparently left the Party apparatus and set up an agricultural company for selected produce. Married a partner's daughter in 1968. Business trips especially to Belgium and Holland. Irregularities of management in 1969. First matrimonial separation. Left for Germany after fraudulent bankruptcy. Contact in Frankfurt. Fraudulent bankruptcy overturned. Returned to Spain. See code-name *Mainz*. New business marketing tropical produce. Irregularities of management. Final matrimonial separation. See code-name *Felt*. Fresh links with the Party under the protection of Santos Pacheco. Code-name *Doubloon*. Training ST 68, Exit Sunflower services. Umbrellas.'

In other words, Carvalho concluded, high-level training, very special service, unlimited protection. He caught Pérez-Montesa de la Hinestrilla looking furtively at the ceiling in one particular corner of the room. Carvalho hurriedly buried the file among the others and made as if to stand up.

'Don't worry. It doesn't always work. You know what things are like in Spain. Sometimes they watch, sometimes they don't.'

Carvalho looked for the hidden eye of the closed-circuit television. He thought he could make it out under the wing of a Murillo angel flying to the top of the *trompe l'oeil.*

'Even I don't know when it's on.'

'But you know it's sometimes on?'

'Almost never, I promise you. I swear it.'

A formal knock on the tall, huge doors followed by a rapid entry. Fonseca stretched out his hand to Carvalho, while Sánchez Ariñó, his head bent but smiling, kept his hands in his pockets.

'I heard you were here, Señor Carvalho, so I thought I'd drop in and say hello. If Mohammed won't go to the mountain, the mountain must go to Mohammed.'

Fonseca put on a most critical look of surprise when he saw the metal box on Carvalho's knees. As his eyes rose questioningly towards Pérez-Montesa de la Hinestrilla, the assistant chief executive's face grew smaller than ever, as though searching for the metaphysical consistency of authority. He beat off the doubt and interrogation clinging to Fonseca's eyes. Carvalho watched them act out their roles of suspicious overseer and hardy administrator, without taking his eyes off Sánchez Ariñó, who seemed lost in the mystery of the new world suggested by the grooved surface of his powerful fingernails. If he sometimes turned his gaze from such a magical preoccupation, it was to fling his boredom and indifference at the other protagonists.

'It occurs to me that . . .'

'What occurs to you is your business,' the assistant chief executive cut him short.

But Fonseca had decided to stop only at the top and he pointed to the box resting on Carvalho's knees. The executive raised his voice on artificial heels and emphatically declared:

'That's enough!'

Fonseca shrugged and gave a wink to Carvalho.

'Well, ours is not to reason why. As far as I'm concerned, you can churn out photocopies and give them to all your pals.'

'I don't think there's any point. Written reports were never your strong point. You've always preferred oral communication.'

'Very clever. Very intelligent. I'd like to have had you here five years ago. Then we'd have seen where your cleverness and intelligence got you. I know very well where they'd have gone: up your arse.'

But he wore a smile, evidently trying to put a brave face on it.

'If you know something and don't inform the legitimate representatives of the government, then you know what can happen to you.'

'I told him that myself,' echoed Pérez-Montesa de la Hinestrilla.

'This isn't a spy film. There are a lot of ugly customers around, as you've already found out.'

'It's also for your own safety,' added the waistcoated executive to ingratiate himself with the other two.

'Of course. That's what matters above all.'

Fonseca was enthusiastic at the discovery of a new argument.

'Your own safety is the supreme consideration.'

'The main one,' Pérez-Montesa de la Hinestrilla said by way of correction.

'Yes, the main one.'

Carvalho stood up and felt a highly charged threat on passing Fonseca, as if the suppressed violence were attempting to electrocute him. He left the zinc box on the table in front of the waistcoated executive.

'You've convinced me. I don't want to find anything out. Here's the box.'

'He's playing games. He's already found what he wanted, and now he's just trying to pull the wool over our eyes.'

'Señor Carvalho, I'd like to warn you for the last time that you are assuming a grave responsibility towards the country, the government and your own conscience.'

The short speech was emphatically supported by the nodding of Fonseca's head. Carvalho was most impressed. He shrugged his shoulders without any sign of defiance, understanding that everything said was for his own good, but he remained the victim of a personal and professional drive which, he well knew, might one day lead to disaster. Perhaps the shrug was not sufficiently eloquent, for Sánchez Ariñó barred the exit by forcefully placing the palm of his hand on Carvalho's chest.

'Is this door yours?'

Sánchez Ariñó pursed his cheek by way of a smile.

'Am I under arrest? Is this the moment when I should ask to see my lawyer?'

'Let him go. But I'm telling you very seriously, Señor Carvalho; you've asumed a great responsibility to the country, the government and your own conscience.'

'There's no need to repeat yourself. I'm sure it's already been taped and filmed.'

Carvalho pointed to the hole in the ceiling. The palm of 'Dillinger's' hand dropped from his chest, and he left the actors to take a breather behind the fallen curtain. This is not moving but being moved, he repeated to himself as he passed through doors, rooms and corridors towards the way out. Once in the street, he was not sure whether to cover his tracks or make them easier to see. He should speak with Santos and others as well, eventually placing the right epithet on the assassination. Yet another taxi-driver disilllusioned with politics, the mayor, the city, the taxi and life. Calle Professor Waksman? Do you know who he was? A fortune-hunter? What do you think? He invented streptomycin, the thing that came after penicillin. And what came then? A lot of concoctions, but nothing really. This time the porter strictly looked the part and was not scratching his balls beneath his uniform. He accompanied Carvalho to the lift, with the submission of an assistant lecturer from the fifties. The detective went up to the flat of James Wonderful, alias Jaime Siurell, walked past it, climbed a few steps to the next floor, and waited. The porter must have told them over the house-phone. They'll wait four or five minutes, then they'll get nervous and the door will open. The door opened. The Central European from the night at Gladys's stuck his head out to make sure no one was on the landing.

'He's not there,' he called back from the door.

'Have you looked properly?'

It was Wonderful's voice. The fair-haired man slowly turned to look again, without taking his hand from his jacket pocket. He ventured as far as the stairs to the landing and then on to the main staircase, where the soles of Carvalho's shoes crashed into his eyes and broke the world into stardust, burning his nostrils with the smell of his own blood. As Carvalho hit him about the ear and neck, he let his body topple gently in an apparent effort to soften the fall and avoid a sharp encounter with the parquet floor. Carvalho jumped over the prostrate body, gripped the door-frame with one

171

hand and pushed his pistol into the flat with the other. The door was open between the entrance-hall and the living room, so that right at the end he could see Wonderful standing attentively and blinking to sharpen the image that approached him.

'Shuster, what's going on?'

Wonderful's hands dropped on the wheelchair as on a parapet, obviously dejected at the presence of Carvalho.

'What do you want here? You're an idiot, a complete idiot. You haven't learnt anything.'

He spoke with greater ease than at their previous meeting, and his eyes even seemed to have returned to their orbits. But as he took his hands from the wheelchair and dropped his arms by his side, tears hung from the ragged lashes of sickly, weather-beaten eyes. Carvalho drew nearer and Wonderful ducked down, concentrating all the strength in his arms to launch the wheelchair like a missile at the detective. Having chosen to contemplete that raging face full of veins, red patches, grimy moisture and mauve wrinkles, Carvalho took the force of the chair on his knees and belly. He fell on his knees, breathed deeply, and let Wonderful regain sufficient agility to move towards a cocktail bar. Just as the old man was about to put his trembling hands on the hidden revolver, Carvalho's neutral voice froze him to a halt.

'You'll never reach the gun. But I've got one, too. Be sensible.'

'Imbecile. You're a real imbecile. What did you come here for?'

'I need a few more pieces of information.'

'And who's going to give you them? Me?'

A flash of hope smoothed the wrinkles on the old man's face. Carvalho swung round and fired before the broken-armed Latin American could do the same. The man fell on his sling arm and uncovered a shadow seeking refuge on the staircase. Carvalho threw himself on Wonderful, seized him by his dressing-gown and forced him to walk in front. With his good arm, the Latin American was trying to hold back the blood that streamed from his chest. Carvalho did not have to say a word, since Wonderful himself cleared a path.

'Careful what you do! I'm coming first.'

Two angry-looking men watched as Wonderful and Carvalho, stuck to each other, took the lift to the ground floor. One of them was the impassive, fair-haired man. He seemed to be smiling.

When they were passing the porter, Wonderful began to exaggerate the difficulty he had in moving. But it was not enough to stop the ill-tempered doorman's eyes from popping at the miracle of the walking invalid. So radical was his surprise that he did not appreciate how firmly Carvalho's arms were placed on Wonderful's shoulders. It did not strike him as odd that Carvalho suddenly left the old man tottering on the pavement, for no other reason than to pounce on a taxi – pounce on rather than hail – in an area where they were certainly not in short supply. But this basic incongruity was as nothing beside the sudden raising of the old man. For a moment Wonderful followed the trail of Carvalho's taxi, but then he let himself be taken in and questioned by the porter.

'I've been able to walk just a little for a few days now. My nephew got very excited that I should see him to the door. Sometimes things like that can boost you more than the best medicine. I hadn't seen him for so many years. He's the son of my little pet sister.'

Similarly, Carvalho looked back to watch the old man allowing himself to be led submissively into the house. Imbecile. You're a real imbecile. You haven't understood anything. And you go around shooting people and breaking their arms. The more powerful your enemies, the more foolhardy you become. You won't reach old age, and nor will you become a young man again. It was true. Imbecile. You haven't understood anything. What do epithets matter to you? Leave them for the politicians. The murderer is so-and-so, and that's that. He grabbed a telephone box, placing his body between it and an agitated woman who had undoubtedly seen it first. While he tried to locate Santos, he listened to the indignant monologue addressed to him through the glass by the woman, who looked like an angry orang-utan.

'Excuse me, but it was an emergency. I had to get a doctor.'

'Well, if you'd told me. I'm only human.'

But Carvalho paid no attention to the moral sermon and got back into the taxi.

'Where to?'

'Take me on a guided tour.'

'A tour? Round Madrid? Aren't you from here?'

'No.'

'That's obvious. A tour of Madrid by taxi!'

But he took him on the tour, from one traffic jam to the next.

'They say it eases up at meal-times. You see?'

Meal-times. For the first time in many years, the appointment

173

with food did not seem important.

'Drop me outside the Ritz.'

The taxi-driver sang softly:

'Ah what pleasure
Dancing a fox-trot
With a young squire
Who talks of love!
If I live to be a hundred years old
I'll never forget the evenings at the Ritz.'

Julio was reading a sports paper propped against the corner of the hotel façade.

'Keep going for two blocks. Carmela is waiting for you. She's not in her usual car. It's a blue Talbot.'

As he walked along, Carvalho worked out what he would say. He looked round twice to see if he was being followed. Carmela opened the door from inside.

'Is your husband safe and sound?'

'The poor guy. They left him crippled for me. He doesn't look too happy. You men don't know how to be ill. If you'd been through childbirth . . . and everything that follows. What headaches! A stomach turned upside down. You're not looking well. Did you meet that riff-raff again?'

'A similar bunch.'

'Santos is waiting for you.'

She stopped on the Gran Via at the corner of the Plaza de España. She pointed to the dull rise of the Madrid Tower towards a dying afternoon sky. Seventeenth floor.

'It's a safe flat. Ask for Pino Betancourt – the flat's in his name.'


He crossed the square behind the dull-witted Don Quixote and Sancho Panza. No one asked him where he was going until he came upon a dark, big-eyed woman with a printed dress that half-covered a pair of high black boots. Santos looked uncomfortable on the low collapsible sofa of a living-room filled with symbols of emancipated woman. The dark woman picked up her bag, nodded to them and went out of the room. Carvalho dropped beside Santos and told him of the flageolet, the special emblem with red paint treated to shine in the dark, the death signal, the Galician and New Zealand kiwi fruits, Esparza Julve, or rather Julvito, the interview with the waistcoated Pérez-Montesa de la Hinestrilla – waistcoated? yes, waist-coated – and Fonseca. Santos rose to his feet as if he were carrying the weight of four bodies. He went onto the balcony to look at the old-town panorama on the verge of nightfall: beyond the autumnal agony of the Plaza de España, between the decor of the Royal Palace and the illuminations of the Gran Via. Seventeen floors between reality and desire, Carvalho thought, without knowing why and without moving from the sofa. Santos Pacheco's white head shone in the sunlight. The animated shadows of doubts were no longer passing through that head – only memories, one, two, three, a thousand episodes from the life of Esparza Julve, Julvito. As Carvalho had spoken, he had seen a prayer steadily taking shape in Santos's eyes. Not that, please; anything, but not that. Santos returned from the balcony.

'For money? Out of hate?'

'Only he knows. But the evidence very strongly points to money. Irregularities of management. Fraudulent bankruptcy. Did you know anything about it?'

'A little.'

'What kind of irregularities?'

'It was after he got married and moved away from the Party. He'd lived the tough life of a Party orphan and communist fighter and he soon became a free man with money in his pocket. No one could help him. I heard of what was happening, but I couldn't give him any financial assistance. I never dreamt that it was so dramatic, that it would lead him where it did.'

'Everything fits. The times. The trip to Germany. No doubt we would discover that he didn't work in a factory, but received special training.'

'So much deceit. I just can't understand it.'

'You can hate what you love, especially if you've been conditioned by a life full of extraordinary events.'

'That must be it. We all surrounded him with the cult of his father. We all wanted him to be like us. We always want new cadres to be like us, talk like us, think like us. Would you mind leaving?'

He went back on the balcony. The sun had moved enough to take the shine off his head. It was now pallid, opaque, abandoned between his shoulders, crestfallen over the void.

'I've finished my work,' Carvalho said without daring to follow.

'Please. Leave me alone for a few hours. I'll track him down before the evening is out. Tomorrow we will settle up and you can be on your way.'

The words came from that motionless head. There could be no doubt.

'I can't be sure that the people from the State Security Office haven't found out.'

'Until tomorrow.'

He was going to say: I'm in torture, Carmela. Do you know where I can get some nice tripe at this hour? But then he realised from her paralysed face that they were not alone in the car. The man he had insulted in the bookshop for being too free with his hands now sat up in the rear seat and expertly searched Carvalho with one hand, while keeping the other out of sight.

'Keep your mouth shut. And you, you already know what to do.'

She did. Having found a way round the España building, she followed the Avenida Princesa down to the Puerta del Hierro and emerged onto the Coruña highway.

'Madrid is like a pocket handkerchief. We've just been near the VIP bookshop, and now you're taking me to another familiar scene.'

'Taking *us*,' Carmela pointed out.

The man did not reply. He had leant back at a distance half-way between Carmela and Carvalho.

'Slow down when you see an advertisement for the Mesón del Cojo. I haven't eaten anything. I'm travelling on an empty stomach.'

'You on an empty stomach? You won't survive. But I don't think this gentleman will let you have a sandwich.'

'Where are we going? Is there a meal prepared?'

The other man closed his eyes and screwed up his nose. They were boring him.

'I'll take bad memories away from Madrid. I've hardly had any sleep. It's a town without doors or private life. They just take you where they like. I wasn't able to go to any fashionable restaurants.'

'I did what I could. Submit a complaint in writing.'

176

Carmela had the voice of a student who is about to sit an exam.

'The Mesón del Cojo,' he said.

Carmela slowed down.

'The next on the right.'

They turned into a street lined with cars and fences.

'Left.'

'And then?'

'Right. Gently does it.'

The man leant towards them, pointing a gun at Carmela's head.

'Shit! Don't scare me like that!' she shouted hysterically.

'Easy, Carmela. It will work out okay,' Carvalho said reassuringly.

'Stop in front of the green lattice-gate.'

Green lattice-gate. What a rich vocabulary, Carvalho thought. The car stopped, and the man leant forward to take the ignition key and put it in his pocket. He gently pushed Carmela so that she should get out of the car. Then he himself stepped onto the pavement and motioned for Carvalho to get out. The three crossed a garden under the acacia trees and came to a door with Andalusian-style iron gratings. Behind it they could see the radiance of a brightly lit house.

A small, thin, bald man was rubbing his hands as if he were cold. Or perhaps the cold came from the cracked walls, spattered with marks of damp and indefinable erosion. Not a single piece of furniture. Maybe that was why the bulk of the fat man seemed rather comforting – a smiling bulk that came out to meet them in the company of the nocturnal visitors to Carmela's flat.

'How nice to see you both! Don't worry. You are my guests. My niece and nephew. I'm sorry this house is so poorly decorated. It's cold and inhospitable. The sooner we get it over, the better. There's not even anywhere to sit.'

'I need to sit down.'

'I can see that, Señor Carvalho. You're not looking well at all. You're too high-spirited, like from a different age. You must have learnt your trade from Klotz novels. Raner is violent and aggressive, always on the move. Things aren't done like that anymore. Look at Le Carré's characters. That's the model. Office work, a lot of office work. Going through files. Everything's computerised, dehumanised. Smiley uses his head, not his fists. Forgive me for always talking about Smiley, but he really does fascinate me.'

'My stomach is empty.'

'There's not a crumb in the house. One more reason to get it over as quickly as possible. You seem to have reached the end of the trail. We'd be very interested to know who you've picked.'

'You already know.'

'I don't think so.'

'May I lean against the wall?'

'No.'

It was a no that condemned him to stay on his feet, like Carmela, like the others who formed a circle around the two pallid faces. Carvalho threw his head back to free his shoulders from a painful, steely tension. The ceiling of broken, flower-patterned plaster surrounded a chandelier whose crystals had gone astray.

'A name is all we want.'

Just a name. A man condemned to death. A few hours gained for Santos Pacheco to prepare a flanking manoeuvre. That was the least thing that concerned him. In the end, though, they were not his clients.

'You must understand. I have a duty to my clients. You also recognise professional secrecy.'

'The name.'

Carvalho said no with his head. The fat man barely moved his arm. His short, thin, bald, shivery companion approached Carmela and hit her on both cheeks until she was dizzy. The fat man and Carvalho looked at each other. The thug had eyes of steel.

'The name.'

Carvalho looked at Carmela, who had covered her face with her hands. She was neither crying nor groaning.

'I must consult my partner. After all, she's got the worst part.'

'Don't tell those bastards anything!' she shouted with a hoarse, false-baritone voice.

Faced with the barrier of Carmela's hands, the bald man landed a punch to her stomach that left her sitting with her legs sprawled and her eyes full of stupefaction.

'You see? The name.'

No, Carvalho's head repeated. The torturer bent over Carmela, pulling her up by the hair. His free hand flew in search of the girl's body, but it found a body that came to meet him and deliver a kick to his shins. Her hands fastened on the little man's face, tearing his eyelids and raising bloody weals of flesh on his cheeks. He let go of her hair in order to protect his face, and Carmela launched into blind hand-to-hand combat. The other two men went towards them, disregarding a mute and tardy instruction from the fat man. Carvalho immediately went for him, even though a pistol was now staring from the cuboid's hand. A kick in his flies demonstrated that he was not insensitive to certain assaults from reality. Two human bodies fell on the detective, undecided between themselves whether to immobilise him or to beat him to pulp. He breathed in splutters, and in splutters, too, he shouted for Carmela to run.

'She's getting away!' one of them said, and Carvalho found himself at the mercy of a lone assailant. He heard the noise of the door being locked. He got to his feet and began moving towards the door, but then someone hit him on the leg and brought him to the ground. He could feel someone on his back. Carmela's legs did not appear against the flaky skirtingboard that formed his horizon. They stood him up and pushed him against the wall. The fat man was in one corner with his hands on his balls; the bald man's face was full of blood, both his own and the blood streaming from Carvalho's nose. The red-haired nocturnal companion was holding a pistol. Only Carmela and the impassive face were missing.

'You're not a professional! You're a kamikaze!'

The fat man was making semi-circular movements around Carvalho, while the other two stood by with the artillery.

'Leave him to us. That's enough of the kid-glove treatment.'

'A kamikaze. I can't stand kamikazes. I hate irrational people.'

The impassive man returned, carefully locked the door, went up to the stout overseer and said something in his ear. The fat man whispered something in reply. The others fell silent, waiting for news that did not come. The impassive man left the room by a side door. Carvalho slid down the wall and sat on the floor. His nose was bleeding and he felt pain from some of the blows he had sustained on his back. He wanted to sleep. He closed his eyes and received a message of warmth from some point of his body. His eyes had been open so long that they actually hurt. His back was grateful for the wall's support. Carmela was not there. He felt happy.

'Take advantage of the five minutes it will take for my friend to get advice. You're through. You will only get out of here feet first. Is it money you want? Set a price for the information.'

Carvalho soon realised that the difference between his persecutors was that some wanted to know what they already knew, while others wanted to know what they didn't know. The previous ones had beaten him and made him feel, but with an extreme sense of assurance. These others obviously had no idea of the murderer's identity.

'Cigarette?'

The fat man held out a packet of Ducado Specials.

'I only smoke cigars.'

'You're out of luck. The Cubans have had two very bad harvests, and stocks of Havanas seem to be finished.'

'I'm used to Canary cigars.'

'Oh, well.'

The fat man leant against the wall and slid down beside Carvalho. As his bottom hit the floor, the shock made him lift his legs and reveal a pair of black knee-length socks fastened by garters. Resting against Carvalho's shoulder, he indulged in a lengthy reflection on who we are, where we come from and where we are going. The important thing is life. It is non-transferable; personal and non-transferable. Carvalho was not sure at which point he fell asleep. He knew these were not the best conditions for sleep, but he surrendered as if his very life depended on it. He was woken by the efforts of the other two to put the fat man back on his feet. The cuboid figure arranged his trousers and jacket and ambled towards the door where the impassive man stood like a tailor's dummy displaying the autumn fashion. They muttered to one another. The fat man returned to the middle of the room, a broad smile on his face. He looked at Carvalho from his all-powerful longitude and latitude, then slowly bent over him and clutched his shoulders. Pulling him up by his arms and elbows, he propped the detective against the wall, yellowed by the light from the ailing lamp. The fat man moved to one side in contemplation of his work.

'Pity we didn't meet under better conditions. You're a brave man. I'd like you to have been my nephew in real life.'

The others whispered with the fat man as if something were nearing an end. They now kept their tension inside themselves, although the guns still lay in their hands like the ashes of a dying fire.

'Maybe this will be my last job. I've already told them I want to retire. I've seven five-year terms behind me. Seven.'

Carvalho watched him draw near. He no longer had the strength to attempt anything, as if Carmela's escape had been his own liberation. The fat man stretched out one hand and, with the other, forced him to shake it.

'It seems we no longer need you to tell us anything. You may leave.'

You may leave. I may leave. From mistrust to acceptance of the situation. Carvalho shook his bones back into their right position, the fleshless frame of a hunted animal.

'You're sleepy. I can see. Sorry I can't even offer you a bed.'

Carvalho left the friendly chatter and walked towards the door, unsure whether to start running or to edge out backwards with an eye for the possibility of a shot. Why shouldn't I run? And he replied: for aesthetic reasons, as a slave to behavioural models he would never be able to rework. It was with such thoughts that he eventually found himself in the cold of the night, with the door closed behind him and life represented by a path through the acacia trees. Half-way along the path, he heard the door open again behind his back. Some steps, a voice that froze him still.

'The car keys. Your companion left the car keys.'

It was the man with the impassive face. He was holding out the keys.

'Where is she?'

'That's your problem,' he replied, turning back to the house.

The car was where they had left it, an object binding him to Carmela without which he would not be able to find her. He leant against the bonnet and waited. Carmela appeared round a corner of the street, hesitant at first, but then running towards Carvalho and staring at him as if he had been raised from the dead. She grasped his hands and put her wounded cheek against his chest. He urged her to get into the car and took the steering wheel. The house remained there, like a distant weight that grew lighter as the car increased the distance.

'Don't worry about it. There was no other solution.'

'I didn't tell them the name. They let me go because it suited them. Either they must know by now or they're not interested in finding out. What about you? How did you manage to escape?'

'I didn't escape from anyone. Nobody followed me. At first I thought one of them was following, but he didn't even leave the garden. I ran like mad, but then I turned back to see if you'd managed to get away.'

'Maybe they were afraid of a scandal. Imagine a chase through the streets.'

'What scandal? All these houses are deserted. I tried to get into one to phone the Party or Julio for help. I didn't want to wander too far in case they let you go. In case you tried to escape.'

'It's all so clear that I don't understand anything. I want to sleep. You drive. Do you feel up to it?'

Carmela took the wheel, and they did not speak until they reached Madrid.

'To hell with sleep! I haven't eaten a thing. I've got an empty stomach.'

'If you go to a restaurant bleeding like that, you will start one hell of a row.'

'But you've got red cheeks.'

'I'll just put on some make-up.'

'Shall we go to El Amparo? New Basque cuisine. Doesn't the name mean anything to you?'

'Basque-style salted codfish, and so on.'

'Don't go on, please. If you're not too shattered, I suggest we eat first and then go dancing.'

'Oh, John darling! This could be our night!'

'Drop me at the hotel for the time being. I want to have a shower. I'll wash my wounds away and be as good as new.'

'Don't be too long,' Carmela said as he got out of the car.

'No,' Carvalho touched her reassuringly. He stood at an angle when he asked for the room key, so that the marks of battle would not be visible, and then dashed off towards the lift.

'Señor Carvalho, one moment please!'

The receptionist was holding out an envelope on which the word 'URGENT' had been written by a nervous hand. Pacing up and down, Carvalho tore open the envelope.


Dear Señor Carvalho,

    I've gone over in my mind the things we have talked about

and experienced in the last few days, and I have come to the conclusion that I am the one truly responsible for all that has happened. My blindness to the main facts and actors is the chief cause of Fernando's death and of the serious damage it may do to my Party and the democratic process in Spain. I take responsibility for the confidence we showed in X, allowing him to get as far as he did and to do what he has done. I thought I could see in him the best virtues of a good revolutionary, but perhaps the only thing I saw was my own image reflected in a convenient mirror.

I have lived through some very painful personal and collective moments, but none was more painful than this. I feel hemmed in by failure. I myself am a failure. I feel I have travelled a long road for nothing, and if I personalise the failure, it is because it applies exclusively to me and affects neither the Party nor its policy. Nearly fifty years of active membership give greater significance to the anguish I feel at what I am now holding in my hands.

Perhaps one of my defeats, one of our defeats, is the great power, the blind faith in the logic and analysis of facts, perceived with insufficient distance and an activist-type alienation capable of petrifying our sense of reality. Using words that do not conjure up what my words have always conjured up, I realise the extreme poverty of my vocabulary now that I'm trying to break out of an 'internal' language. I don't know if I'm making myself clear, or even how much I want to make clear. History did not allow us a normal existence. For better or for worse, we have always been in an exceptional situation: we saw the light of day as an alternative to social-democratic revisionism; we immediately had to wrestle with the struggle against fascism; we became a fiercely persecuted underground movement, conditioned by national repression and a bipolarisation of world politics; we entered legality declaring freedom to be a revolutionary instrument, but we were culturally weighed down by a history filled with exceptional situations and various relics. Maybe it would be necessary to make a clean break: to give a sense to the future of the communist movement beyond the alibis of a generation educated in resistance and self-repression, instead of in a process of building socialism in freedom, with the weapons of democratic liberties and the historical energy of the masses.

The gods are dead, but we priests have remained. We respond as priests to the priesthood of counter-revolution now on the defensive. But perhaps that is not the way we should respond; perhaps the only way is to lose our own priesthood so that the other priesthoods will be thrown into relief. I look around me and am anguished to find not only that we have not taken this road, but that we have striven to reproduce ourselves as priests in our own heirs. Having no epic or ethical alibi, those heirs will end up believing that socialism is the result of eight hours of solid, though badly paid, labour. But bad pay is itself an alibi so long as power is not held, and that alibi has disappeared among the priests of the socialist countries, where power entails material privilege.

Fortunately socialism remains as the process and objective of human emancipation, and the mistakes committed by parties such as ours are instrumental errors that do not invalidate the progressive meaning of history, the progressive meaning of human emancipation from all restrictive burdens. This meaning is preserved in every nameless militant capable of understanding the collective significance of the struggle and the long march, of sacrificing part of his or her individual liberty in the struggle for collective liberty and, if necessary, sacrificing his life for a juster history. We have to purify egoism in order to understand the evil derivatives of primary, animal egoism or the rationalised egoism of capitalist culture and civilisation.

If the goal is so clear and its subject so self-evident, what prevents us from reworking the method and the instrument? A culture, a false consciousness of ourselves as a collective, a consciousness that is both methodologically and instrumentally conservative. What I am saying to you is the product not of the boundless depression that has gripped me, but of many reflections and conversations, including those with Garrido himself. Both of us knew we were being driven forward by the tongue of our accumulated historical glacier, but neither he nor I was capable of initiating the scandal of an internal cultural revolution through a break with the statutes and the cremation of old relics.

Now I am facing the corpse of Fernando, murdered by my

own godson. I feel like a stupid, empty old failure, with nothing left but to embalm the corpse and patch up the Party so that the images will be safe. I have no wish to be in charge of the election, this false election, and I would like to give an exemplary significance to the act of my self-destruction. I owe you this explanation because, in the end, it was to you we turned to give us the absolution that I assumed to be impossible. In the use that the counter-revolution has made and will make of everything that has happened, our own dramaturgy will itself be of some advantage. I hope that my exit will at least produce a respectful silence.

Greetings,

Madrid, 12 October 1980                    José Santos Pacheco


Carvalho put the letter in his pocket. He immediately caught himself moving towards the lift, then towards the street door and back again to the lift. He re-read a chance fragment of the letter: 'We have to purify egoism in order to understand the evil derivatives of primary, animal egoism or the rationalised egoism of capitalist culture and civilisation.' A fine sentence, but hard for a dying man to utter, however good his lungs. Carvalho had to struggle against a defensive incredulity. He found himself on the pavement. Carmela was parked on the corner, gesturing towards him and surprised at his lack of decision. He automatically walked up to the car. Who am I to deny him the role of scapegoat?
'Where does Santos live?'
'His family lives in Calle Legazpi. But he has a flat of his own.'
'Where?'
'It's a secret. Very few people know.'
'You know.'
'Yes.'
'Let's go there.'
'No. I need authorisation.'
Carvalho walked round the car and sat next to Carmela. He held out the latter and showed her two or three fragments. She started up the car and began to sob when they reached the third set of traffic lights.

185

'Yes, I won't deny he's in.'

The concierge still had the look of suspicion with which she had met the strange, hurried couple who asked whether Santos was in his flat. She eventually let them go up only when Carmela showed her Party card.

'There are so many fascists around.'

Carvalho and Carmela pushed so hard on the bell that they almost broke it. No answer. They went back to the resistant concierge, who became suspicious at the incongruity of it all.

'He's definitely in.'

'Well, if he is and doesn't answer, then something must have happened. Do you have a key?'

The woman looked hard at Carmela and Carvalho, apparently convinced by her but not by him.

'Are you also from the Party?'

'This is a very important gentleman who has come a long way to see Santos.'

She arched her eyebrows, sighed resignedly, went into the office and returned with a bunch of keys. As they were climbing the wooden stairs, the woman searched for the key to Santos's flat and said almost to herself.

'I've known him for thirty years and nothing like this has ever happened before. Come rain or shine, Ventura – that's what I still call him – always has the same character. Something like this is very difficult, particularly in a man. Because where there's a man, there's a lunatic. I'm not exaggerating.'

The concierge strode across the landing, sized up all the aspects of the door, and pressed the bell with all the simplicity, assuredness and familiarity of an expert who belongs to the same tribe. She looked at Carvalho and Carmela as if to say: He'll answer for me all right. But he didn't answer for her. With a sudden nervous apprehension, she faced the door and cut into the lock with a well-aimed key. Before the three-man expedition lay a reception room with nothing to receive them and a corridor more obscured than brightened by a naked light-bulb.

'Señor Ventura, are you there? (He's been Ventura for twenty-five years and Ventura he'll remain.) Señor Ventura, are you there?'

He was there, half asleep on a wicker chair against a background of unpolished pine bookcases.

'He's fallen asleep.'

Carvalho pushed the concierge aside in his hurry to reach Santos. He felt his pulse and opened one of his eyelids.

'Coffee. As much as you can make, Carmela. Or rather, would you make it, señora? You ring a Party doctor to come at once; if not, call an ambulance.'

The concierge repeated Carvalho's gestures. She took his pulse. Raised an eyelid. Stared open-mouthed at the man and woman.

'A clot?'

'Coffee. Make some coffee or he'll die.'

'Oh my God!'

She assumed the position of the black American holder of the hundred metres record and immediately showed the rubber soles of her velvety slippers. Carvalho pulled Santos's head back, opened his mouth and put two fingers down his throat, producing such a nervous reaction that the sleeping man seemed to be coughing from his stomach. Carvalho persisted, his hands full of saliva. Finally, the retching took material shape in a thick white mucus that spread over Santos's unshaven white-and-black chin. The body bent forwards. One bout of retching followed another, as if an internal piston were driving to his lips the hidden illness of the sleep of death.

'Coffee.'

It was too hot. Carvalho cooled it with water, tore the cloth cover from a book on Mayakovski's theatre, and used it as a funnel into Santos's gasping mouth.

'Hold the funnel.'

The concierge held it with one hand and stroked the sleeping man's white hair with the other. Carvalho let some coffee trickle into the funnel, and Santos's head began to shake in refusal of the potion. When Carvalho insisted, Santos tipped forward spitting out the coffee. A white milk emerged from his mouth, punctuating the fits of choking that sounded like the reports of a blocked organ-pipe.

'Poor man. It's like Chinese torture.'

The concierge looked accusingly at Carvalho as he again inserted the funnel into the mouth of a convulsively sobbing, babbling and slobbering Santos. The action of vomiting once more became an uncontrollable implosion of his whole body. A little later, Carvalho's tired eyes watched a young doctor attend to Santos while he carefully took in Carmela's attempts to think rationally about the situation. Tell the Party. What for? Tell his family. What for?

'What do you mean, what for?'

'This man tried to commit suicide without seeking permission from the Party or his family. Don't turn it into an item for the agenda of the next central committee or a reproach on the part of his would-be widow. Besides, all the papers would find out.'

The newspapers were the convincing argument. Carmela agreed and returned to the doctor's side.

'I won't be responsible if he isn't taken to hospital. He has good reactions, but there may be complications.'

'We can't take the political scandal upon ourselves,' Carmela argued as Carvalho kept his eyes on Santos.

What does a political scandal matter to you now? It wouldn't be fair if you appeared in your underpants on the pages of History. Much better if you're there in your prison costume, in one of your conspiratorial disguises, in your marble suit of armour. Santos's eyes were two tear-filled outlines. His body lay on a metal bed scattered with pieces of plaster: a chair beside the headrest, books on a floor covered with sheets of newspaper, a window looking onto a back-yard. The closest thing to a cell. Nothing else but a corridor leading north to a kitchen with ragged white tiles and an iron stove. One of those 'economic kitchens': coal, heavy white coal bins with blackened calves. To the south, a clean bathroom delivered to the conspiracy of rust on the mirror, the bath-taps, the shower, the low-wattage electric heater. A dining-room with a pine table in the middle, three or four rush-bottomed pine chairs, bookcases, Lenin, Lukács, Stalin, *Storia del Partito Communista Italiano* by Paolo Spriano, Togliatti's *Political Writings*, Bukharin's *ABC of Communism*, Rosa Luxemburg's *Scritti Politici*, Isaac Deutscher's *Stalin*, the *Anti-Dühring*, Thompson's *Making of the English Working Class*, Mehring's *Karl Marx*, Cole's *History of Socialist Thought*, the *Manual of Political Economy* of the USSR Academy of Sciences, Berlinguer's *La Alternativa Communista*, Lafargue's *Right to Idleness*, Fourier's

*Theory of the Four Movements*, Hobsbawm's *Primitive Rebels*, Lichtheim's *Marxism*, four or five Lefebvres, three or four Garaudys, London's *On Trial*, Mao's *Selected Works*, Serge's *Memoirs of a Revolutionary*, Arrabal's *Letter to the Spanish Communists*, Semprún's *Autobiography of Frederico Sánchez*, Mayakovski's *Complete Works*, Ostrovski's *How the Steel was Tempered*, Labriola's *Essays on Historical Materialism*, Fernando Buey's *Getting to Know Lenin*, Abendroth's *History of the European Workers Movement*, the volume *Socialist Humanism* by Fromm and others, Ramsay MacDonald's *Socialism*, Gramsci's *Selected Works*, Carr's *The Bolshevik Revolution*, Balzac's *Complete Works*, Della Volpe's *Critique of Taste*, López Salinas's *The Mine*, López Pacheco's *Electric Power-Station*, José María Castellet's *Twenty Years of Spanish Poetry*, Manuel Sacristán's *Writing on Heine*, Della Volpe's *Rousseau and Marx*, Jean Jaurès's *Socialist Studies*, Jean Kanapa's *Socialisme et Culture*, Claudín's *The Communist Movement*, Marcuse's *Eros and Civilisation*, the *History of the CPSU*, Deutscher's Trotsky trilogy, *The Secret Correspondence between Stalin and Churchill*, Broué's *The Moscow Trials*, Norberto Bobbio's *Which Socialism?*, Bahro's *The Alternative*, *Bury my heart at Wounded Knee*, *Bury my heart at Wounded Knee*. *Bury my heart at Wounded Knee*.

The last of the Sioux war chiefs now became a reservation Indian, disarmed, dismounted, with no authority over his people, a prisoner of the Army, which had never defeated him in battle. Yet he was still a hero to the young men, and their adulation caused jealousies to arise among the older agency chiefs. Crazy Horse remained aloof; he and his followers living only for the day when Three Stars would make good his promise of a reservation for them in the Powder River country.

Late in the summer, Crazy Horse heard that Three Stars wanted him to go to Washington for a council with the Great Father. Crazy Horse refused to go. He could see no point in talking about the promised reservation. He had seen what happened to chiefs who went to the Great Father's House in Washington; they came back fat from the white man's way of living and with all the hardness gone out of them. He could see the changes in Red Cloud and Spotted Tail, and they knew he saw and they did not like him for it.

In August news came that the Nez Percés, who lived beyond

the Shining Mountains, were at war with the Bluecoats. At the agencies, soldier chiefs began enlisting warriors to do their scouting for them against the Nez Percés. Crazy Horse told the young men not to go against those other Indians, far away, but some would not listen, and allowed themselves to be bought by the soldiers. On August 31, the day these former Sioux warriors put on their Bluecoat uniforms to march away, Crazy Horse was so sick with disgust that he said he was going to take his people and go back north to the Powder River country.

When Three Stars heard of this from his spies, he ordered eight companies of pony soldiers to march to Crazy Horse's camp outside Fort Robinson and arrest him. Before the soldiers arrived, however, Crazy Horse's friends warned him they were coming. Not knowing what the soldiers' purpose was, Crazy Horse told his people to scatter, and then he set out alone to Spotted Tail agency to seek refuge with his old friend Touch-the-Clouds.

The soldiers found him there, placed him under arrest, and informed him they were taking him back to Fort Robinson to see Three Stars. Upon arrival at the fort, Crazy Horse was told that it was too late to talk with Three Stars that day. He was turned over to Captain James Kennington and one of the the agency policemen. Crazy Horse stared hard at the agency policeman. He was Little Big Man, who not so long ago had defied the commissioners who came to steal *Paha Sapa*, the same Little Big Man who had threatened to kill the first chief who spoke for selling the Black Hills, the brave Little Big Man who had last fought beside Crazy Horse on the icy slopes of the Wolf Mountains against Bear Coat Miles. Now the white men had bought Little Big Man and made him into an agency policeman.

As Crazy Horse walked between them, letting the soldier chief and Little Big Man lead him to wherever they were taking him, he must have tried to dream himself into the real world, to escape the darkness of the shadow world in which all was madness. They walked past a soldier with a bayoneted rifle on his shoulder, and then they were standing in the doorway of a building. The windows were barred with iron, and he could see men behind the bars with chains on their legs. It was a trap for an animal, and Crazy Horse lunged away like a trapped animal, with Little Big Man holding on to his arm. The scuffling went on for only a few seconds. Someone shouted a command, and then the soldier guard, Private William Gentles, thrust his bayonet deep into Crazy Horse's abdomen.

Crazy Horse died that night, September 5, 1877, at the age of thirty-five. At dawn the next day the soldiers presented the dead chief to his father and mother. They put the body of Crazy Horse into a wooden box, fastened it to a pony-drawn travois, and carried it to Spotted Tail agency, where they mounted it on a scaffold. All through the Drying Grass Moon, mourners watched beside the burial place. And then in the Moon of Falling Leaves came the heartbreaking news: the reservation Sioux must leave Nebraska and go to a new reservation on the Missouri River.

Through the crisp dry autumn of 1877, long lines of exiled Indians driven by soldiers marched northeastward toward the barren land. Along the way, several bands slipped away from the column and turned northwestward, determined to escape to Canada and join Sitting Bull. With them went the father and mother of Crazy Horse, carrying the heart and bones of their son. At a place known only to them they buried Crazy Horse somewhere near Chankpe Opi Wakpala, the creek called Wounded Knee.

'What are you reading?'

Carvalho closed the book and handed it to Carmela.

'One about Indians. Well, this is the moment. He's awake.'

Santos moved his head on the pillow to follow Carvalho's approach.

'The others can go.'

Carvalho sat on the edge of the bed, while the others obeyed the old man's orders.

'I'm very tired.'

'Me too. I've spent three days on the run. Since I arrived in this town, I haven't known sleep or been able to tell north from south. But now it's over for me.'

'And me. I thank you for what you have done. I can't say that I'm glad.'

'The central committee will be meeting in a few hours.'

'I'll send a message that I'm sick. They'll have to start operating without me.'

'They want to acclaim you as their general secretary.'

'I won't let them.'

'I don't make or break the king. It's your business. There's just the little matter of what should be done with the murderer.'

'I've already sent suitable instructions.'

'I don't want to miss the ending. If possible, I'd like to be there before the start of the central committee.'

'Talk to Mir. He'll sort out any problems you may have. He'll also pay you.'

Carvalho stood up and stretched out his hand. It was held more than shaken by the two rapidly shrunken white hands of a man who had descended into old age within the space of a few hours.

'The letter I sent you.'

'Yes?'

'Destroy it.'

'I already have. I don't keep correspondence, and sometimes I don't even read the letters that people send me.'

Santos closed his eyes with a smile.

'You still don't seem sure what is the rule and what is the exception.'

'It's well known.If you abandon Marxism, you end up believing in astrology and unable to tell good from evil.'

'Someone who abandons Marxism has lost his sense of good.'

'*Kyrie eleison.*'

'I suppose they'll all come today.'

The secretary winked sceptically. Mir made a guess at the number of files left by the corner of the display-table, which was full of fresh folders in which the members of the central committee of the Communist Party of Spain would find the agenda, an outline of the political report collectively drafted by the executive committee,

192

and a proposal to convene an emergency conference between the second and sixth of January 1981.

'The sixth of January? What about the epiphany?'

Leveder sought an explanation from all the executive committee members present among the various groups of comrades.

'How will we normalise our relations with society if we can't share with our sons the joy of receiving toys from Their Majesties the Three Magi?'

'Come on, don't be silly.'

'Well, more than one of us will have our ears boxed by the missus. It really is the limit to be doing politics on the feast of the Three Magi.'

'My wife will ask whether I'm married to her or the Party.'

Leveder was provoking miniature dialectical storms.

'Mir, I've got an idea how we can solve the problem of the Magi.'

'It's not a problem for me.'

'What about the kids? They'll be excitedly looking forward to their presents.'

'Mine are grown up. Anyway, they're republicans from birth.'

Leveder went away laughing and Mir winked at the secretary.

'He thinks I was born yesterday.'

'He's always in a mood for joking.'

'He's a great guy, but I saw him coming this time.'

Mir smiled left and right, happy to have won the cut-and-thrust at Leveder's expense.

'I heard that Santos is ill. Nothing serious, I hope. Who will take the chair?'

'The Party organiser,' Mir replied to Sepúlveda Civit.

A ring of people were noisily laughing at one of Leveder's remarks.

'Mir, come over here. You're being talked about.'

'What did that euroanarchist say about me?'

'He suggested that, on the epiphany, our children should come to the congress and receive their presents from you dressed as one of the Magi.'

'Good idea. Dressed as a black. I've been doing it all my life. As a black. We'll propose it at the end. What's he doing here?'

Mir's voice rose in surprise as he saw Carvalho enter alongside a steward. The detective went up to him and read in his eyes a certain irritation at his presence.

'Santos gave me permission and said you would sort out my problems.'

'That's my job. What problems?'

'I'd like to collect what's owing to me and look around until the meeting begins.'

'You can collect through there. Go out to your right and ask for Cespedes. He's in charge of finances and has been told all about it. There's no problem with the other because you're already here.'

'Has Esparza Julve arrived?'

Mir stared into his eyes.

'Why shouldn't he?'

'Was he informed in the usual way?'

'Like everyone else.'

Neither man dropped his eyes.

'I'll go and collect, just in case.'

Royo from finances was a bald, wary, light-skinned Aragonese. Carvalho attributed his opening remark to the proverbial rectitude of the Aragonese peasantry.

'That's a nice packet you're taking away.'

'Do you resent it?'

'Me? Why shoud I? Pay is pay. What I do resent is the Party's unserious attitude to finances. Whenever I give a report, they just nod off or go to have a piss. Royo has to plug all the holes, and sometimes there aren't enough hands for the job. Some of them seem to think a revolution can be made for nothing. Shall I cross it?'

Carvalho nodded. He put the cheque in his pocket and returned to the large ante-room. As soon as he entered, he felt there had been a major change. A near-total silence mummified the still compact groups. The rigidity of their bodies was belied by the fact that their heads tried to look anywhere except at the spot where Esparza Julve was collecting his folder and chatting normally with the secretary. The two voices grew ever louder against the background of silence.

Esparza Julve put the folder under his arm, went up to a group of comrades and said something that was greeted with monosyllables. He tried his luck with another group. Then another. His steps became heavy with fatigue. From his position in the room, Carvalho guessed that Esparza was trying to draw near the door without giving the impression of flight. But now Mir was in front of him with his eyes averted, giving the order for the meeting to begin. Esparza tried to slip by Mir, but the chief steward took him by the arm and gently pushed him towards the main room. Esparza put on a wan smile and attempted some jocular remark. Carvalho followed the pair until they entered the meeting. He stood in the doorway watching their backs as they went up to the first row of tables. Mir then left Esparza, who went to take his usual place.

As if at a signal, the members of the central committee plenum of the Communist Party of Spain rose to their feet, noisily pushed aside the chairs and formed a compact circle around Esparza Julve. They stood silently at a distance, as if to create a zone of pure air around a putrified mass, their nail-like eyes hard, sometimes tearful, red, wild, contemptuous. Esparza Julve rose slowly, picked up his file and took a few steps forward. Apparently obeying a secret order, the circle opened at the point where he reached it. Then someone shouted in a choking voice: 'We see, we feel, Garrido is here!' Esparza Julve walked past Mir without looking at him. Carvalho moved away from the door, and the man passed alongside looking out of the corner of his eye, with a sweaty nose and the eyes of an animal afraid of death.

'Keep your fear for outside. Here they've just morally executed you. But outside, you'll have a gun pointed at you for as long as you're alive. You're the most troublesome accomplice in the world.'

'What are you talking about?'

But he did not stop. He escaped as if he were slipping through a tunnel of perspiration. The door to the main room was closed. The central committee had begun. Carvalho followed Esparza Julve, allowing him to draw some distance ahead. Down the marble stairs with the feigned agility of legs that felt as painful as his heart. Carvalho held back so that his presence would not be interpreted as persecution. Run, rabbit, run. And he let the rabbit leave, some thirty metres in front of him. The glass doors opened automatically, as if they were part of the stage-setting. As soon as they shut again, a burst of machine-gun fire turned them into a spider-web canopy against which the distorted silhouette of Esparza Julve fell like a wineskin drilled by a thousand deaths. Carvalho threw himself to the ground, while the Hotel Continental lounge filled with shouts and voices. He stood up and ran to the doors, which still had a battered consistency to them. Carvalho's approach activated the photoelectric cell, so that the doors opened as if nothing had happened.

Then they disintegrated into powdered glass, revealing the bloody Punch and Judy show on the steps to the street. The corpse of Esparza Julve could have been an empty dinner-suit for all the attention Carvalho paid it. Carmela looked at him inquisitively from the crowd held back by the police. The detective made her walk with him to the car. He got inside, waiting for her to react and take the wheel.

'Who was that?'

'Garrido's murderer. They killed him.'

'It was from a car. I was phoning the nursery from the box on the corner. A car was parked on double lines, like many others, and suddenly it drove off spouting machine-gun bullets. Who was he?'

'Esparza Julve.'

'Are you mad? Do you know who you're talking about?'

'He was already a corpse when he left the hotel. They killed him with their scorn.'


The Madrid end of the air route always seems like a dress rehearsal of repatriated Catalans in the context of a star-wars film. Carvalho put the blue ticket in his jacket pocket and, without any enthusiasm, tried to persuade her to go back to Madrid. She did not say yes or no, but she remained by his side as they walked up and down a stupid, narrow corridor that led from a shop selling atrocious plain sandwiches towards the most absolute nothingness. Desire was impossible, and they had also run out of words. Maybe for that reason Carvalho suggested that they have something like a beer, to the tee-totaller Carmela. *An Aguila, always cool with its oh-so-natural taste*, she sang softly.

'Two beers, double quick. And a pork patty.'

'Will this one do?'

'It's just symbolic. A monument to the unknown pig.'

But he ate it. He apologised to his neighbour while trying to find a more comfortable position for his elbows. Just a few inches away was Cerdán's sad face, with its drooping eyebrows, its sunken eyes

196

and its sagging lips.

'So many years without seeing each other, and now it's every other day.'

'That's true.'

'Have you finished in Madrid?'

'Completely.'

'I'm off to Barcelona.'

'I guessed as much.'

'There's a lot to do there. Do you still keep in touch with old comrades?'

'No.'

'I do. They're nearly all disillusioned: it's the result of a revisionist, reformist policy. I'm going to try to do something. The task is to achieve a minimal unity in action, and from there to force the historical parties to react by ditching a petty-bourgeois leadership.'

'I wish you every success in your work.'

'We are few. Slandered. Driven off our feet.'

'You people remind me of the joke about the Galicians.'

Cerdán sighed resignedly at having once again to face Carvalho's rationalist incongruity.

'Which one?'

'The one about the five thousand Galicians who wandered around the Casa del Campo and sorrowfully complained: We's lost!'

'It makes me cry more than laugh.'

'That's up to you.'

'We're still living through times in which we cannot be on friendly terms. Where have the smiles of neo-capitalism led to? Aren't the smiles of eurocommunist reconciliation a slap in the face for the working class and the oppressed peoples of the world?'

Cerdán turned with little enthusiasm to chewing a horrible, Madrid-style ham sandwich: bread like stone, plastic ham, an unappetising appearance.

'How's your health?'

'It's not keeping up with me.'

'Despite the exercises and strict diet?'

'Despite everything.'

'Have you tried a regime of salted codfish, iced champagne and screwing like mad?'

'I'm on a modest assistant lecturer's salary, whereas you're not involved in politics, a university career or anything like that. Still, things are going well for you. You seemed rather shy but really you're a man of resources. Of course . . .'

'What?'

'I've forgotten what I was going to say. Let's drop it.'

'You haven't forgotten. The other day, you were on the point of asking me after the bookshop do. But the question stuck inside you like a cyst. Shall I ask it for you?'

'Okay. Let's see.'

'What were you doing that day in Via Layetana, the den of the Barcelona police? Why was a red like you walking calmly down the steps?'

'That's not quite it, but my question was quite similar.'

'I'm tempted not to reply.'

'You don't have to.'

'We could agree to meet again in another twenty years, at this airport. During one of your stops in the postponed revolution and at the end of another one of my business trips. I'll tell you then.'

'I won't live another twenty years.'

'Can you swear?'

'Almost.'

'Okay, then, I'll take pity and let you in on my secret. I'll confess my guilt. I'm more or less Galician, and there's hardly anyone there who doesn't have a maid-servant, a civil guarder or a policeman in the family, however close or distant. There's no escaping it. As soon as I was born, I realised that I'd arrived in a family of maid-servants, civil guarders and reds condemned to death in 1936 or 1939. The proletariat, too, is pluricultural.'

'A relative?'

'A relative.'

'You could have said so.'

'I was a young aesthete.'

Cerdán finally gave up the struggle with the ham sandwich. Carmela was reading *El País*, detached from the conversation between the two men.


At the bottom of his glass, Carvalho could see his cousin Celestino: a strapping young man with Celtic features who knew little about anything; a decent guy whose hands were dirty with fascism.

'I don't like it, Pepino, but they'll use it against me if I refuse. There's no way round it. I'll try to keep out of it as much as possible.'

Either hands dirty with earth or hands dirty with human flesh.


'We'll be boarding soon.'

'So it seems.'

'Are we on the same plane?'

'I don't think so.'

Cerdán thought it was a scientific answer, although Carvalho had not bothered to check the colour of the boarding cards.

'Goodbye.'

Carmela raised her eyes from the paper.

'That wasn't a very friendly meeting. You obviously think very highly of him.'

'I owe him fifty per cent of what I used to be and absolutely nothing of what I am now.'

'He's an honest enough man.'

Carvalho shrugged his shoulders. *Will passengers with blue cards please prepare for boarding.* Carmela took him by the arm and they walked towards the boarding-lounge like a properly married couple.

'Come back some day. When you've resolved the contradiction between the abstract and the concrete arse of women comrades.'

'You'll have to put on five kilos. My conscience stops me from going to bed with women under fifty kilos.'

'But I weigh fifty-three!'

'What a pity. Why didn't you tell me?'

Carmela kissed him on the lips with her small, soft mouth. He tried to put a hundred passengers between himself and Cerdán, who climbed up to the plane and took a seat without looking round.

Although Biscuter assured him that Charo was well and although he was tempted to have a proper lunch near the office, Carvalho decided to ring Charo and then go straight to his house in Vallvidrera. To sleep or not to sleep, that is the question. All the more so after his display of nodding and snoring for the dozens of Madrid–Barcelona mongrel executives who had watched his desperate, gluttonous sleep with smiles, laughter and even clicks of the tongue.

'Will I see you tonight?'

'I'll sleep all day and wait for you in Vallvidrera.'

'I love you very much, Pepe.'

'That's your look out.'

It was her look out. One day when he had nothing to do, he would mark a day for his marriage with Charo in some diary of the future. Before the year two thousand, of course. Or in the next fortnight. He could not remember where he had left the car in the huge airport parking area, and so he had to look for it as one scans a crowd for a particular face. Here I am, the deserted animal growled, showing all the marks of bad weather and neglect. It was the first contact with a part of his mobile den and he greeted it by asking how it had been. He received a tardy, mulish reply from the starter, but the engine lost patience several times and was on the point of seizing up as he waited to pay. In the end, however, it went cheerfully along the road to the Castelldefels motorway.

It was a sunny day and the looming hills of Tibidabo and Montjuic seemed to be propped up by the Mediterranean, a sea which carried the blood of its shore-dwellers out to the most suitable four corners of the earth. A mediterranean faith in life gripped his weary muscles, and when he reached the ring-road exit at the Travesera de la Corts, he intentionally missed the way home and headed for the Diagonal with its solid lunches of roast meat and finely matched wines. After a good meal, sleep would be a precisely controlled pleasure rather than the flight of a lost, beaten, collarless dog. He went into La Estancia Vieja with the air of a man about to eat the world, to eat and drink it.

'An aperitif?' the owner Juan Cané suggested.

'A sour pisco, for the two of us.'

Cané went off to order a tapa de bife for Carvalho, not an entraña because it was too tough that day. After the second pisco, Carvalho decided that the world was all right and gave in to Cané's tempting solicitude: assorted pâtés, a piece of grilled steak, a sweetbread pâté, green vegetables, a little of everything. Some chinchulines? Carvalho could not remember what they were. Lean, braided intestines cooked over charcoal. Right, chinchulines. How about roast sweetbreads? Also. Cheese fried with aromatic herbs? Why not? And tapa de bife as well? Of course. Cané began to grow alarmed at the dynamic he had unleashed. He sat at Carvalho's table to witness the spectacle of an unleashed meal. A 1959-vintage Paternina. And now, tell me, even if it's in Argentinian, what these marvellous words mean: asado de tira, tapa de bife, entraña, chimi-churri. The Argentinian took a ball-point pen from his pocket and began to draw dissected four-legged animals, showing the difference in cuts between the continental Spanish culture, short on meat, and the Argentinian culture in which meat is everything.

'Here you slice the beef horizontally and use it for stews. There we cut it vertically and that is the asado de tira or roast strip. The fineness of the asado comes from the slow roasting. Tapa de bife? Entraña? Here you only cut the steak in one way. But what goes by the name of steak is really a number of different meats with distinctive texture and taste. According to how it is cut, this part of the bullock will provide tapa de bife or entraña. Entraña is a bit of a problem, because the meat will be tough if the animal is not a soft, well-constructed bullock. But when everything is all right, it is the best part of the animal. As for that ocean of chimi-churri in which you bathed the meat and the serving-dish, it is a roasting sauce made from garlic, parsley and peppers, something like the Mexican chillies but not so crude, aromatic herbs and oil. Are you still hungry enough to scrape up the chimi-churri?'

'It's not hunger but sleepiness.'

The second bottle of Paternina '59 was Carvalho's exclusive property. Whereas Cané ate in the restaurant every day, Carvalho only did so from time to time: if he didn't keep himself under control, he would end up with his liver in his gullet. Where have you been? Madrid. How are things shaping up? Will I also have to leave

Spain with the restaurant on my back? Who was the character that went for Garrido? What did you think of Garrido?

'What are they eating at the table over there?'

'Do you still feel like looking at other people's plates?'

'One should always desire other people's women and food.'

'It's roast breast of lamb.'

Some other time. What were you saying? No. Nothing is going to happen. You won't have to leave with the restaurant on your back. Garrido? It's still not clear. What do I think of him? I don't know. Only time will tell. Either an Indian chief or a revolutionary in transition between the assault on the Winter Palace and a socialism as clear and self-evident as ripe figs. But I'm no good at politics. It doesn't interest me. Just as I'll never make the slightest effort to learn the Watutsi language, so I won't lift a finger to learn politics. I used to read the papers, but now I don't even do that.

As Carvalho spoke, Cané noticed that he had not taken his eyes off the table with the roast breast of lamb. He was about to repeat his offer of a trial taste when he realised that Carvalho was looking not at the food, but at a woman with hair between red and chestnut-brown, a wonderful rosy skin, a perfect mouth and bones that would win an architecture prize. It even seemed that the woman's eyes met Carvalho's after each piece of conversation or mouthful of food, looking over the three men acompanying her and even the restauranteur himself.

'Anything else?'

'Some coffees.'

'How many?'

'Five.'

'Didn't you want to sleep though?'

'I've got the whole evening in front of me.'

He followed Carvalho's eyes as they hung on the table, the girl or the breast of lamb eaten slowly as a delicacy.

'Cigar?'

'Yes.'

'Something to drink?'

'Do you know how to make a bajativo?'

'It's on the menu. But it's Chilean not Argentinian. It's an excellent after-dinner drink: cognac, crème de menthe.'

The waiter brought the bajativo. Carvalho picked it up, examined the green topaz in the gloomy half-light and raised the glass as if holding it out to someone. In fact, Cané could see that he was offering a toast to the rosy woman and that she was furtively returning the toast with a glass of wine as she went on talking with her table-companions.

'A pick-up?'

'No, I know her. She's called Gladys, a Chilean woman. She's the one who first gave me a bajativo to try.'

"Montalbán does for Barcelona what Chandler did for Los Angeles—he exposes the criminal power relationships beneath the façade of democracy." —*THE GUARDIAN*

## THE ANGST-RIDDEN EXECUTIVE
978-1-61219-038-9

In this, the third of nineteen Pepe Carvalho novels written over a period of more than twenty years, scrupulously cynical detective/gourmet Pepe Carvalho is asked to investigate when a womanizing industrialist is murdered, but the police—and powerful friends of the dead man—prefer that he accept the official version.

"A writer who is caustic about the powerful and tender towards the oppressed."
—*TIMES LITERARY SUPPLEMENT*

## THE BUENOS AIRES QUINTET
978-1-61219-034-1

In Buenos Aires to investigate the disappearance of his cousin, nihilistic gourmand Pepe Carvalho quickly learns that the city is "hell-bent on self destruction" and that he'll have to confront the traumas of Argentina's "Dirty War" head on if he wants to stay alive.

"An inventive and sexy writer... Warmly recommended"
—*THE IRISH INDEPENDENT*

## MURDER IN THE CENTRAL COMMITTEE
978-1-61219-036-5

The fifth novel in the series combines a classic "locked-room" murder mystery with a soul-searching odyssey through the thickets of post-Fascist Spanish politics.

"Splendid flavor of life in Barcelona and Madrid, a memorable hero in Pepe, and one of the most startling love scenes you'll ever come across."
—*SCOTSMAN*

## OFF SIDE
978-1-61219-115-7

Barcelona's most promising new soccer star is receiving death threats and Pepe Carvalho, gourmet gumshoe, former communist, and political prisoner under Franco, is hired to find out who's behind it.

"Carvalho is funny ... scathingly witty about the powerful. Like Chandler's Phillip Marlowe, he is a man of honor walking the mean streets of a sick society."
—*INDEPENDENT* (LONDON)

## SOUTHERN SEAS
978-1-61219-117-1

Barcelona detective Pepe Carvalho's radical past collides with the present when a powerful businessman—a patron of artists and activists—is found dead. A mystery as eccentric as its cast of characters, *Southern Seas* was awarded Spain's Planeta prize (1979) and the International Grand Prix de Littérature Policière (1981).

"Montalbán writes with authority and compassion—a le Carré-like sorrow."
—*PUBLISHERS WEEKLY*

# Ⅿ MELVILLE INTERNATIONAL CRIME